The Last of The Greatest Generation

A WWII Mystery That Divided Two Nations

J Robert Gould

The Last of the Greatest Generation

Published by

RebelBooksPress.com

A division of The Jersey Tomato Press, LLC

Copyright © 2023 by J Robert Gould

ISBN: 978-1-0880-9037-4

Front and back covers by Dreamtime Entertainment

Manufactured in the United States

First Edition

DEDICATION

This book is dedicated to my father-in-law, John Abplanalp, who passed at age 96 on March 8, 2023, and who told me many stories of his time on the USS Ticonderoga, some of which are used in this novel. His love of country was remarkable, and when asked about his service, he would humbly say.... "It was no big deal." For him and those World War II veterans past and present, your service was a big deal, and the country cannot thank you enough.

CHAPTER

1

John Anderson was in the South Pacific on the aircraft carrier *USS Ticonderoga* looking through binoculars as he scanned the skies for Kamikaze pilots from the ship's control tower. It was a boring task, but the fear of an attack lingered on the crews' minds. As he lowered his binoculars and looked along the horizon he reached into his pocket and removed a black and white picture of a young girl; she was beautiful with light hair and a lovely smile. They had fallen in love and planned on getting married until the Japanese bombed Pearl Harbor and changed their plans.

"What's her name?" came a voice standing next to him. John hadn't noticed that the ship's captain had joined him on the bridge.

"Sir, sorry, I was just looking at my girl," John said, as he showed the picture to the captain.

"She's beautiful. What's her name?"

"Evelyn, Evelyn Hunter. I call her Evy. She's back in Buffalo."

"You're lucky to have her son."

"I agree sir. Probably too good for me."

1

The captain chuckled. John put the picture back in his pocket, raised the binoculars and looked to the empty skies.

"Keep your eyes open. These damn Kamikazes will come from nowhere and I don't want to be caught with my pants down; so stay focused, got it!"

"Yes sir."

John continued looking through the binoculars scanning the empty skies.

Suddenly the Captain grabs a bullhorn and yells to a number of sailors setting up 2 large military cannons. "Watch what you're doing. We don't need those damns things rolling off the ship!" He looks over to John. "I can't believe we put those on deck. This is the first for an aircraft carrier." A few minutes pass when the captain leans on the railing. "Anderson."

"Sir."

"Are you ready?"

"Sir, about as ready as I will ever be."

"Good, because this ship and crew lives are at stake. Do you realize that?"

"Yes sir, I do. We won't disappoint you."

The captain nodded. "I hope not," he paused. "Son, for now I'm reassigning you to the seventh deck. I need someone down there to manage the steam thrusters, so head down there when your shift is done."

"Yes sir." John lifted his binoculars and took another scan across the empty horizon, but the captain's words kept echoing in his mind.

John was walking the flight deck before heading down to his new assignment. He stopped and closed his eyes to feel the mist of the ocean breeze blow and the warmth of the sun across his face. Despite being at war, the moment felt like he was somewhere in the islands with no worries in the world. Suddenly, he felt a thud.

"Shit Anderson, watch where you're going," said the large burly marine named Butch.

John looked up and squinted. "Sorry Butch, just taking a walk."

"Just keep your eyes open so you don't find your skinny ass flying around the deck," came the stern reply.

2

"Yeah, well just keep your fat ass out of the way so you don't block out the sun."

Butch's expression took a serious turn and his eyes burned through John until he couldn't contain it; he burst out laughing. "Well, you know Anderson, it's good that you have at least a few pounds on you, or you'd blow right off the deck."

John put his hand over his eyes to block out the sun that peered over Butch's shoulder. "Nah, I'd just grab your ass and hang on."

Butch chuckled, then asked. "Where you headed?"

"Seventh deck."

"Steam room?"

"Yeah."

"Take care, as skinny as you are, they'll probably just find you in a puddle."

John laughed and shrugged. Butch patted him on the back and headed to the hatch leading to the lower decks. He turned, "Anderson, you did well in training, give'm hell......Hooyah!"

John smiled and gave a salute. Butch returned the salute, winked, and disappeared through the hatchway.

There was no hurry to report to his new assignment, so John continued walking around looking at the planes lined up with their wings pointed upward as if preparing to fly.

A few hours passed as John was rummaging through his trunk in search for a set of lighter clothes to wear in the steam room. Suddenly, he heard the alarm of 'battle stations' signaling that the ship was under attack. In the chaos he forgot where he had been reassigned and out of habit started up the ladder to the tower. He could hear something hitting the deck and explosions reverberating throughout the ship. He reached for the last rung which would have led to the flight deck when Butch grabbed his belt and pulled him down.

"Get out of the way Anderson! I need to get to the deck!" he yelled.

John gave a glare. "What the... "

John held onto the side of the ladder as Butch shot up to the overhead latch leading to the flight deck. As soon as he popped open the door and started up to the deck, a piece of shrapnel flew by and decapitated him. John simply hung there in shock as Butch's body fell. *Shit that could have been me!!*

Suddenly it hit him. *Gotta get to deck seven!!* He managed to get his balance and started down to the ladder. He yelled at a sailor who was heading up in the opposite direction, "Move it!! Move your ass!!"

He made it to his assigned deck in the engine room, it was hot and damp with the fog of steam hovering all around him. He wiped the sweat from his brow, his clothes were dripping wet, and he had a tough time breathing as he inhaled the thick moist air.

Okay, they're okay, at the right level, as he tapped the pressure dials for good measure. He glanced up at the sign above the dials, it was labeled THRUSTERS.

He looked around the room. *Damn, I'm the only one down here.* He ducked when another explosion roared above him. *Shit, when are they going to stop!* He turned the pressure handle increasing the steam to the thrusters and tapped the dials again. *Still good, still good.* He rubbed his head with both hands grasping the enormity of his responsibility. *I gotta keep this pressure level or we'll be a sitting duck.*

He could hear the bending of metal as more explosions shook the ship. The sounds pierced his ears, and his nerves were at their end. *Stop already!!* he yelled in a frantic voice as he put his hands over his ears: *just stop!!*

The main bridge communication radio rang, John picked it up. "Anderson here!!" he yelled over the sound of the alarms.

"Sailor, we're flooding you in!" came a voice.

"What, come again? Did you say you're flooding me in?!" John yelled.

"Decks five and six are on fire and that's where the munitions are; if they catch fire the ship will blow, so we're flooding all the decks from five through seven!! Just hang in there son!!" Then the phone went dead.

He closed the hatch, spun the handle that sealed it and sat down on the metal steps. The sounds of the explosions hitting the ship, mixed with the alarms, were deafening. He heard the water hitting the door and it creaked from the outside pressure. He pulled a picture from his pocket and stared at it. *This is it, Evy. I love you so much; I will always love you. I hope you have a good life. I'll miss you.* He put the picture to his lips, kissed it and then closed his eyes. The sounds of the explosions and alarms slowly faded.

CHAPTER

2

"Papa John, can you hear me? Papa John?" came a faint voice. Music from the television was playing Frank Sinatra in the background.

"I can hear you; I can hear you. I just had my eyes closed for a minute. Geez, I'm not dead you know," John said, as he pulled himself up in his bed. He was still sharp and could remember many details of his life, but his age had finally caught up with his body, and his mobility was limited.

John glanced over to a framed black and white photo, the same picture he had carried with him during the war. "I miss you Evy."

"Papa John, can I get you anything?" Cindy asked.

"You look just like your grandmother," he said. "You have the same blue eyes and blonde hair that she had; she was a looker, just like you."

Cindy smiled, looked over at the photo of her grandmother and rubbed his cheek. "You're so sweet."

"You know I was one the first." John said.

"The first for what?" Cindy had heard him say this same thing several times but never got tired of hearing it.

"The first to step foot in Japan."

"Wow, Papa John. That had to be something."

John smiled and winked. "I'm kinda tired, I think I'll take a nap." He was starting to sleep more than usual and would mumble things. He was still 'with-it', but he often drifted off and start talking about his service in the war, especially the *USS Ticonderoga*. Cindy found his tales interesting but figured they'd be lost when he passed.

Cindy was proud of her grandfather but never understood the significance of what he was telling her. She wondered how many others were around like him, veterans of a war long ago. She was finishing up his laundry when she quietly walked into his room to pick up a few more things and noticed him awake and looking at a tattered piece of paper. It appeared old and was taped together.

"What's that Papa John?"

"It's an old war article that I've kept over the years," he replied without looking up.

"What's it about?"

"Nothin' important." Then he quickly folded up the paper and put it back in the nightstand.

Cindy had seen him pull that same paper out on several occasions, unfold it, look at it, fold it again and put it back in the drawer. She left the room to finish folding the last of John's clothes when she started thinking about having someone write down his war stories that he's told her over the years. She remembered that her neighbor across the street had someone associated with a newspaper up north, and reached for the phone.

"Hello?" came a garbled reply.

"Hey Chris, this is Cindy."

"Cindy? Wow, it's great to hear from you," Chris said after finishing the remainder of his sandwich.

"I'm sorry, did I interrupt your lunch?"

"No, no, not at all. Geez, I've been meaning to call to see how things are going with you and Papa John, but I guess time got the best of me."

"Yeah, I know it's been a while. I've been busy too."

"Is everything okay?" he asked.

"Yeah, everything's fine." She paused. "I wanted to get your opinion on something."

"Sure, what is it?"

"Well, from time-to-time Papa John tells me stories about his time in World War two and I thought that perhaps you would know someone who might be able to give me some ideas on the best way to document them."

"Wow, that's right, I remember that he was in the Navy back then."

"Yeah, he was. Anyway, he's a hundred and six now, and I'm not sure how long he'll be with us, and I'd like to have some record of his stories."

Chris rubbed the side of this face. "A hundred and six? Wow, I didn't know he was that old."

"Yeah, it's just that I think his stories are so good, but I'm not sure if anyone would really care about them."

"Well, I can check with my brother, he runs our family newspaper back home in Vermont. I'm not sure if he'd have interest, but it doesn't hurt to ask."

"Thanks Chris. Like I said, I'm not sure anyone would care about that war anymore, but I feel like I should document something, if nothing more than to have it for me."

"Let me see what I can do."

"Thank you so much."

Chris put his cell phone down and stared out his office window. *A hundred and six, man.* he mumbled. He was curious about John and the surviving veterans from that war and started Googling military sites. Then he pulled up documents from the Bureau of Veterans Affairs.

It took him a few weeks of plowing through hundreds of on-line files that he pulled from the Department of Defense, the Veterans Administration, and public records. He even accessed files from Arlington Cemetery to see what information that would yield. He enlisted his husband, Robert, to do some digging into several media sites that had obituaries of deceased veterans from all the wars to-date. Through a parsing tool that Robert developed, he was able to focus on just World War II veterans. They worked together to delve into anything and everything that they could find until late one evening they looked at each other in shock. After all their research and scrubbing of data, they couldn't believe what they had found.

Piles of paper were strewn all over the office floor. Chris leaned back in his desk chair. "HOLY Shit! This is amazing!"

"Yeah, I'm thinking the same thing you are," Robert said, as he leaned forward in his chair across from Chris. "All the data that I've found points to the same thing."

"I'm not sure but I think this could be really big," Chris said.

"If this is what we think it is, I believe this could be beyond big," Robert replied. He started clicking on a few more computer keys and then sent the file to his printer. "I've put everything in a spreadsheet and sorted it so I could alpha and date range, and this is what I've got."

Robert stretched a large spreadsheet on the desk that went from one end to the other. It contained thousands of lines and columns that listed all known veterans of World War II. The spreadsheet was organized with the veterans' names, their branch of service, what unit they belonged, the dates they served and when they passed. He looked over to Chris with a grin and pointed to the only line that was highlighted. The name was John Anderson, Navy, *USS Ticonderoga*, Service 1941 to 1946, Living. They did several data dumps to verify their conclusion, and everything pointed to the same thing, John was the last living World War II veteran.

CHAPTER

3

C hris and Robert sat silent and stared at each other for a moment. What had started out as a simple gesture for a friend had resulted in what became an almost a full- time job. They were happy to help, but when they started doing the digging on John, they became obsessed with finding out whether their hunch was right.

Chris reached for his cell phone. Cindy answered.

"Hello Chris, how are things going?" she asked.

"Going well. Listen, I know that I was supposed to call my brother about your idea on getting someone to help with your grandfather's stories but..." Chris started.

Cindy interrupted. "Yeah, I hadn't heard from you for a while, so I thought that he didn't have any interest."

Chris's leg was shaking in excitement. "Well, actually, Robert and I started doing some digging after you and I talked. We think we've found something on Papa John that may be a pretty big thing."

"What is it?" Cindy asked.

Robert interjected. "Well, digging isn't the right word, we've been plowing through every record we could get our hands on."

"Really, what were you looking for?"

"We've run a number of spreadsheets from the data that we pulled from all Veteran sites, and we believe that your grandfather is the last World War two veteran alive," Robert replied.

Silence lingered in the air; they couldn't believe that the time had finally come where those words would have so much meaning.

"Cindy, he's the last of his generation," Chris said.

Robert and Chris looked at each other, there was no response from the other end. Robert shook his head. "Cindy? Are you there?"

Cindy wondered if she had heard correctly. "The last! Oh my God, is this true? Are you sure?"

"Everything points in that direction. We've double-checked our data, and haven't found anyone still alive from that period, so, yeah, he's the last," Chris replied.

Cindy was shocked, she hadn't thought a lot about the war her grandfather fought in, she just liked listening to his stories. She enjoyed how animated he got when he told her about the *Ticonderoga* and described the showboating, he would do to get everyone's attention.

Suddenly she had a sense of urgency envelope her. "Chris, do you know if your brother has anyone that can document Papa John's stories? It's more important now, don't you think?"

"Yeah, you're right. Let me check and see what I can find out," Chris said.

"Thanks, I appreciate that."

"No problem." Chris hung up the phone and looked over at Robert. "This isn't going to be easy for me."

After the call, Cindy walked into her grandfather's room. He was asleep, she stood there looking at him. She wasn't certain if she should say anything when he awoke but she felt that he would want to know. *How do I tell him?*

Chris looked at the phone and hesitated.

"How are you going to ask him? You two haven't talked for some time," Robert asked.

"I know, Anthony and I don't particularly get along that great. You know, ever since I came out and moved away from Vermont," Chris said.

"Listen, you two need to get over that."

"Yeah, I know, but I had no interest in working for the newspaper and neither did my sister. That along with my being gay, well, I think he was pissed when I left to come here."

"He's been the editor of the *Town Register* up there since your mom and dad retired. It's been a while and things must be going well. I think you're overreading things. He's your brother for Christ's sake. He loves you no matter what."

"I know, you're probably right. It's just that it's been a long time. I don't know."

"Well, listen, if we're right about this thing with Papa John, I think your brother will appreciate that you gave him a heads-up first."

Chris looked at his watch. "It's late, I shouldn't bother him."

Robert shook his head and stared. "You're stalling, call him."

Chris dialed the number.

Anthony had his hands on his chin with his arms leaning against the desk shaking his head wondering what he was going to do as he watched his top reporter stumble out of the office and head home. He was startled when his cell phone rang. He looked down at the number and answered. "Chris?"

"Hey, Anthony, how are things going?"

"Going good, how are things going there with you and Robert?"

Chris looked at Robert who gave him a thumbs up. "Everything's going great with us, thanks for asking. Listen, I hope I'm not bothering you."

Anthony paused; a level of guilt came over him. "No, you're not a bother. I, I, you know, I guess it's been a while."

"Yeah, but I can understand. I get it…," Chris said.

"No, no, I should've…." Anthony paused.

"Listen, you don't owe me anything."

11

Anthony paused again, and then said. "Well, it's great to hear from you."

Chris smiled, it felt good to hear his brother's voice. "Hey, I think I have something for you."

"Okay, I'm listening."

Chris went on to explain what they had found and how he thought that it might make for a good story.

"Hey, listen, I appreciate you calling me on this. It might be a great story, or it might be nothing, regardless, I really appreciate you thinking of me."

"No problem, you were the first person I thought of."

"You know, it's been too long. We need to get together. I mean, really, it's been too long," Anthony said.

"I know. I miss ya Anthony."

"Love ya Chris. Tell Robert that I love him too."

Tears welled up in Chris's eyes, he stuttered, "Love you too." He looked down at the phone, ended the call and looked up at Robert. Robert smiled. "Time heals all wounds"

CHAPTER

4

I t was 10 in the morning in the old Irish bar that had dark wooden walls with an odor mixed from cigars, cigarettes, and beer. The glow of a green neon light in the shape of a four-leaf clover buzzed above the pinball machines. The columns were covered with stapled dollar bills each with the dates and names of who had been there and who was in love with whom. The long rustic wooden bar had several worn leather stools neatly tucked under the counter. The place was eerily quiet, contrary to the cacophony of noise that burst from the doors every evening. The only sound was the distant television with the local Middlebury news.

Austin Paige was alone at the bar twirling a full glass of Woodford Reserve bourbon from a bottle he took from the back of the bar. He was disheveled. Once athletic, he was 10 pounds heavier. His clothes looked like he had slept in them, but it didn't matter; actually, nothing mattered to him. He lived above the bar called *The Shamrock* in a one-bedroom apartment that his friend and bar owner, Shannon O'Neil, had rented him. It was convenient as it made getting a drink easy, and he was making a habit of it.

Shannon was his sounding board, as bartenders tend to be, but in this case, he knew Austin was headed off a cliff unless he did something. He came around the corner and noticed that one of his bourbon bottles was missing. "Listen man, you can't keep coming down here in the morning and getting buzzed. What's your boss going to say if you keep going in smelling of booze?"

Austin leaned on the bar, and his shirt was half in and half out of his slacks. "He won't give a shit."

"You know, you have to get it together, you can't keep doing this to yourself."

"I know, I know, I get it, but this helps me get going."

"Whatever, but this won't make things better."

"Sure it will, it always makes things better my friend, watch this," Austin said, as he chugged the rest of his drink and then reached for the bottle.

Shannon grabbed it, "Enough man! Come on, it's only ten in the morning."

Austin stared at him with blood shot eyes, "Don't push it."

"You're doing this every day. First, it was only during the evening but now you're plowing through half a bottle every morning. This isn't good."

Austin brushed his hand through is graying unkept hair and used his sleeve to wipe his running nose. "Just give me the bottle!" he grunted under his breath.

Shannon relented. Austin grabbed it with his shaking hand and filled the glass. "Thanks," he said. Then closed his eyes and tipped back another drink.

Shannon leaned in and in a low compassionate voice said. "You know this won't bring them back."

Austin opened his eyes, stared ahead and slowly poured another drink.

"I know," he whispered.

CHAPTER

5

Austin left *The Shamrock* and headed to his office. As he walked out the door, he sprayed a mist of mouthwash from a small bottle that he kept in his coat pocket in an effort to conceal the smell of alcohol. When he got to the office parking lot, he turned off the car, rolled down the window to let the blast of cold air sober him up. He waited a few minutes and then headed into the building. He quietly snuck into the office hoping that he'd be inconspicuous but was unsuccessful.

Anthony was waiting for him. "Seriously, you can't keep coming in here like this. You're my brother-in-law but I can't have you stumbling in here every morning."

Austin took off his coat and reached for the wall then plopped down behind his desk. "I'm fine," he insisted, as he straightened his clothes.

"Really, you gotta use the wall for balance? Listen, I've been making excuses for you, but I'm running out of things to say. The others around here are looking for me to do something. Shit man, you gotta get your ass together."

Austin rubbed his unshaven face, "I know, I know, I'll be fine."

"Well, you need to do it quickly or I'm going to have to make some tough decisions. Please, don't put me in that position."

"No problem, I'll take care of things."

Anthony started out of the office, turned, and whispered. "I love you man."

Austin looked up, his expression was worn and solemn; his voice trailed as he spoke. "I know, love you too."

Several hours had passed. Austin was scrolling through his computer when he noticed a social media post about an article that Anthony had completed. It had gotten a number of hits and had accumulated a lot of followers, especially from the media outlets in the state. He looked at the top of the post where the columnist credits are given and noticed his name at the top. He got up and walked into Anthony's office with a copy of the article. "Hey man, I appreciate what you did for me."

Anthony wrinkled his face. "What are you talking about?"

Austin held up the article. "You didn't need to give me any credit. You're the one that did all the work on this."

"No, you're the one that did all the heavy lifting and found out about the graft going on in the State House. Shit, those two representatives had to be one brick short of a full load to think they could skim millions of dollars from that road contract and get away with it. So credit goes where credit's due."

"Well, just sayin', you didn't need to do that."

Anthony shook his head. "No worries, listen, you're the best investigative reporter I have." Then he motioned for Austin to sit across from his desk, paused, then smiled. "You remember when we were kids, we were so competitive? Then in high school we used to see who could get the best story when we worked on the school newspaper."

Austin chuckled and nodded. "Yeah, I remember getting the scoop on you when I found out the captain of the football team had the answers to the finals and was selling it to anyone who was willing to pay."

"Yeah, probably not something that you'd print in a school newspaper."

"Maybe, but he didn't know that."

"Well, it's good that you didn't print anything; he would've pounded your brains in!"

"I know but, he looked out for me after that, and I never had any trouble with anyone for the rest of the year."

Anthony laughed. "Yeah, blackmail helps, I guess."

"Guess so." Austin paused, smiled. "You know you didn't do so bad at Duke when you headed up their paper. You nailed some pretty compelling stories."

"Just dumb luck I guess," Anthony said.

"And you, you old coot, I paled in comparison to what you did at Princeton. You were one hell of a reporter up there. If you hadn't exposed the graft going on with the administration, the whole university funding apparatus would have been compromised."

"Yeah, dumb luck too," chuckled Austin.

Anthony leaned forward on his deck. "You know, I'm just glad I was able to talk you into coming back here to help me with this fledgling newspaper."

"You didn't need my help. The *Town Register* would've done just fine without me," Austin replied.

"Well, you married my sister, so I guess coming back here wasn't all that bad."

Austin's expression changed and he sunk in the chair. Anthony knew he had hit an emotional subject.

"Again, I want to thank you for what you did for me on this article, you didn't need to do that." Austin got up and slowly walked back to the office, his head hanging.

Anthony saw his brother-in-law sit back at his desk and stare out the window. He knew he had done the right thing by giving him the credit for the article and wondered how he could help him turn his life around. *Shit*, he said out loud, got up and headed to his office.

Austin saw Anthony approaching, swung his chair around and started pecking on the computer.

"Nice Try. Hey, I got something for you if you're interested."

"Sure, you need me to get the scoop on the latest recipe from the diner?"

Austin replied.

Anthony slowly shook his head. "Seriously man. Chris has a lead on something that may be up your alley."

"Chris, really, is he still with Robert?"

"Yeah, they're still together."

"Aren't they in Florida?"

"Yeah, Fort Myers specifically. Here's what he's got. He believes that he's found the last World War two veteran. He and Robert did some research and believe that their neighbor is the last living person who fought in the war, the guy's name is John Anderson."

"Wow, sure, I'd love to do a piece on that, you know I'm into that kinda stuff. It sounds like it could be an interesting story."

"Okay, I'll send you down there. I'll have Chris hook you up with the contact and we'll go from there."

Anthony turned to walk out of the office, stopped, and turned back around. "Listen Austin, I'm saying this as your boss, not as your brother-in-law. I know you've gone through a lot, and I care for you, but I can't have you work like this anymore. I'm sending you down there because you were good at what you did at one time. You need to figure out how to get your head back on straight and come back here with a new focus. Don't fuck this up; do you understand what I'm saying?"

Austin nodded; the tone was clear. "Yeah, I get it," he said.

He also picked up on the *'once'* being a good writer. He knew that he'd done some good work, but his focus had been on forgetting, not writing. Now he was going to interview an old man; if he was the last World War II veteran alive, that alone would make for a good story, even if John Anderson's real war stories weren't that interesting.

CHAPTER

6

The winter snow had come in a fury as Austin was putting the last of his things in a small backpack and the bag he planned to check for his trip to Florida. *This should do it,* then he took a few sips from a bottle of bourbon, then twisted the top back on. He wrapped the bottle with towels and stuffed it in his bag hoping it would make it past the security check before loading it on the plane. He took one more look around and then headed downstairs.

He slowly walked up to the bar and plopped down on a stool. "Fill'er up with my favorite."

Shannon took the Woodford Reserve bottle and poured a shot in a glass. "Where you off too?"

"Florida," Austin replied.

"Wow, where in Florida."

"Fort Myers."

Shannon slid the shot glass over to Austin. "You going to be okay to fly?"

Austin smirked. "Well, I'm not the pilot so I think I should be fine."

"What ya going to be doing in Fort Myers?"

Austin tipped his head back finishing the drink, flinched, shook his head, then slammed the glass on the counter. "Man, that hit the spot!!" He coughed a few times and wiped his mouth with his sleeve. "Well, I'm goin' down to talk to an old man about a war that no one's interested in."

"Well, you never know, you might go down there and come back with a new perspective on life."

"Yeah, right."

"Just keep your head on straight and don't drink the bars dry."

"Thanks for the words of advice my friend, but I don't think I'll find any peace that I want or need down there." He turned, waved, and walked out the door and into the awaiting cab.

The driver looked in his rearview mirror. "Where you off to?"

Austin looked up, he had a few in him and didn't realize his short staccato tone. "Airport, Florida." The driver got the hint and didn't say anything further. Austin glanced out the window as the snow and cold wind whistled by. He leaned back in his seat and looked in the rearview mirror. By all appearances the driver was happy. He was wearing earbuds, bobbing his head, and quietly singing to himself.

How content. He has no pressures; a simple life and probably a happy family. "Hey, do you have any family?" Austin asked.

The driver pulled an earplug from his ear. "What?"

"I said, do you have any family?"

"Yes sir. I have a beautiful wife and two wonderful kids, a boy, and a girl."

Austin turned and looked out the window without saying a word.

The driver looked back in the mirror and noticed the empty expression on his passenger's face. He had seen many a solemn person while driving a cab, but he'd never seen anyone that looked as if life had handed them a bad hand.

The cab pulled up to the airport. The driver got out and opened the trunk and pulled out the bags.

"Have a great time in Florida," he said. Austin nodded and headed into the terminal.

He was in his seat on the plane looking out the window hoping that his bourbon bottle made it through the baggage security check when an older woman sat next to him.

"I guess you're heading to Fort Myers too!" she said with excitement.

He looked over and gave a quick insincere smile. "Yep, headed to wherever the plane is taking us," he said in a sarcastic tone. *I hope she's not chatty.*

The lady got the message, shook her head, and sat quietly in her seat as the plane took off.

Austin saw the flight attendant walking down the aisle and raised his hand to get her attention. "Bourbon, please."

"Can I get a ginger ale," asked his seat partner.

Austin turned and gave a half smile.

"My name is Gladys by the way, what's taking you to Fort Myers?" She asked.

"Going to do an interview for a story."

"Oh my, that's wonderful, who are you interviewing?"

"Someone named John Anderson."

"John Anderson? He's a legend in Fort Myers."

Austin leaned over. "You know him?"

"Well, I know of him. He's been in Fort Myers for a long time. Several years ago, he was recognized for his service in World War two."

"Really, that's interesting."

"His granddaughter takes care of him, she's very beautiful," Gladys said, and then winked.

Austin smiled. "Well thanks for that information."

The flight attendant came back after a few minutes with their drinks. She handed one to Gladys and the other to Austin. Gladys raised her glass, "Here's to finding a great story and to your happiness."

Austin lifted his glass and touched it to his seat mate's. *Happiness? Are my emotions that obvious?* He took a sip of his drink. "Thanks, nice to have someone to talk to. I'm Austin Paige."

Gladys sipped her drink. "So do you have a family, wife?"

"No." he quietly whispered.

Gladys noticed Austin's demeanor change. "Well, no worries honey, when you get into that Florida weather it'll make you a new person."

The flight was long, but their conversation made time seem to pass quickly. The plane taxied to the terminal. Austin helped Gladys with her bags, and they chatted until they reached baggage claim. Gladys was met by her friend who she introduced to Austin. They left to go their separate ways but not without Gladys coming back giving him a hug. "You'll find happiness," she said.

He was taken by her kindness. "Thank you," he said. Then Gladys smiled, waved, and walked away.

Gladys was right, as soon as he walked into the Florida sunshine, he felt better. *Maybe there's something to this weather.* He looked back to the baggage claim area thinking about what Gladys said about being happy and hoped to see her smiling face again, but she was gone. He turned back and noticed several drivers holding up signs with names on them, and one had his.

He walked over to the person in a suit holding his name. "I'm Austin Paige."

"Pleasure to meet you Mr. Paige. I'm Jay, I'll be driving you today," he said, then grabbed the bags and headed to the car. "First time in our town?"

"Yeah, first time."

"Well, welcome to Fort Myers."

Jay walked to a black sedan and loaded the bags in the trunk, opened the rear door for Austin and then started out of the airport.

"Where are we headed?" Austin asked.

"I have instructions to take you downtown to the Indigo Hotel. It's really nice, old but new, you'll like it there," Jay replied.

Austin looked out the window and noticed that it was the antithesis of Middlebury: no hills and no snow. He leaned forward and crossed his arms on the back of the driver's seat. "Hey, what's there to do in Fort Myers?"

"Well, I guess it depends on what you want to do."

"Any good bars or places to hang out down here?"

"There's a few spots close to where you're staying, but there's not a lot. We're pretty much a little town."

Austin paused and glanced out the window. "It's pretty flat here."

Jay looked in his mirror and chuckled. "Welcome to Florida."

Austin gazed at the passing palm trees with dangling coconuts. As they approached downtown, he noticed people walking around in tee shirts, flip flops, holding cans of beer. *Exactly as I thought Florida to be.*

"Here you go," Jay said, as he pulled up in front of a brick building that had the letters McCrory's etched into the block above the entrance.

The location used to be a popular store back in the late 50's and 60's where the kids could sit at the soda fountain and get a cold root beer float. Now it was a hotel, called the Indigo. The streets were brick as well, and it gave the town a rustic turn of the century feel. Jay pointed to a few restaurants and made a couple of suggestions. Austin handed him a few bucks, grabbed his bags, and went inside.

His room was nicely appointed with new furnishings and paintings that juxtaposed the old, rustic exterior appearance. He put his bags on the bed and unzipped the larger piece. *Jackpot!!* he said, holding up the bourbon bottle. *Now we're talkin'.* Then he uncorked the bottle, found a glass, poured a drink, and took a sip. *Okay, pace yourself buddy.* But old habits die hard.

He polished off a few more glasses of bourbon and then made his way to a small restaurant and bar called Bruno's which was within walking distance of the hotel. The place was small but popular given the number of people that were squeezed in. The walls were lined with pictures of New York, specifically Brooklyn. Small bags of pasta and jars of red sauce were scattered about but strategically placed for people to buy. There were tables peppered about and a counter served as an optional dining area where people could sit and watch the chefs prepare meals. Everyone at the counter was in a daze, as if they were watching a reality show, complete with the occasional flames shooting up to the ceiling followed by oohs and awes. The distinct aroma of Italian spices, sauces, and boiling pasta lingered in the air. The owner, Cal, had jet black hair, boundless energy and an accent that definitely pointed to being a New Yorker. He was expressive, waving his hands back and forth when speaking, and he was speaking a lot. He saw Austin walk in and waved for him to sit at the bar.

Austin nodded and slid onto a bar stool. *Well, this is convenient. Close enough to walk to.*

Cal came over, smiled, and leaned on the bar. "Welcome! What can I get for you tonight?"

"Bourbon, Woodford Reserve, would be perfect, thanks," Austin replied.

Cal nodded, disappeared, and returned with a bottle. He opened it and poured a shot. "Can I get you anything, we have a great pasta dish tonight."

Austin looked down at the glass. "Nope, this will do."

After a period of time, Cal came back to check on him. "Pour me another," Austin mumbled. He had long forgotten about pacing himself.

"Are you sure you want another? Like I said we have a great dinner menu."

Austin raised his glass. "Nope, bourbon's fine."

Cal reluctantly poured another drink, took the bottle, and put it under the counter. "What brings you to our town?" he asked.

"I'm here to do a story on one of your locals," Austin replied, then took a sip from his glass.

"You a reporter?"

"Yep, Austin Paige is the name. I'm from a paper called the *Town Register* in Middlebury." He reached out and shook Cal's hand.

"Where's Middlebury?" Cal asked.

"Vermont."

"Very nice to meet you. Who are you doing the story on?"

"John Anderson."

"Papa John, how nice is that. He's somewhat of a celebrity down here you know."

Austin tipped his head back and finished his remaining drink. "So I've heard." He didn't make the Papa John connection.

"He's been recognized for his service in World War two and has been interviewed a few times about his experiences on the *USS Ticonderoga*."

"Didn't know he was on a ship," Austin stuttered.

"You okay?" Cal asked.

Austin didn't say anything and just sat staring at the counter. Cal waited a few minutes then turned and headed to the kitchen but looked back to see Austin head hang.

Several hours passed and the bar was closing; Cal came over to check on him. "You need any help getting back to your hotel?"

Austin squeezed his eyes together. "Nope, just around the corner."

Cal watched Austin leave. *What a shame.*

Austin made a premature turn down a side street to find himself walking along the river that ran through town. He leaned against the railing to take in the calmness of the water as it passed by. The cool evenings in Florida were so much better than the frigid weather he left in Vermont, and despite the amount of bourbon he consumed, was able to appreciate his surroundings. The evening lights glittered on the river. He remembered what Anthony said about getting his life straight. *I can't keep doing this.* He stumbled back to his hotel, fell into bed, looked at the rotating ceiling until he slowly drifted off to sleep.

CHAPTER

7

Anthony arranged for his brother to pick up Austin at the hotel for the morning meeting with John's contact. Chris knocked on the hotel room door. "Austin, it's Chris." There was no answer. He knocked again. "Hey, Austin, it's Chris…are you in there?" There was still no answer. He looked down at his phone to ensure that he had the right hotel and room number; everything checked out. He banged a few more times but with emphasis. "Austin!" he shouted.

Finally, the door unlocked, a disheveled person slowly opened the door.

"You look like shit!" exclaimed Chris.

He was taken by Austin's appearance. He wasn't what he remembered when he last saw him. Austin stood there for a moment gathering his wits, wiping the sleep from his eyes, and trying to figure out who was at the door.

"Chris? Hey, buddy, nice to see you again."

"Nice to see you again too but, man, you look terrible! Geez, did you sleep in your clothes?"

Austin looked down at himself. "Yeah, I guess I did."

"We need to get you cleaned up," Chris said. He put Austin in the shower and unpacked his luggage to find some clean clothes. He glanced over at the end table by the bed and saw the bourbon bottle with three quarters of the contents emptied. He figured that was the elixir Austin used the night before.

Chris pulled the clothes out of the suitcase and hung them up in the closet. Austin came out of the shower wrapped in a towel, clean and shaven and looked to be more with it. "Sorry Chris, I guess I wasn't ready for you this morning."

No problem, I guess I was a bit early." Chris tossed him a dress shirt and slacks. "Hey, I have breakfast set up with Cindy Davis. She's John Anderson's granddaughter who takes care of him."

Austin put on the shirt and slacks. "That's great, but first I need some coffee, really bad."

Chris chuckled. "I bet you do."

"Listen, I'm sorry about this. It's been a long time since we saw each other last. I just….." Austin stuttered. "I guess I haven't made a very good impression."

"No problem."

Austin's expression changed. "Come on over here, brother." They hugged one another.

"Let's get out of here," Chris said. They walked out the door and into the car then headed for their meeting.

"So how have things been going with you and Robert."

"Actually, things have been great. We've been doing interior design work down here and won a few awards for our work."

"No kidding, well, I'm not surprised. You've always had great taste."

"Thanks. Robert's really good too."

Austin grinned. "I bet he is."

Chris paused. "Listen, why don't you come over to our house this evening. I know Robert would love to see you and he'll cook up something that will blow your mind."

"You know, I'd love that." Austin looked out the front window. "You know, I'm sorry that I haven't stayed in contact. Well, with everything that's happened," he paused, cleared his throat, his voice sounded far away. "Anyway, I should've have called or something."

Chris glanced over with a sympathetic look. "Austin, it's alright."

Austin nodded.

Chris pulled up to a restaurant and into a gravel parking lot. "We're here."

The place was small and quaint. Austin was impressed by how rustic it looked. It was on a river with a porch that wrapped around the building. It was once an old fishing lodge that had been converted into a Southern style restaurant. It had large family style tables covered with checkered tablecloths. There were pictures of cotton farms and old buildings that could have been from the 1860's. A large Confederate Flag was displayed inside the entrance. They sat down at a table and waited for their appointment.

"This is a nice place," Austin said, as he glanced around. "Clearly you all haven't gotten the message that the Civil War's over."

Chris laughed. "Well, it's been here for some time as you might guess." He waved over at the server to get her attention.

"Do I have to eat grits?" Austin chuckled.

Chris laughed. "Yep, and collard greens too." He got the waitress's attention and asked for two cups of coffee.

"I guess Anthony told you that Robert and I did a bunch of research on John Anderson. Everyone calls him Papa John by the way. Anyway, it appears that he's the last living World War two vet. Robert and I did more research to verify everything, and it checks out. I don't know but we thought this could be a really big deal."

"That's what your brother said and you're right, if he's the last living survivor of the war, it could be a big deal. That alone, I think, is a story but if there's nothing compelling about this guy's life outside of the last vet thing, I'm not sure it will capture the attention of anyone. If he did something cool during the war, that may be of interest but otherwise this may not go anywhere beyond a quick interest story."

"Well, you'll have to see what you can find out," said Chris, as he noticed Cindy coming through the front door. Austin had his back to her as she approached the table.

28

"Austin, this is Cindy Davis," Chris said, as Austin turned around. "Cindy, this is Austin Paige."

Austin was immediately struck as his eyes caught hers. Chris picked up on the connection and grinned. Austin reached out to shake Cindy's hand.

"Very nice to meet you Mr. Paige. I understand that you work with Chris's brother up in Vermont," she said, as she smiled and sat down next to Chris.

"Yeah, sure, Vermont, right, yeah I work with Chris's brother," Austin stuttered. *Shit I can't even speak straight; get it together.*

"Well, I'm so happy that you took the time to come and meet with Papa John and listen to his stories. I hope that you'll find it worth your trip down here."

"Yeah, me too, hope it's worth it," he said. *Damn, did it again, that was a stupid thing to say.*

Cindy turned and smiled. Chris picked up on Austin's behavior and thought it nice to see him clearly captured.

"I think we should set up a time for Austin to stop by and have a quick introduction to Papa John, don't you think, Cindy?"

"I agree," she replied.

"Yes, that would be great," Austin said. *Thank God, I didn't screw that up.*

"I can arrange that for tomorrow morning. Papa John gets up early and has his routine of coffee and a paper so sometime around ten o'clock should work out fine if that'll work for you Mr. Paige."

"Please, call me Austin, and yes, ten o'clock will be fine." *Okay, now I'm talking straight.*

Cindy and Chris started talking to Austin about Fort Myers and about Chris and Robert's interior design work; he listened but everything was just garbled noise.

All Austin was focused on was Cindy. *She's beautiful. I can't believe I'm sitting here thinking about this.*

It wasn't long before they all finished their breakfast.

"So Austin, what do you think of our little town?" Cindy asked.

"What, huh?"

Chris chuckled.

"Fort Myers, what do you think of it so far?" she asked.

"Nice, really nice. Like it," Austin stuttered.

Cindy looked over at Chris. "Well, thanks again for setting this all up for me." She looked back to Austin. "It was nice to meet you." She got up, shook his hand.

"Yes, it's nice to meet you as well. I look forward to meeting Papa John," Austin said.

Cindy left but not without Austin watching her walk out.

Chris chuckled as he noticed Austin's stare. "Are you okay?"

"I'm fine," Austin replied.

"Yeah right."

They headed back to the hotel. Nothing was said on the trip back. Austin stared out the car window as the large palm trees that lined both sides of the road passed by. Chris glanced over. *Well, well, Mr. Paige; someone's caught your attention.* He knew what it was, he just wondered if Austin did.

CHAPTER

8

Austin spent the rest of the day walking around Fort Myers and admiring the small-town feel. He especially liked walking along the river that he found out was named the Caloosahatchee. He talked to some locals who told him that Thomas Edison and Henry Ford built winter residences in town that people can tour. The weather was beautiful, with a nice breeze coming off the water that whistled through the large oaks and palm trees that dotted the banks of the river. He wondered why the town hadn't taken off like so many other places in Florida but thought that perhaps it was best to remain small, where everyone seemed to know everyone else. *I could be happy here.*

It wasn't long before he realized that Chris would be picking him up for dinner and he quickly darted back to the hotel to get ready. He finished getting dressed and looked over to the bourbon bottle that had a bit left.

I don't think it would hurt to have something to get me going, he reasoned and with that poured a shot of bourbon into a glass and chugged it.

He felt the warmth of the liquor as it went down and justified that it was what he needed to get him primed for the evening. He put the glass down and started to go out the front door when he looked back.

A little more won't hurt me and finished what remained in the bottle. When Chris arrived, it was clear that Austin had had too much to drink; he tried to disguise it, but he didn't do a very good job of it.

Chris started driving to his house. "You okay?"

"Yeah, fine," Austin replied. He didn't say anything further during the trip and it was obvious why. When they arrived, they started up the stairs that Austin gingerly maneuvered.

"Robert, you remember Austin," Chris said, as they entered through the front door.

"Of course, I remember Austin. It's great to have you here," Robert replied.

"Great to be here. Thanks for the invitation," Austin said. "Hey, do you both mind if I sit on your front porch for a few minutes. I just need to get a little fresh air." But everyone knew why.

Chris came out with a glass of water. "Here you go."

'Thanks," Austin muttered, his hands were shaking.

Chris went back in the house to let Austin sit it out.

Robert nodded in Austin's direction. "Is he okay?"

Chris looked back to the front porch. "Yeah, I think he'll be okay in a few."

Robert was concerned for Austin, as was Chris, but both knew why he was the way he was. Austin was sitting out on the porch when he noticed Cindy through the window of the house across the street. She was working in the kitchen and was in an apron likely working on a dinner for her and her grandfather. He was captured by her and wondered what it would be like if she cooked for him. Austin was in the middle of his 'make believe dinner' when Chris came back out to the porch.

"Are you okay?"

"Yeah, I am fine, thanks for the water," Austin replied. "Feeling much better, thanks."

"No problem, we have dinner just about ready, do you want to come in?"

"Sure," Austin said, as he gathered himself and walked into the house.

Chris and Robert's house was extremely fashionable with a contemporary flair that contradicted age of the house. As were many houses in Fort Myers, theirs was built in the 1920's. The rooms were small but the furnishings and restoration that they completed made it look modern inside.

Austin looked around the room. "You guys are really good; this place looks fantastic."

"Thank you. It was certainly a work of passion," Robert said. "We're pretty proud of what we pulled off here."

"I'd love to have you do some work on my place if I ever get one," Austin said.

Robert glanced over at Chris; their expressions showed pity. Dinner went well, and in addition to being incredible interior designers, Chris and Robert were outstanding cooks.

"I don't think I have eaten this well in years. I guess your tastebuds are more acute without alcohol," Austin said, as he polished off his last bite of food.

Chris's eyes widened with surprise. "Uh, yeah, tastes different, doesn't it."

"Yeah, it does. Hey, listen, I really appreciate you guys having me here tonight. It feels good to be with family again."

"Well, we appreciate you coming down here," Chris said.

Everyone got up and walked to the living room. They sat down as Austin looked around; he knew he didn't make a good impression with Chris and didn't do so well with Robert. The silence, albeit momentarily, said everything.

"Listen, I am sorry about how I came off earlier. It's just that I've had a tough time with things. I guess I just haven't really figured out how to deal with it," Austin said.

Robert and Chris glanced at one another and let him continue.

"You know, I thought I could handle things. I try not to drink but it helps keep the pain away."

"You mean it helps mask it," Chris said.

"Yeah, I guess you're right. Your brother's been really patient with me, and quite honestly, I don't know why he hasn't gotten rid of me."

"Well, you're family, and we don't give up on family," Chris said.

"What would make you happy Austin?" Robert asked.

Whether it was a reflex or driven by something else, Austin stared out the front window to see Cindy standing in her kitchen. "I don't know," he said. He didn't turn back and continued staring out the window. "I wish I knew."

"Well, you need to find that out," Robert said.

Chris noticed what Austin was looking at and smiled, *perhaps he's starting to figure that out.*

CHAPTER

9

The buzzer went off at 9:00am which startled Austin. He hadn't awakened to an alarm clock for some time. He rolled over and clicked on the television to the local news. He felt better than he had in a while, it was the first time he'd had a good night's sleep without the room spinning. He slowly got out of bed recalling what Robert had said about finding out what would make him happy. He also remembered seeing Cindy in the kitchen window. He smiled as he thought about their first meeting; *I hope I don't come off like a babbling idiot again,* he thought as he headed for the shower.

Chris knocked on the hotel door wondering what he would see. When it opened, Austin looked like a different person; he noticeably had more energy. "Hey Chris, great to see you this wonderful morning. Can we stop on the way for a cup of coffee?"

"Wow, sure, I know a place. Geez man, you look way different then yesterday."

"Yeah, sorry about that. I feel a lot better this morning but getting a few cups of coffee in me will certainly help."

Austin noticed that Chris was driving a different car than the one he had the day before. "What's this?"

"Anthony rented this car for you while you're here." Chris handed Austin the keys. "I can't be shlepping you around all the time."

"Makes sense, it'll allow me to see more of the town."

"Well, that won't take long," Chris chuckled.

They arrived at Cindy and John's place just before 10 am. Chris got out of the car, and waved at Cindy who was standing on the front porch, then headed to his house.

"Thanks for the wheels," Austin said.

Chris turned and shouted from across the street, "Thank Anthony, not me."

Cindy smiled as Austin waved and started walking up the sidewalk. *He's definitely good looking.*

"Hi Cindy, thanks for arranging everything with your grandfather," Austin said, as he bound up the front stairs. He noted the large front porch similar to Chris and Robert's place. Cindy's house, however, looked to have been built in the 70's given the block construction. He glanced over to the kitchen window, where he had seen her the night before.

"Thank you again for taking time to talk with Papa John. He's in the living room waiting for you," she said.

John Anderson was sitting in his favorite place; a large gray plush, cushioned recliner that appeared to have been worn over the years. He was watching the television that was tuned to a Pandora station that was playing Frank Sinatra music. It had the title of the song and a picture of the singer that would change each time a new song came up; it was the music of his generation.

Cindy came into the room followed by Austin. "Papa John, this is Austin Paige. He's a reporter from up north who's come to talk with you," she said. John looked up and motioned for him to have a seat of the adjacent sofa.

"I'll let you gentlemen alone to talk for a few minutes." Cindy turned and left the room.

"Are you married?" John asked.

"No," Austin replied.

"Cindy isn't married either, maybe you two should hook up."

Austin wasn't sure if he was blushing, but he could feel the warmth in his body come to the surface. "Well, I guess that's for another day," he said trying to get control of the moment.

The room and furniture looked to be from the 70's as well. It was large and bulky but looked comfortable. There were wooden plank floors that creaked as you walked across them. The walls were peppered with paintings of flowers and mountain scenes with a style that echoed Vincent Van Gogh. The place had an interesting feel almost as if you were immersed into a Disney themed experience, waiting for Laverne and Shirley to pop out of the kitchen.

Austin noticed a large bookshelf in the back of the room from wall-to-wall and floor-to-ceiling. "Wow, you have a lot of books over there. There must be hundreds of them. Are you a big reader?"

"Well, I used to be. Most of those go back to the nineteen forties. I guess I've collected a lot over the years," John said.

"Do you mind if I take a peek?"

John gave a dismissive wave, "I don't give a damn, nobody really looks at em anymore."

Austin got up to look through the titles and noticed that all the books looked to be on World War II. "This is impressive, you've got quite a collection here."

"You think so?" John said. "Glad someone appreciates them. I brought these over from my house when I moved in with my daughter and her husband. These books and a trunk of stuff is all I have left to my name."

Austin was pulling a few books from the shelf when he noticed that John had strolled up next to him. "Are you okay to be walking?"

"I'm old, not dead!"

Austin chuckled and looked down at John, "I'm glad, otherwise this whole trip would've been a waste of time."

It only took a few seconds before John got it and started laughing. "Yeah, guess you're right, it would've been a waste of your time and mine if I just died standing here."

It was only a few moments and a few comments, but Austin and John started to bond.

Cindy came around the corner to see them both standing looking through several books that they pulled from the shelves. Austin looked to be having a great time with John who was equally excited to finally be able to share his collection with someone.

"Wow, these are something," Austin said, as he started to return the books to their proper places.

"I'm glad you like'm, I've had'm for so long that I forgot what's here," John said. He turned and strolled back to his chair using his walker. "They're in order from the beginning of the war to the surrender of Japan," he said, as he maneuvered back to his chair.

Austin turned and started back to the sofa. "Well, it's impressive for sure. I've been a World War two enthusiast since I can remember. I enjoy looking for things about the war, specifically the Pacific conflict. You must have a treasure of information over there."

"Gotta a lot of stuff for sure," John said.

Austin sat down, opened his briefcase, and pulled out a pad of yellow note paper. "John, I wanted to come down here and take a few minutes to talk about your time in World War two and anything that you can remember from that time. Do you mind if I take notes of our conversation, so I don't miss anything?"

"I don't mind…. and Austin."

Austin looked up. "Yes sir?"

"Call me Papa John. That's what my family calls me."

"Thanks Papa John. I feel honored."

"Son, what do you want to know about my time in the service? I don't have much to say about it and it's probably not very exciting."

Austin grabbed his pen and flipped the page on his yellow pad. He figured that the interview would likely be quick and contain much of what was already known about the war, but perhaps John could add some personalization to the story. What he could not have imagined was that he was about to become involved in one of the biggest investigations of his life.

CHAPTER

10

J ohn had made himself comfortable in his chair and leaned over for his coffee mug. Austin reached for his pen and pad to start and capture John's tales. He still had doubts as to whether the trip would be worth the time, and even more, concerns that there wouldn't be anything of interest to write about.

"So, let's start with how you got into the war," Austin said.

"I knew that I had to get in and do my part," John began. "It was nineteen forty-one when I enlisted, I was a little older than most, but it didn't matter. I didn't know when the war was going to end, shit nobody did, but I wasn't going to let any time pass, I had to get in. All I knew is that I wanted to kick some ass, especially the Japanese. So, I went down to the place where they were enlisting people. The Marines and the Navy military guys were there. I wanted in the Marines, that's where I knew I could see action. My dad was a hunter and showed me how to shoot a gun. Good thing too because it wasn't long before I could hit the middle of a target from 100 yards, and I figured that'd get me into the Marines. I wanted to get into the Pacific action and perhaps be part of the forces to invade Japan. I was pissed at 'em for Pearl

Harbor. When I tried to get the Marines to take me, they said it 'd take a few days before they could get me signed up. I didn't want to wait anymore so I went over to the Navy guy, and they took me right away; that 's how I got into the Navy."

"So, I guess that being in the Navy never gave you the opportunity to shoot a gun," Austin said, as he was jotting down his notes.

John looked at Austin, shrugged but didn't say anything.

"Okay, did they send you to a ship right away?"

"No, not at that moment, it was about a week after that I was assigned to basic training in San Diego. But I was also suddenly torn about leaving too."

"Really, why?"

"You see, I met a girl, Evelyn was her name, Evelyn Hunter. I called her Evy."

Austin noticed John's smile. He had a faraway look as he talked about her. "She was beautiful, blonde, blue eyes." Papa John looked up at Cindy and smiled. "She looked a lot like Cindy."

Cindy was taken. "I never knew you thought I looked like grandma," she said.

John smiled. "Yes, she was beautiful, and I knew that 'she was it'. Have you ever experienced that, Austin?"

Austin was caught off-guard. "Well, no sir… maybe I have, I guess." He looked at Cindy hoping he wasn't too obvious as to the timing of John's statement and the glance at her.

"You'll know it when it happens. I'll tell you son, my heart started pounding when I met her, and I was a bumbling idiot. I couldn't even talk to her, I just mumbled words," Papa John chuckled.

Cindy gave a demure smile. Austin figured that she was recalling their first interaction and was putting two and two together.

"Evy's brother invited me to the house for dinner. I couldn't eat that night, all I could do was stare at her," John said. "I didn't know what to say to her. I knew that I was heading out to war and figured that I wouldn't be coming back. We went out to the porch and talked until the sun came up. Neither of us knew that time had slipped away. Well, we fell in love that night." His expression looked as if he was back in the moment. "It was a night I'll never forget."

The silence lingered for a moment when John perked up and returned to the story. "I told Sunshine, which was my nickname for Evy, that if I returned, I was going to marry her. She grabbed by face, kissed me, and told me to come back to her. I guess that made me more determined to live through whatever I was going to experience. She was certainly worth living for."

Austin looked over at Cindy, *I get it,* then came back on topic. "I guess you went to San Diego after that," he said.

"Yeah, Evy and I spent the next couple of days together and then I was shipped off to San Diego for bootcamp," John said. "I was flown in for training, but I didn't know what I was specifically training for."

"Well, you were in the Navy, so I guess it was something to do with ships," Austin said. He felt embarrassed by the simplicity of the question. *Navy, ships, duh you idiot.*

"Well, they have you go through some testing and then set you up based on what your good at. After they did that, they took me to the side and had me train on a few things. One was the ship steam systems, the equipment used to keep the ship running and the other was special weapons training."

"Special Weapons? What was that the big guns on the ship?"

"No, I was put with a few other new naval recruits and trained with military arms, rifles, machine guns, grenades, mortars and a bunch of weapons like that."

"Was that normal training back then?" Austin asked. "It seems odd for a Navy steam room recruit."

John coughed a few times. "All I know is what they told me. They said that when we got close to Japan, we'd be a team to be used for a special military function."

Austin perked up. "Special military function, what was that?"

"You know, I am a bit tired," John said. He started getting up from his chair. Cindy came over and helped lift him to his walker and then they went to his room.

Austin was intrigued by what he had heard so far and walked over and randomly pulled a book from the shelf.

"I've never heard that story before," Cindy said, as she entered the room.

Austin turned. "Well, it is certainly interesting," he said. "I'd be interested to learn more about that."

"Me too. Would you like a bite of lunch?" Cindy asked.

"I'd love it," he replied as put the book back on the shelf and followed Cindy to the kitchen. But his mind wasn't currently on the interview, it was on her.

CHAPTER

11

A breeze blew across the porch and the shade of the trees made it feel several degrees cooler than it actually was for an early Florida afternoon. Austin and Cindy had retired to the front porch with a small high-top table in the corner that allowed them to see the huge oak trees that lined the road. Cindy prepared tuna salad sandwiches with southern sweet iced tea, a typical Southern drink.

"Wow, you know this is really good." Austin said, as he put his glass of tea down on the table.

"Thank you. My grandmother taught me how to make it. You get a gallon glass container, put a bunch of tea bags in it and then set it out in the sun for a day."

"Hmm, never had it this way before." Austin gazed around the porch and then to the street. "I'll have to say, I can understand why people would come down here, this is really something."

"Yeah, I think this is a little bit of heaven; a lot of people reference this place as Paradise."

"Well, I can certainly understand why, it's probably in the twenties or colder in Middlebury right about now."

"So, tell me about yourself," Cindy asked.

Austin hesitated for a moment. "Well, there isn't much, I went to school at Princeton and majored in journalism. I ended up working for my friend Anthony, you know, Chris's brother, at the local newspaper back in Middlebury where I grew up. I've done some investigative work up there and had some success which is why I was sent down here to talk with your grandfather."

"Do you have any family?"

Austin paused. "No, no family." He cleared his throat.

Cindy noticed a sudden change in his expression that belied the truth of a family.

"So, besides taking care of Papa John, what keeps you here?"

"Well, it's not much of a story either. I went off to college in Georgia and got a finance degree and moved back here with my parents after school to take care of them when they became ill. When my grandmother died, Papa John moved in with us. Then my dad died of cancer and mom died not too long afterward from a heart attack. I guess, as they say, she died of a broken heart. Papa John took that pretty hard; he didn't think that he'd outlive his wife and kids. Anyway, I've been taking care of him ever since."

"It must be hard to lose your parents and then have the responsibility of your grandfather."

"Well, I miss them every day. And Papa John's really sweet and loving so it's not really that hard at all."

"You're being modest but I'm sure he's glad that you're here for him."

"I think so. Anyway, I guess my life's pretty boring in comparison to being an investigative reporter."

Austin gave a quick chuckle. "It's not all it's cracked up to be."

Cindy smiled. "Why don't I believe you."

"By the way, have you told Papa John about why we're doing the interview with him? About being the last living veteran?"

"No, not yet. I'm really not sure how to tell him. All I've told him is that we wanted to document the stories that he's told me over the years, so we have a record of it. Although so far there's a few things that I haven't heard before."

"Yeah, I'm a bit curious about his special military reference. I guess that it wasn't unusual back then, but it certainly is interesting. Maybe they just did something special on the ship. I don't know," Austin said.

"Well, that's something that he's never mentioned to me before." Cindy got up to gather the plates and return to the kitchen.

"Please, let me help." Austin got up and collected the remaining glasses.

They both walked back to the kitchen and started putting the dishes in the dishwasher. As they entered the kitchen, Austin looked out the window to see the chair he had been sitting in across the street when he first saw Cindy in her apron that evening. Then memories of Middlebury started flooding in. "I should be going," he said.

Cindy wiped her hands with a towel. "I enjoyed our lunch. I assume you'll be returning tomorrow?"

"Sure, I should be here around the same time tomorrow if that's alright with you."

"That'd be fine. I'll have Papa John ready; I think he likes talking to you."

"Me too." Austin walked to the front door and turned to find Cindy behind him, he stopped and stared into her eyes. There was an awkward silence as each looked at each other. Time slowed as they stood there. Finally, Cindy coughed, Austin's sign that it was time to leave. He turned and walked out to his car. She looked out the front door as he backed out of the driveway. It was an unforeseen connection that each didn't expect, even as fleeting as it was.

John had gotten up and walked to his bedroom doorway when he saw them both at the front door. *Well Sunshine, I think she's finally met someone.* He smiled and went back to his bed.

CHAPTER

12

Despite his new surroundings, Austin was still fighting the demons. His past kept following him and his natural resolve was to numb his feelings, which he was very good at. His ritual set a pattern that he knew could find him in a compromising position, but he hoped that his anonymity would help him stay under the radar. Bruno's now replaced the Shamrock as his drinking retreat.

Austin pointed to an empty glass. "Pour me another."

"Are you okay?" Cal asked.

"Yeah, I'm fine, thanks."

Austin was sitting at the bar sipping his drink and didn't notice that someone had come up and sat beside him.

"Ginger ale," they ordered.

Ordinarily Austin could care less who was next to him but had heard that same order placed before.

"Nice to see you again," the occupant said.

"Gladys, right?"

"Yes, that's right, nice to see you again," she said.

"Wow, small world." *So much for the anonymity.*

"So how do you like our little town?"

"Very nice, I certainly like the people."

Cal came back with Gladys's drink. "Would you like to join me for dinner?" she asked.

Austin rubbed his half-shut eyes. "I don't think I'd be a very good dinner guest."

"Well, have you eaten yet?"

"No."

"Well, let me tell you, you need to get something in your stomach and the food here is outstanding. So, come join me," Gladys said in a tone that was more of an order than a request.

"Sure, I guess, but I don't want to be a bother."

"You won't."

They both walked to the table that was set up in the corner. Austin had difficulty finding the chair without first having to look for it.

"So, how are things going with your interview with Papa John." She motioned to Cal for a glass of water.

"It's going okay so far. We're just getting started."

"Well, he's an interesting character."

Austin rubbed his forehead trying to clear the brain fog. "Yeah, he's interesting alright."

Cal came back with a glass of water. "Here, drink this." She handed Austin the glass. "And what about his granddaughter." Gladys motioned to Cal to keep the water coming.

"Well, she's more than what I expected."

"What did you expect?"

"I really don't know, but she's something."

Cal returned with a pitcher of water. Austin took it, and after a few more glasses Gladys could see his focus begin to appear.

"So, how are YOU doing?" she asked.

"I'm better now, thanks," he replied.

"That's not what I'm asking."

Austin stared at her with a furrowed brow. "What?"

"I said, how are YOU doing?"

"I don't understand."

"I'm pretty good at reading people."

Austin shook his head. "I still don't know what you're talking about."

Gladys pointed to the glass of bourbon. "That stuff you're drinking doesn't help you know."

Austin stared at his drink.

Gladys reached over and put her hand on his. "Trust me, I've been down this road."

Austin looked up and shook his head. "What do you mean?"

Gladys sat back in her chair and took a sip of her ginger ale. "I never liked this stuff but it's better than the alternative."

"Alternative?"

Gladys adjusted herself in the chair. "It's been so long it's hard to remember the date anymore." She took another sip of her ginger ale. "Anyway, I was at a card game with my friends. We were having a great time and we all talked until late in the evening. When I got home there was a police car in my driveway. I figured that my son probably did something; he was always doing something wild. I told him that he'd get in trouble if he didn't straighten out, but you know kids. He was a teenager and figured he'd rebel against the 'establishment', as he called it. Anyway, when I got in the house, I saw my husband sitting there with the police officer. I knew immediately that something was bad."

Austin sat in silence.

Gladys looked down at the table then back to Austin. "When my husband got up, I saw his expression, he didn't need to say anything, I knew. My son was hanging around with his friends when they decided to take a joy ride. The driver lost control of the car and my son was killed when the driver crashed into a telephone pole."

Austin felt a pressure in his chest as if someone was putting a fist to it.

"I didn't know how to cope with the loss, so I started down a road that I think you're familiar with."

Austin listened.

"I guess it helped me forget about things, but it really didn't help. My husband, bless is soul, tried to help but I thought I had a handle on things."

"Where's your husband now," Austin asked.

"He passed away a few years ago but not without seeing me come to terms with my loss and getting my life together. Thank God, because losing him before I got it together would have been too much for me. He always supported me and told me that I had to accept what had happened and when I did, I'd finally knew what to do."

Austin said nothing.

"I know that it's hard and you may have a tough time understanding it, but whatever pain you have will fade in due time. You just have to accept that whatever it is, is history now and that's the toughest thing in the world to do. And that..." Gladys pointed to the glass of bourbon again. "That won't change a thing." She looked up at him. "Hopefully you'll find someone to help you like my husband helped me."

Austin's eyes started welling. "Why are you telling me this?"

"I don't know what you're going through, but I saw signs when we were on the plane together. And when I saw you at the bar, I figured you needed someone to talk too. You seem like a nice person and... you remind me of my son."

Austin choked a few times. "I'm so sorry about your son."

Gladys smiled, reached over, and patted his hands. "Are you hungry?"

He wiped his eyes. "I'm famished."

CHAPTER

13

The bright sun was something that Austin was unaccustomed to seeing in the winter mornings in Middlebury as he woke up. The evening with Gladys kept echoing in his mind; it was the first time anyone had confronted him with a compassionate argument about his problem.

Austin was heading to the shower when his cell phone rang, he noted the number. "Hey Anthony."

"Hey, how is it going down there?" Anthony asked.

"Actually, things are going well."

"So, how's the interview progressing with John?"

"It's going great, we just started, not sure what we'll turn up when it's all said and done."

"How are you getting along with Cindy?"

"It's goin' great."

"Glad to hear that everything's good. How long do you think you'll need to complete the story?"

"I don't know but I'll get back to you on that."

"Okay, don't take too long. I could use you back here."

"Got it."

"Talk to you soon."

"Likewise." Austin clicked off the call and got into the shower.

Anthony leaned back in his chair. *I hope I made the right decision.*

Austin finished his shower and headed out to his car. He looked up to the sky which was deep blue with no clouds. The morning was cool and comfortable.

As he drove down the street, his mind kept running the scene of the evening dinner with Gladys. He couldn't shake the feeling that she knew him better than he knew himself.

Cindy was up early and was in the kitchen making coffee.

"Why are you pacing around so much," John said.

"Papa John, I didn't know you were up yet."

"Couldn't sleep; all I heard were your slippers back and forth on that damn floor," he said. "You nervous about something?"

Cindy glanced out the window. "No, I'm just waiting for Austin to arrive."

John smiled. *I bet you are*, he whispered.

The sound of the car driving up grabbed Cindy's attention. "He's here!" she said with excited anticipation and darted to the front porch.

John shook his head. *Hope she figures it out.*

Austin drove up the driveway and parked the car. He smiled when he saw her standing on the front porch waving at him.

"Hi Austin, how's your morning going?"

"Absolutely wonderful," he said, as he exited the car.

"Can I get you a cup of coffee?"

"Sure!"

They went in the house and into the kitchen. Cindy poured the coffee and handed it to Austin. He grabbed the cup with her hands still around it; neither moved.

"Can you two lovebirds get me a cup of coffee?!" came a crackling voice from the living room.

Cindy's face blushed. "Okay! It's coming!"

"I'll take care of it." Austin took the coffee mug and went into the living room. "Here you go."

"Thanks," John said. He smiled and winked.

Austin sat on the sofa and opened his briefcase. "So, I think we should start with that special military training you were involved with."

"Nah, let's talk about something else, that's not important," John said, as he sipped his coffee. Cindy came into the room and sat down. John looked over at her and then to Austin who was pulling out his notepad.

"Let's talk about love," John said.

Austin and Cindy looked at John with astonishment.

Cindy felt a warm rush go through her body.

"Evy and I were separated by a war which made our relationship very difficult at the start. She knew that we were going to be together, but I wasn't so sure that I'd be coming back. All I knew was that I wanted to be with her for the rest of my life; I guess that may be what got me through some tough times."

Austin reached for his pen and pad. "Tough times, what tough times did you have?"

"It was this picture that got me through it all," John said, as he pointed to the black and white framed photo.

"Through what?" Austin asked.

"I was stuck in the hull of the *Ticonderoga* for three days. They flooded me in when those damn kamikazes hit our ship. It wasn't long before the water started slowly seeping through the hatch that I thought I had secured. It was at my waist, all I remember thinking was, I'm gonna drown and die. I remember staring at Evy's picture and praying that I'd make it back to her.

"Three days? Was there anyone there with you?" Austin asked.

"Nope, just me and Evy's picture. I hadn't heard anything the whole time I was down there until I finally heard a banging on the door. I turned the latch and opened the door to see my buddies staring back at me. I figured my prayers had been answered."

"Shit, I can't even imagine that," Austin replied.

"Well, that's when I knew that Evy and I were going to be together forever."

"You and grandma had been married for a long time." Cindy said.

John smiled and looked down for a moment as if he was reliving the years with his wife. "Yes we were. There was one thing that we both knew; never spend time living in the past."

Austin looked at John; *I've heard this before.*

The morning turned to afternoon. John had regaled them of his life with Evy. Austin did little to change the subject or take notes.

Finally, after John ran out of stories he paused. "I'm getting a bit tired." He got up and grabbed his walker. "Austin?"

"Yes sir."

"I want to give you something." John strolled over to the bookshelf and reached into a corner. He pulled out old leather covered journals that were tied together with twine, blew off the dust and stood there for a moment. "I haven't looked at these in years," he said staring at them. Then he turned and worked his way back and handed them to Austin.

"What are these?"

John waved off the question and headed to his room.

Austin looked at Cindy and shrugged.

"I don't know what those are," she said. "I've never seen them before."

Austin carefully slid them in his briefcase. "I guess I should be going."

He got up and headed to the front door. As he got close, he turned. "I know this is probably premature, but would you join me for dinner some time?"

Cindy smiled and touched his arm. "I'd love to."

"Great, I'll plan something for us." Austin turned and left for his hotel.

Cindy placed her head against the door and smiled.

John climbed into bed. His mind was on Evy. He laid there looking at the ceiling fan slowly turning above him. *I miss you Sunshine, I'll be with you soon.*

CHAPTER

14

T he hotel room was lit by a single lamp as the dark evening skies filled the seams of the partially opened blinds. The sound of the television softly echoed in the room. Austin was sitting at the corner table as he poured another shot of bourbon in his glass. His eyes were glassy, and the calm of his morning was replaced by the pain of the evening.

I'm so sorry, he quietly uttered to an empty room. He tipped his head back and finished what was left in his glass, then wiped the tears from his eyes. He looked at the empty bottle and glanced around the room for another; there was none. He got up and stumbled his way to bed and quickly dozed off.

The morning sunrise peered through the blinds filling the room with bright strips of light. He squinted his eyes as he slumbered out of his stupor. He glanced at the table and noticed a pizza box with a few lonely wedge pieces along with an empty bottle of bourbon. He rubbed his pounding head and reached into his suitcase and pulled out a bottle of aspirin. He got up, staggered to the bathroom, popped a few pills, and washed them down with a glass of water. He made his way back and sat at the end of the bed rubbing his head, something he's done so many times before.

A portable coffee maker was in the corner of the room, by the looks of it, it hadn't been used for some time. He struggled but finally got it working and plopped a Styrofoam cup under the dispenser.

He took a sip, his face wrinkled, and he shook his head then looked in the cup to figure out what concoction was being pawned off as coffee. After letting what little caffeine was in the coffee to kick in, he decided to go through the journals. He walked over to the table, grabbed them, and looked at the binder. Each was labeled with a number, 1 through 4. He picked up the first journal and began skimming through the pages; he was specifically looking for any special military training reference but could not find anything, instead he found John's notes about boot camp and about how much he was looking forward to getting back home. He noticed a written entry; *I hope this training is worth the risk,* but there was nothing more about it.

The fog from the evening's binge slowly started to clear. He turned a few more pages when a picture fell out. He moaned as he reached down and picked it up. It was a photo of a beautiful young girl standing on a front porch, he turned it over and noticed a written name: Evy. He continued flipping through the pages and stopped now and then to read some things. As he wiped the sleep from his eyes and found another black and white photo of what looked like, a storage trunk with a written note on the back that said, *'I'll never do that again'.* He continued through the journal when he noticed something wedged in the crease.

Hmm, what's this? He pulled out an aged yellowed folded paper. He slowly unfolded what was a map of Tokyo, with a red line drawn from the coast to an area marked with a circle. Several little towns were within the area but the one in the center seemed to stick out... *Chiyoda District.* Then he looked at his watch. *Shit, I gotta get going!* And launched himself from his chair table and headed for the shower.

The drive to Cindy's seemed shorter, but he was now familiar with the traffic pattern, and it didn't take long before he was parked in Cindy's driveway. He reached for his pocket to see if he had any of his breath spray, but there was none. Then he held his hand to his mouth and gave a quick huff of breath to see if he could pass the bourbon smell test, he failed. He got out of the car and gingerly walked up the stairs; his first cup of caffeine hadn't completely done the trick. He shook his head to release the remaining cobwebs and rang the doorbell.

Cindy opened the door to see Austin a bit haggard. "Hi, Austin, glad to see you this morning. How did you sleep last night?" she asked, as he walked in.

"Good to see you too Cindy... Slept well, thanks," he said with a noticeable lack of sincerity.

Cindy noticed a distinct alcohol odor as he passed. She pointed to the living room. "He's waiting for you," she said.

Austin slumped down in his usual place on the sofa, took the journals from his briefcase, and set them aside. John was sitting in his chair sipping his morning brew.

"Cindy, if you don't mind, can I get one of those?" Austin asked, as he pointed to John's coffee mug.

"Sure," she said, and disappeared into the kitchen.

Austin took his pad out and searched for a pen. The fog from the morning had cleared but the aspirin hadn't done it's work yet.

"Here you go son," John said, as he passed him a pen. "Are you okay?"

"Yeah, Thanks." Austin took the pen. "Well, I was going through your journals this morning and came across some interesting things that perhaps you can shed some light on."

John took a sip from his cup. "What do ya want to know?"

Cindy walked in with a steaming mug of coffee. "Here you go Austin," she said. "This should help."

He smiled and simultaneously cocked his head; *I wonder what she means by that*. He took a sip and let out an *aww*. Then he reached for the journal and pulled out the picture of Evelyn that he had found earlier. "Your wife was certainly beautiful."

John smiled and nodded. "Yes she was. Looks like Cindy, don't ya think?"

"Sure does." Austin glanced down at the picture then handed it to Cindy.

"This other picture is interesting too especially the comment on the back; *I'll never do that again*." Austin handed John the photo. "What's this one all about?"

He chuckled. "Well, I was trying to play a prank on my shipmates and thought it would be funny to jump out of this trunk and scare'm. So, I got in, sucked in all the air, and then the damn lid slammed down and locked."

"What! Are you kidding me, you locked yourself in a trunk?"

"Yep, fortunately, I had the key in my pants pocket and was able to squeeze my arm back and get it." John painstakingly demonstrated how he maneuvered himself to get the key. "Then I slowly pushed the latch and opened the lid."

"How long were you in there?"

John chuckled again. "I don't know, I guess, maybe about ten minutes."

Austin shook himself. "Shit! I'm starting to feel claustrophobic."

"Yeah, didn't work out so well. I kept the picture as a reminder of some of the stupid things I did."

"Did you keep the trunk, or did you give that up when you left the ship?"

John shrugged and never gave an answer.

Austin moved on. "I was looking through a journal and found a map of Tokyo with lines and a circle drawn around an area. Not sure what it means but it's interesting. Anything that you can tell me about?"

Austin started looking for the map and didn't see John's expression turn serious. He found it and started unfolding it.

"It's nothing, just something that I found back then," John replied, but his expression said differently. Austin took note.

"I know we just started but I'd like to stop for now. Maybe we can catch up later," John said.

"Sure, whatever you'd like to do," Austin replied. He looked over at Cindy and shrugged his shoulder. John got up, used his walker to head to the bedroom and slowly closed the door.

"Did I say something wrong?" Austin asked.

Cindy shook her head. "I don't think so. He's been feeling weak for the last several days but he's usually engaging," she replied. "His expression changed though when you asked him about that map. Do you have any idea what that's about?"

"No, not really. The map was stuck in one of the journals as I was looking through them this morning. It looks like one of those treasure maps we used to get when we were kids. I haven't really studied it. I just thought it was interesting."

"Yeah, not sure but that map seems to have struck a chord," Cindy said.

"I suppose we're done. I'm sorry that things went south like this. I don't know what I said but I hope I didn't say anything to upset him." Austin started collecting everything. "I guess I'll head back and start going through these journals."

John laid in his room thinking about the map that Austin had discovered. After all these years, he had forgotten about it. He rolled over on his side wondering if the decision to share that part of his life was worth the risk he would endure if the truth emerged. He closed his eyes and slowly fell asleep.

CHAPTER

15

Austin collected everything and closed his briefcase when the doorbell rang. He heard Cindy open the door and greet a familiar sounding guest. "Morning Chris."

"Hey, listen, I know it's short notice, but Robert and I wanted to see if you two would like to join us for dinner this evening." Chris asked.

Cindy came around the corner. "Austin, do you have plans for this evening?"

"Nope. I'm open."

Chris popped around the corner and joined Cindy. "Hey, buddy, how things goin'?"

Austin chuckled. "All good brother."

"Well, ya know Robert's one hell of a cook. Be good for you two to stop by and get some grub."

"Love it, that is if Cindy would like to join me."

She smiled. "You know, you do owe me a date."

Chris raised his eyebrows. "Well well. We're dating already?"

Austin shook his head. "No, well, not yet but we'd both love to join you tonight."

"Okay, will seven work for you?" Chris asked.

"Yep, that's great," Cindy said. Austin nodded.

"Good, see you both tonight. We'll make it special since it's your first date."

Austin rolled his eyes.

Chris winked, headed to the front door and then back across the street.

Austin started toward the front door when Cindy turned. "Well, I guess I'm off the hook for our first date now," he said.

"Yes, I think you got off easy on this one," she giggled.

"Maybe I can make it up in some way."

Cindy stopped in front of the doorway, put her hands together. "Since you don't have anything to do right this moment, do you have a minute?"

Austin smiled and perked up. "Sure, what do you have in mind."

She turned and grabbed a sweater that was hanging on a coat rack next to the door. "Come with me, I'd like to show you something." She grabbed Austin's hand and headed out the front door.

"Where we headed?"

"You'll see."

It was a short walk, and it didn't take long for Austin to figure out where he was going.

They walked over to a bench on the bank of a large river. A huge oak tree cast a shadow and the surrounding red and purple bougainvillea's created privacy for anyone who sat there. A gardenia bush in full bloom gave a sweet odor that waft through the air. The sun glistened off the water and even in the daylight made the waves look like they were dancing with diamonds.

"This is my favorite place to reflect on things," Cindy said, as she sat down.

"This is the Caloosahatchee, right?" Austin asked, as he joined her on the bench.

"Very good Mr. Paige."

"Well, I'm an investigative reporter you know."

"And a good one, I'm sure."

"So, do you come down here a lot?" Austin asked.

"Not as much as I would like, you know, with Papa John and all," she replied.

"Well, it's certainly a beautiful spot."

They both gazed at the river as the water passed by; they said nothing but heard the small waves lap against the side of the sea wall, the sound created a calming effect.

"You know, you do a wonderful job of taking care of your grandfather," Austin said, breaking the silence.

"Thank you, I love him so much," Cindy replied. "It's just…"

Austin adjusted himself and turned toward her. "Just what?"

Cindy shook her head. "It's nothing."

"No seriously, what are you thinking about?"

"It's crazy and stupid."

"Listen, nothing's crazy or stupid. Trust me, I've probably heard it all."

Cindy paused and looked across the water. "I don't know, I always wanted to have some excitement in my life. I thought I'd get to do something that had meaning. Like you, I bet you get to do things that are exciting."

Austin leaned back on the bench and looked back across the river. "Not really, I'm just a reporter."

"But see, that has to be fun and exciting."

"Truthfully, it was at one time but then…"

Cindy turned, "Then what?" she asked.

Austin paused and looked down. "I don't know, just that sometimes things happen and your focus changes. Funny, I was once on my game, but

I guess I kinda lost my edge."

"I don't know, I don't think you lose that. I just think things happen."

Austin nodded. "Maybe."

Cindy patted his hands. "You know, I think you're going to get your edge back."

He tried to smile. "I don't know if I'll ever get it back again, it's been a while."

"I believe in you, and I'll be here to help you get it back." Cindy said.

Austin cocked his head; he wasn't sure what she was alluding to but felt her words touching; he patted her hand. "And I'll be here when you start your exciting adventure," he responded.

Cindy squeezed his arm.

After a few minutes, he looked down at his watch. "You know, I guess I'd better get back and do a little work."

"Yeah, me too."

They walked back to the house and up the front porch. They stopped at the steps, Cindy on the top looking down at Austin on the bottom.

"I enjoyed our little talk," she said.

"Me too. I'll see you at seven," Austin replied.

Neither moved, and for a moment, they just looked at each other. Austin cleared his throat. "Uh, guess I better get going."

"See you soon," she said, as she turned and went into the house.

Austin sat in the car for a moment staring at the front door. He recalled the dinner with Gladys where she hoped that he'd find someone to help him deal with his issue. He started the car, turned around to back out of the driveway then looked back at the front door of the house – *maybe?*

CHAPTER

16

A ustin had returned to his hotel room and taken the day to take a nap, something he needed and seldom did in Middlebury. He awoke and looked at his watch, he needed to get ready. He stretched and then started thinking about the brief interview with John and wondered why it had ended so abruptly. As he was pulling out clothes for the evening, he glanced over at the bourbon bottle that the housekeeper had left... it was empty. The temptation to find an alternative elixir tugged at him. He paced the floor feeling uncomfortable then shook his body trying to shake the jitters that were clinging to him. He couldn't immediately put a finger on why he was so edgy, but it didn't take long to register... *I haven't had a drink all day.*

To take his mind off things, he strolled over to the corner table, opened the map, and stared at it. *This is important, I can feel it*, he said. Then he sat down and looked at it again; *this has to be relevant to something.* He quickly flipped through the journal to see if any reference was made as to its purpose; there was none. He looked over at the digital clock by the bed, it was time to go.

Austin arrived at the house just before 7:00. Cindy was waiting for him on the front porch. He got out of the car and started toward her, "You look fantastic," he said.

"Why thank you Mr. Paige." She curtsied. "Do you like my dress?"

"I love it," he replied. It was a beautiful melon colored dress that accentuated her thin figure.

"Seriously, I've never seen anything as beautiful as you before." Austin felt a blush come over him."

"Why, Mr. Paige, you do say."

Austin realized what he had said and could feel the heat of embarrassment wash over him. "Geez, sorry, that was probably the wrong thing to say on our first date."

Cindy laughed again, smiled, and grabbed his hand. "Well, it was very sweet."

They strolled across the street and knocked on Chris and Robert's front door.

"Come on in!" Chris yelled from the kitchen.

"Wow, something smells fantastic," Austin said, as they entered the house.

"We hope you like it. It's Robert's famous chicken dish that he's perfected over the years," Chris said, as he walked from the kitchen to greet them. "First, what can I get you to drink?" he asked. He reached for a bourbon bottle from his liquor cabinet.

"I'll have a red wine," Cindy said.

Austin looked at the bourbon bottle. The urge was overwhelming, but Gladys's advice was echoing in his head.

The pause was noticeable. Cindy turned. "Austin?"

"I'll have soda water with lemon," Austin blurted out.

"Come again?" Chris asked, as he stood there holding the bourbon bottle.

Austin repeated. "Soda water and lemon would be great."

Chris smiled and winked. He replaced the bottle and poured Cindy a glass of Cabernet. He turned and headed to the kitchen. "Soda water and lemon, coming up!"

Cindy could see the sweat on Austin's forehead. "Are you okay?"

"Yeah, fine," he said. He took out a handkerchief and wiped the sweat from his face.

Cindy took Austin's arm. "Sure you're okay?"

"Yeah fine." He put the handkerchief back in his pocket.

Chris walked back to the kitchen. "Austin wants a soda water and lemon."

"What, no bourbon?" Robert asked.

"Nope, just soda water and lemon."

Robert leaned his body and looked out to the living area where Cindy and Austin were talking. "Well, maybe he's turning over a new leaf now that he's met someone."

"Well, that's pretty premature, don't you think?"

Robert nodded his head for Chris to look around the corner.

Chris took a peek. "Maybe you're right."

Cindy and Austin were sitting on the sofa in the living room. She leaned in and took his hand. "It's okay," she said.

"Thanks." He knew that whatever veil he thought he successfully conceived was now lost. "Sorry, just got a bit flustered for some reason."

Cindy smiled. "That happens sometimes."

Chris and Robert came from around the corner. "Dinner is served," Robert announced.

Chris came over and handed Austin a soda water. "This will help," he whispered.

The dinner went well as everyone chatted about their day. Chris and Robert filled the conversation about their design work.

The small talk was a relief for Austin as it took his mind off things. He leaned back in his chair. "I can't believe I ate so much."

Robert pointed to what was left on the table. "I have more."

"Are you kidding me, I couldn't eat another thing."

They all were sitting at the dining table when Robert looked at Austin and Cindy. "So, what are you two up to?"

"Well, we're having a good time talking with Papa John," Cindy replied.

"How's the interview going?" Chris asked.

"Well, I thought things were going well but then he got really quiet this morning for some reason," Austin responded.

Chris shook his head. "What do ya mean?"

"Well, I found something in the journal that I thought was interesting, but it didn't appear that Papa John wanted to talk about it."

"What did you find?" Robert asked.

"A map."

"What kind of a map?" Chris asked.

"Specifically, it's a map of Tokyo with some lines and a circled area."

"Maybe it's just something that he collected when he was on the ship," Chris replied.

"Yeah, that's what he alluded to but his whole demeanor changed when I unfolded it and showed it to him," Austin said.

"Yeah, I noticed that too. His expression almost gave the impression that he was surprised to see it," Cindy said.

Robert chimed in. "Well, again, maybe it's nothing but a souvenir of some kind."

Austin leaned forward with a serious expression. "Yeah, but it has his writing on it."

"What does it say?" Chris asked.

"There's a date with words written across the top, but it's definitely his handwriting."

"What's written on it?" Robert asked.

"Honestly, I glanced at it, but the date is nineteen forty-five and the top says something about Sundown," Austin replied.

"So, on the map, what's circled," Robert asked.

"It's a large circle that encompasses a few towns, but the Chiyoda District is in the center, so I think that's the reference point."

Robert shrugged his shoulders. "Well maybe there's a simple answer."

Austin shook his head in agreement. "Maybe, but I have a feeling that there's more to this story than meets the eye."

"Why do you say that?" Cindy asked.

"I can't put my finger on it, but something seems off. I just think there's more to him then we know," Austin replied.

Chris chuckled. "Really? You don't think he was part of something clandestine do you? Papa John, seriously?"

Austin shrugged. "Maybe you're right. I guess it's the reporter thing in me, but he did mention a special military training in boot camp but every time I bring it up, he changes the subject."

Robert got up and started clearing the table. "Well, it's probably nothing. Anyway, he's the last living veteran of World War two and that's a big story in and of itself."

Austin looked at Cindy. "Has Papa John ever said anything to you about Japan or anything special he may have done while he was on the *Ticonderoga*?"

"Nothing that I can remember. He just talks about some of the battles he was in and about working with a special group of men, but I never really paid much attention to anything in particular."

"Special group of men?" Austin asked. "What special group of men?"

"He never said much, just that he was part of a special group when he was in the Navy. I figured it was while he was on the ship in the engine room. He never elaborated on anything, so I didn't pursue it," she replied.

"Interesting," Chris said. "You don't think he was more than what he's been saying for all these years, do you?"

"Who knows, but I think the journals will tell us more," Austin replied.

Chris frowned. "If he wanted to keep everything a secret, then why in the world would he have given you anything that would expose him?"

"Good question, maybe he didn't think that I'd really do any digging or maybe he wants to tell us something that he's never told anyone, to tell you the truth, I really don't know."

"Well, if he wanted to clear his conscious, I'd think he'd just come out and tell you," Chris said.

"I get it but sometimes it's not that simple. People hold things back for various reasons; maybe it's because they don't think it's a big deal or maybe they'd feel embarrassed if something came out."

"Wow, wouldn't that be something if there was more to Papa John than we know."

Cindy was trying to recall all the discussions that she's had over the years. *Did Papa John say anything that would help Austin?*

Robert was looking down at his phone as he came out of the kitchen. "Hey, I was curious about the Chiyoda District and decided to look it up."

Chris winked at Austin. "He's always the consummate researcher," he said.

Robert looked up from his phone. "Austin, did you look this place up?"

"No, actually I was going to do that but haven't gotten to it yet, what did you find?"

"Well, it's interesting. You said that Papa John had a map with a line and a circled area, correct?"

"Yeah, not sure what it means."

"Well, it's a sacred place. It also happens to be where the Emperor of Japan's palace is located."

Everyone looked at one another; the room suddenly went silent.

CHAPTER

17

ustin's mind was flooded with emotions as he drove back to the hotel. He was taken by Cindy's compassion and felt she knew more than she was letting on about the burden he was carrying. He was also thinking about John's connection with the map and the emperor's palace. As he entered his room, he was joined by a companion he had thought he could ignore – a bottle of bourbon he had purchased.

He unbuttoned his shirt then reached for the bottle and unscrewed the top. He grabbed a glass and clenched the bottle. It had always been easy to pour a drink in a glass, but he knew that one led to another and then to another.

Austin stared at the ceiling, *please make it go away*, he whispered as he closed his eyes in prayer. He looked back down, put the glass on the table and resealed the bottle; *not now*, he said to himself in a defiant voice. Then he looked over at the journals and refocused. *Chiyoda District, there must be something to all of this*, he mumbled.

He walked over and picked up the journals and laid down on the bed. He started looking through the pages, now more focused on what each was saying. He pulled out the map, opened it and laid it beside him. *There must be something in here that would make sense.*

The first journal was much of what John had told him; information about his boot camp training and about Evelyn. But he was still puzzled by the map. *Come on, give me something,* he whispered.

He finished the first journal and opened the second one hoping to have something jump out, but John's notes continued to talk about his shipmates and his daily routines with chow and drills. *Maybe there is something here and I can't see it.*

Then he started to scrutinize each page to see if John's notes had any subtle change. He was about halfway through the second journal when his phone rang. It was Anthony. "Hey Anthony, what's up?"

"I know it hasn't been that long, but how are things going with John?"

"Things are going along fine, why'd ya ask?"

"Well, I need you back here. We have more things happening with the state investigation. Apparently, some of the things you initially uncovered led to the discovery of some irregularities by a few politicians in the governmental contracting processes. Shit Austin, this could ultimately lead to the governor's mansion. I need you to get things wrapped up down there and get your ass back up here."

"Well, I think there's a bigger story to John beyond being the last living veteran," Austin said.

"Listen, I get it, but don't try to find something that's not there. Face it Austin, he's just an old man that fought in a war that few will likely remember. If he weren't the last living vet, then there wouldn't be any story at all. I don't want to be an ass about this, but just get a few quotes from him, write a quick story, and get back here."

"I get it, but I still think there's more to John's story."

"Listen, man, you gotta get real. You're trying too hard to find something that's not there. Just wrap it up and pack your bags."

"But Anthony…"

"Austin, just get it done."

"Okay. Just give me a few more days so I can get what I can from John, and I'll send you a draft."

"Thanks, by the way, how are things going down there? Are you keeping yourself focused?"

"Yep, staying focused." Austin understood the inference.

"Okay, take care of yourself and we'll talk soon."

Austin sat at the edge of the bed. *Damn, I know there is something here, I just have a feeling.* He had gut feelings before, and he was usually right.

Austin changed into his shorts and a t-shirt and made some of the hotel's terrible coffee. He figured he was going to spend a good part of the night looking through the journals. He got up from the bed, grabbed the journals, sat at the worktable tucked in the corner of the room, clicked on the light, and slowly started reading every page. The content didn't vary much and mainly focused on the daily routines on the *Ticonderoga*. He was beginning to think that Anthony was right; there isn't anything here. He was at the end of the second journal when he noticed an interesting note that John had made about a small group of men. He thought about what Cindy said and figured the group were his shipmates in the engine room, but something stood out. He read the entry: *This evening we were given our orders and will start training tomorrow.*

Austin rubbed his chin. *What orders could they have been given?* He continued reading; *we'll be training for an amphibious landing tomorrow and then special weapons next week. I hope everything goes well. This could be big.*

Austin started running his fingers through his hair. *Why would an engine room operator need to be trained for a landing with a small group of men and why special weapons training?*

He continued reading: *We're meeting with the CO tomorrow for mission clarification: Smitty, Ghost, Jaws and I will be provided more detail on the landing. Operation Sundown will either make a difference in the war or we'll be dead."*

"What the…!" he said, then walked over to the bed and grabbed the map. He looked at the faded writing that was at the top, he squinted to see the words that had faded over the years. He pulled the map closer to the light to get a better look and there they were…*Operation Sundown*. His heart started racing; he opened the third journal when there was a knock on the door.

73

CHAPTER

18

Austin's attention was focused on the journals when he opened the door. "What!" he yelled. There she was, standing there. Austin was shocked and surprised - pleasantly surprised.

"I'm sorry Austin, but I was out for a drive and just…"

Austin interrupted. "Cindy, uh, I mean, I wasn't expecting you. I'm sorry, please come in."

The weather was chilly by Florida winter standards and a cold breeze rushed in.

"I am so sorry to come here. I know that this was the last thing that you were expecting," Cindy said.

"No, please, I am happy that you're here. I just wasn't expecting anyone, so I apologize for my attire." He glanced down at his t-shirt, shorts, and no shoes.

Cindy started pacing. "I am so sorry, maybe I should leave. I don't know what I was thinking. This was a bad idea. I can't believe I came here."

Austin could sense how uneasy she was feeling; he wanted to calm her down. "Seriously, it's great that you're here...." he paused. "Truly, I'm glad that you came this evening."

Cindy stopped pacing but was visibly uneasy. "I don't know what I'm doing here. I've never done anything like this in my life."

Austin reached for her hands and held them. "Please, I'm actually glad you're here. I don't know but this evening at Chris and Robert's was one of the most enjoyable evenings I've had in a very long time."

They stood there for a moment looking at one another. Cindy could see the sincerity in Austin's face.

"Where's my manners. Can I get you a cup of coffee?"

"Sure, I'd love some."

"Gotta warn ya, it's pretty bad."

Cindy smiled and sat down by the table; she noticed the full bourbon bottle on the table.

He poured some coffee in a Styrofoam cup and handed to her. She frowned and shook her head in disgust. "You're right, this is terrible."

He laughed as he sat next to her. "Told ya, never doubt a reporter."

Silence lingered as each tried to form their thoughts. Austin broke the uneasiness; he leaned forward putting his arms on his knees holding the coffee with each hand. "Cindy, I want to thank you for your understanding this evening at Chris's, I know I made things uncomfortable for you."

Cindy gave a puzzled expression. "I don't know what you're talking about."

Austin lowered his head and looked at the floor. "I don't know how to put it; I guess I haven't had someone that I've felt comfortable with in a long time and - I don't know - I guess I've been trying to hide from the world for so long that I forgot what it was like to be with someone like you."

She leaned forward, held his hands, and whispered, "it's alright, I understand." She leaned back and inadvertently glanced again at the bourbon bottle.

Austin took note. "Yeah, that, well, I guess that's been my only friend for the last few years. It's always been there to help me forget things."

"Does it work?"

Austin slowly shook his head. "No, but it doesn't judge."

"No one's judging you Austin. Sometimes it helps if you have someone to talk to."

"Maybe." He paused, something started to stir inside, an emotion he kept buried. "You know it's really nice that you came here this evening."

"I shouldn't have bothered you... I.. I really should be going." Cindy got up.

Austin reached over, "No! please don't."

"Okay." Cindy slowly sat down, caught by Austin's insistence.

He looked over at the bourbon bottle and then to Cindy. She noticed him starting to choke up. "Are you okay?" she whispered.

Austin sniffed and rubbed his nose with his sleeve. "Sorry, not very gentlemanly like."

"That's okay," Cindy said.

"You asked me if I had a family once, I did. Back in Middlebury, I was married to my boss's sister – and Chris's sister – her name was Teresa. We met when I came back home from college and married shortly thereafter; things were nice. After a few years we had a beautiful daughter; we named her Mandy." Austin paused for a moment. Cindy could see emotion starting to emerge.

"She was an angel." He smiled as if she was standing in front of him. "She was an only child and was a daddy's girl. I used to call her sweet pea." He chuckled. "She hated that when I called her that as a teenager. She'd say 'quit that daddy, I'm not a baby anymore'," Austin chuckled again. "You know, never tell a father that because we'll continue doing it." He gave a reflective smile.

Cindy sat in silence as he continued.

"Well anyway, Teresa and I were worried about her. Her mood seemed to change when she entered high school, but we wrote it off as a teenager thing. We never really probed into why she was so sad all the time." Austin cleared his throat. "I was stupid, I just was too naïve to figure it out," he said emphatically.

Cindy sensed Austin's manner change to self-anger.

"I should have asked! Why didn't I ask!" he said looking at Cindy. She said nothing, it wasn't a question.

Austin pulled a tissue from a box on the table and wiped his nose. He looked down recalling the moment as he spoke. "One night we tried to get Mandy to join us for dinner, but she was holed up in her room and wouldn't come out. I didn't do anything and figured she wasn't hungry. After a while, Teresa told me to go check on her. She had the door locked so I knocked on it a few times, she never answered. After a few more times, I got pissed that she was ignoring me so I busted the door open." Austin paused again; Cindy could see that he was having a hard time reliving that moment.

"Mandy was lying in the bed, motionless. I shook her a few times thinking she was asleep but I could tell by her color that she wasn't breathing. I tried CPR and we called 911. The paramedics came and took her away, Teresa was screaming, and I didn't know what to do."

Austin looked at Cindy. She had an understanding expression and one of sympathy. "It's okay," she said.

He paused to catch his breath. "She died at the hospital." He sat silently.

Cindy reached over and held his hands. "I'm so sorry," she gently whispered.

"When we got home from the hospital, we found an empty bottle of pills on her bed table that she must've taken some time that night. We also found a note that she wrote telling us that she couldn't take life anymore. That her sadness was too much. That she loved us and for us not to blame ourselves, that she was in a better place." Austin rubbed the tears from his eyes.

It was a few minutes before he could say anything more. He took a deep breath and exhaled. "Anyway, it was about a year after that, that Teresa and I divorced. Our relationship was never the same and we just stopped living for one another. I guess, that happens, and it was really my fault. I started drinking heavily and couldn't focus on anything anymore. I guess I never really stopped trying to numb my feelings. I can't get the thought of Mandy in that bed out of my mind, except when I use my friend here." He pointed to the bourbon bottle.

"I can't imagine what you're going through. I just..." she stopped.

Austin leaned back in his chair. "I haven't told anyone this before. I don't know, I guess I thought that keeping it inside was the manly thing to do."

Cindy reached out and took his hands. "No, you did the manly thing. You took the step that I think you always wanted, but never thought you had the strength to do."

Austin squeezed her hands then rubbed his eyes. "Whooa, that was tough," he said, as he exhaled.

"I'll be here for you, whenever you need me."

He reached over and caressed her face. "You have no idea..."

Cindy reached up and held his hands to her cheeks.

"Thank you," he said.

Cindy smiled, took another sip of coffee, gave a repeated frown, and choked.

Austin laughed, "Didn't get any better did it."

Cindy shook her head and coughed, "No."

CHAPTER

19

C indy put the coffee down. "I should be going,' she said, as she stood to leave. Austin got up and took her hands. "Please, I'm happy you're here… look, let me show you something." He took her over to the worktable where the journals and the map were laid out.

"Look here," he said, as he pointed to a page. "Here's an entry about Papa John and three men that were being trained for a special operation. Check out the reference."

Cindy looked at what he was pointing to. "*Operation Sundown,* what do you think that is?" she asked.

Austin pulled the map under the light so she could see it better. "Look here at the top, it says the same thing, *Operation Sundown,* and in small print it has the date, May twenty-fifth." Then he pointed. "See this line and the circle here?"

"Yes?"

"It goes from the coast of Tokyo to the Chiyoda District. Remember? Robert found out that that's the location of the emperor's palace."

"You don't think Papa John was involved with anything bad, do you?" Cindy asked.

"I don't know but I think that he had something to do with either capturing or killing the emperor," Austin replied.

"Papa John? He couldn't hurt anyone. He's so gentle, he couldn't do anything like that!"

"I don't disagree, but times were different then. I don't know what he had to do with anything, but he has this map, it's his handwriting on the top. What else could it mean?"

Cindy stood there in astonishment. "Seriously?"

"Yeah, my hunch is that John was more than an engine room worker, I think he was in a unique special ops group of some kind. This could be big! Can you imagine what this would uncover? There's nothing in US history that indicates that we tried to take out the emperor. This could really change things if people knew what we were trying to do. Maybe, just maybe, this was an option that the US thought could end the war early. Just think, if we captured or killed the emperor, the war would have been over," Austin said.

"Yeah, but wouldn't that make the Japanese even more determined to continue fighting?" Cindy asked.

"Maybe, but the emperor was the head of the Japanese people; whatever he said would be taken as gospel. If he said the war was over or if he were dead, the Japanese army would have little reason to continue fighting."

"I don't understand, wouldn't someone just fill his spot like when Roosevelt died?"

"The Japanese culture is different. I doubt that anyone would have replaced the emperor; he was the head of state, so without him there's no rallying cry for the people to follow."

Cindy shook her head. "I don't know, it seems strange that the US would put their hopes on four men from a navy ship. I just can't see Papa John being part of a group like that, especially if they were to actually kill someone; he just wouldn't do that."

"I get it. I don't see him as someone that would be part of a mission as gutsy as this one either, but things aren't often as they appear," Austin said. "Well, I've got to talk with him tomorrow, maybe I can find something out."

Cindy's expression changed. "Austin, I am worried about him. He seems to be declining and getting weaker every day."

"I hope that I am not putting pressure on him, I mean, I don't want him to feel compelled to tell me anything or…"

Cindy interrupted, "No, he enjoys talking with you. I think he wants to tell you something. I haven't said anything to him about being the last veteran of the war yet, but he really likes you and so do I."

Austin paused for a moment and looked at Cindy. He felt the same way although he had a stronger word. He leaned in and kissed her. The kiss was soft and gentle; they continued until the moment became passionate. Austin picked her up and gently laid her on the bed. They continued kissing one another as they undressed. The evening went on as they made love to one another late into the night. They finally fell asleep after several hours.

It was early morning when Cindy awoke and looked over at Austin, who was fast asleep. She kissed him on the forehead and slipped out of bed and got dressed. She walked over to the table where a journal laid open. She flipped a few pages to see if there was anything that she could make out beyond what Austin had told her; she didn't see anything. She opened one of the other journals and noticed that at the top righthand side of the inside cover, in small print, were the letter and numbers, J - 3 - 5. She didn't know what it could reference and closed the book. She looked over at Austin again, she knew that she was falling for him and hoped he felt the same way.

She bent over and picked up her shoes and gently opened the door and closed it behind her. She had a sick feeling in the pit of her stomach thinking that what she had done by coming to Austin's room was wrong. She had never done anything like it, but then again, she never had feelings for anyone as she had for him. She got in her car and headed home.

CHAPTER

20

C indy arrived home and looked in on her grandfather; he was asleep. She began to think about what Austin had said about the special operations team. *Could it be true?*

She went into the kitchen and prepared a pot of coffee then walked into the living room, sat down, and started recalling the evening. She still felt guilty about surprising Austin in his room but smiled when she thought about their evening together. She wasn't certain about Austin, but she knew how she felt.

Austin awoke to find himself alone in bed. *Cindy?* he mumbled as he rubbed his eyes. He gathered himself and figured that she had slipped out. He laid there looking up at the ceiling. It had been a long time since he had the feelings for someone as strong as he did for her. He pulled himself up, looked at the other side of the bed and smiled, then reached for his phone.

Cindy's cell phone rang. "Hello?"

Austin was balancing his phone to his ear as he hurriedly got dressed. "Cindy?"

"Oh, hello Austin." She hadn't yet recognized the number and was startled by his early morning call.

"Do you mind if I come over now? I want to get started talking with John about the stuff we found in the journal last night."

"He's still asleep but I am sure that he'll be happy to talk with you."

No one said anything. Neither wanted to be the first to address what had happened.

Austin finally broke the silence. "Thanks. I should be there in about an hour."

"Okay, I'll get Papa John ready for you." She was surprised by Austin's business-like conversation. *Did last night not mean anything? Was it just a one-night stand for him?* She started thinking that she had made a horrible mistake.

Austin clicked off the phone and started putting everything in his briefcase. He walked around smiling with more pep in his walk then he had in years. He felt compelled to come clean about how he really felt about Cindy but was worried that she might think things were happening too fast. *Wait, we just slept together, how can she think that things are happening too fast.*

He pulled everything together and hurriedly walked out the door, then looked down and noticed that he hadn't buttoned his shirt correctly.

CHAPTER

21

Austin drove to Cindy's house and pulled up in the driveway. She was on the front porch as she had been in the past. Austin could see her standing there but she looked anxious. *This doesn't look good*, he said. He put the car in park and headed up the driveway. The excitement that he had when he left his hotel room was now tempered by her expression.

Austin slowly walked up the stairs. "Hey, is everything okay?"

"Can we talk?" Cindy asked.

"Sure."

"Austin, about last night. I am not sure what we did was a good idea. I mean, I just don't know what I was thinking. I shouldn't have come to you like I did. I just wanted to say…"

Austin sensed her uneasiness and interrupted. "Can we talk over here?"

They walked over to the corner table on the porch and sat in adjacent chairs. Austin gently took Cindy's hands.

"Last night was the most wonderful thing. I never thought I'd ever feel that way again," he said.

Cindy's expression changed from concern to hope.

"I guess, I've been upset at the world for a long time, but I don't know, something's changed in me since I arrived here, and I know it was you," he continued.

Cindy smiled.

"My heart stopped when I first saw you and I couldn't even carry on a coherent conversation; I felt like a bumbling idiot."

Cindy laughed.

"Listen, I haven't felt anything in a long time, and I always just seem to push people away."

Cindy squeezed Austin's hands.

"I am not very good at this." He paused. "I guess what I'm trying to say is that I can't imagine being without you."

Cindy's eyes started welling.

"I feel the same way," she said. "I was so scared. I didn't know how you felt and then after last night; well, I felt ashamed of myself. I've never done anything like that before. Then this morning you didn't say anything. I don't know, I guess I thought you didn't have feelings for me."

Austin laughed and pointed to his shirt. "Are you kidding, you should've seen me this morning. I couldn't even dress myself; the buttons were all screwed up. I looked like some kind of idiot. When I rolled over and you weren't there all I could think of was getting here this morning."

"I am so happy being with you. I can't imagine being without you," she said.

"Ditto."

Cindy lightly punched him in the arm. "You're a writer and that's the most romantic thing you could come up with?" She got up, pulled Austin from the chair, and put her arms around him. "I guess we should head inside and talk with Papa John. He's up and having his morning coffee."

"How's he doing?"

Cindy took on an anxious expression. "Like I said last night, I am worried about him. I'm not sure but he appears to be getting weaker."

"Well, I'm here to help in any way that I can."

"Thank you, that's so wonderful of you to offer."

They started toward the front door. Austin was happy that he finally had the courage to tell Cindy how he felt, but then he started to remember his conversation with Anthony. *I need you back here*, were the words rumbling around in his head.

Austin followed Cindy inside to see John sitting in his chair sipping his coffee using both hands. She was right, he looked frail. Austin sat in his usual place on the sofa and started to pull out the journals and his pad. John looked over but didn't smile as he usually did when they got together.

CHAPTER

22

Austin was concerned about John's demeanor. He looked much more serious than he had in the past and wasn't certain what to make of it. He pulled the journals and map from the briefcase as sat them to the side then flipped the papers on his yellow pad to begin taking notes.

John looked at the journals and then to Austin. "What did ya' find in the journals?"

"Well, there's a lot I don't understand based on what you've told me so far," Austin replied.

John looked down and took another sip of his coffee.

"For example, the map that I found that has a line and circle over an area in Tokyo called Chiyoda District, that I've since learned is where the emperor's palace was located during the war. And the map has the words *Operation Sundown* written on it."

John continued sipping his coffee as Austin pushed on.

"You referenced an operations military team." Austin flipped back a few pages on his pad.

Cindy came in from the kitchen and sat next to Austin as he continued. "John, I'm not sold on the fact that you spent all your time as an engineer in the engine room when you were on the *Ticonderoga*. From what I'm gleaning from your journals so far, I get the feeling that you had something to do with a special mission in Japan, specifically in the Chiyoda District. There's also a date in small print, written on the map." Austin started asking more direct questions. There was no time to wait for John to volunteer information that he needed to get the story done. He pressed on.

"John, who were Smitty, Ghost and Jaws? And what's the importance of May twenty-fifth, nineteen forty-five?

John remained motionless in the chair, looking down at his coffee cup. Cindy and Austin looked at one another. It was unusual for him to be so quiet. He coughed a few times then took a napkin and wiped around his mouth and then around his eyes.

John gazed forward with a faraway look. "Petey, Jimmy and Franky were great men. I haven't heard those names since the war," he said. "We made-up nicknames for everyone for various reasons, it was a label that stuck with you throughout the war."

Cindy reached over and put her hands on Austin's as John continued. "We named Pete 'Smitty' because his last name was Jones, not sure why we did that, but it was funny at the time. We called Jimmy Peterson 'Ghost,' because his skin was so white that we figured that he hadn't seen the sun in a long time. Franky Balboa was nicknamed 'Jaws,' because he never stopped talking." John smiled and continued looking straight ahead as if they were all standing in front of him. He looked over to Austin and Cindy; he noticed she was holding Austin's hand.

She looked at her grandfather. "What did they call you?"

"Bullseye," John replied.

"Bullseye.... why Bullseye?"

"I was the sharp-shooter."

"Who was in command of your group?" Austin asked, as he was quickly jotting everything down on his yellow pad.

"Captain Burton." John paused and looked at the bookcase and then back at Austin. "He was a great man, one of the best leaders I've ever known, he was such a great man," he said, as his voice quivered.

Cindy looked to Austin with a puzzled expression. She had many conversations with John about his war time experiences but he never said anything like this before.

"So, you weren't an engine room guy in the navy, were you." Austin asked.

John looked over. "I gave you the journals so that you could write your story, I don't think that it's important what I did during the war. There are others that can give you a better story than I can."

Cindy slid over to John, knelt next to him, and put her hands on his. "There aren't anymore," she said in a quiet tone.

"What do you mean?"

Cindy looked at Austin; he nodded.

"Papa John, you're the last living World War two veteran. After you, there's no one that can tell us a story," she said.

John looked at Cindy trying to take in the words. He knew he had been around for a long time but being the last living veteran made him feel confused and sad. "I'm the last?"

Cindy slowly rubbed his hands. "Yes."

There was silence, no one wanted to say anything. They had just laid something on John that he hadn't expected, who could have imagined being the last of the greatest generation. Cindy and Austin looked at one another wondering what was going on in John's head.

"The last," he mumbled.

Austin waited a moment to let the news sink in. "John, are you okay?"

He cleared his throat. "I'm fine."

"John, from what I understand so far, it appears that you were a lot more than an engineer. There could be a great story here but I need to understand what you did during the war so I can get it in print."

"I don't know if it would be a good idea for anyone to know about what I did," John said in a defiant voice.

"Why?" Cindy asked.

John didn't say anything and just sat there. Cindy and Austin looked at one another. They knew that they had just laid some heavy news on him.

Austin waited a moment and continued. "John, were you really assigned to be an engine room sailor on the *Ticonderoga*?"

"Yes....and No," he replied.

"What'd you really do during the war?" Austin asked.

John glanced at the journals and noticed that there were four of them. "It was a difficult time back in those days. I had enlisted because I wanted to be a part of something big. I was young and impressionable. When I was in training, I was asked to take a test. I didn't know what it was, but I figured it was to see what I was good at. I didn't really have any experience in anything in particular. I guess the test was something about intelligence and other things. I don't remember much of it but all I know is that I was pulled aside and asked to take more tests."

Austin was quickly writing down everything John was saying.

John coughed a few times and cleared his throat. "I was told to go see this Colonel about some training with a special group. I had no idea what was going on, but I did what I was instructed. I went through some more training, and I guess I must've impressed them because they made me go through more tests."

"What were these tests? Do you remember?" Austin asked.

"There were some geography tests and physical things I had to do like run through obstacle courses and jump out of planes."

"Jump out of planes?"

John shook his head, "Yep, they trained us to parachute out of a plane."

"Were there others?" Cindy asked.

Austin grinned remembering what Cindy had said that day by the river about wanting something more in life. *So, nothing exciting in your life, huh.*

"Yes, but only a few of us were chosen," John continued.

"Chosen for what?" Austin asked.

"All I knew was that they told us that we were going to be part of a group that no one knew existed," John replied. "They said it was for a special mission."

"Wait! A special mission; would that have been *Operation Sundown?*" Austin reached over, grabbed the map, and held it up. "Was this what you were being trained for?"

There was a long pause as John stared at the map. "Yes," he replied.

Austin put down the writing pad and leaned in. "Do you know what the group was?"

"I was told that it was part of a new organization that had been formed a few years back and that I was not to tell anyone about it."

Cindy leaned in. "Do you remember the name of the organization?"

John paused as if he was reluctant to say anything, but he did. "It was called the OSS."

"OSS, you mean the Office of Strategic Services!" Austin exclaimed. He looked at John who sat emotionless. "Shit, you were with the OSS?!"

Cindy's face noted that she was clueless. "What's the OSS?"

Austin stared at John as he answered Cindy's question. "OSS was an intelligence agency for the US during the war, it was ultimately dismantled but it set up to what was to become the CIA."

Cindy straightened up as if jolted. "CIA! Papa John were you a spy?"

John looked at Cindy and then at Austin and remained defiant to answer the question that by his actions, he answered.

"Holy Shit!" Austin mumbled.

CHAPTER

23

nthony received an outline of what Austin had uncovered about John. He wasn't certain whether he was reading fact or fiction. If what he was reading was correct, it would be compelling and equally interesting for the public to learn. But for the moment, time was of importance and clarity as to some of John's story would take time to evolve. What was paramount, was that he needed Austin back in Middlebury. Anthony took out his phone and punched in the number.

Austin picked up the phone. "Well, what'd ya think?"

"I'm not sure. It looks like you have a start to a pretty interesting story. So, John was part of the OSS?"

"Well, that's what we uncovered so far but we think there is more to it," Austin replied.

"We?"

"Well, Cindy's been helping me uncover a few things."

"Cindy? That's John's granddaughter, right?"

"Yeah, she's been very helpful."

"I bet she has," Anthony chuckled.

Austin chuckled as well.

"I'm not sure how this is going to unfold. The OSS thing could end up being nothing or it could be something. But I thought you were focused on John being the last survivor of the war, wouldn't that be more significant at this point?"

"Yeah, but there could be an even bigger story. Just think, the last survivor is an OSS agent and perhaps was a part of something that could redefine some part of history."

Anthony picked up on Austin's enthusiasm. "Okay, try to get this wrapped up quickly because I need you back here soon. I'll give you another week to get things buttoned up. And Austin?"

"Yeah?"

"Good job."

"Thanks." He smiled and hung up the phone. He hadn't heard those words in a long time.

Austin was sitting at the end of the bed reading through his notes. He knew that he was on to something, he could feel it in his bones, but he also knew that John was not going to easily divulge anything. He wanted to make sure that he would be asking the right questions. He also was thinking about having to return to Middlebury. Suddenly his cell phone rang.

"Hello?"

"Austin, I think there's something wrong with Papa John," Cindy said in a panicked tone.

"What is it?"

"I don't know, he's weak and having difficulty breathing. It's scaring me."

"Call 911! I'll be right over!"

Austin arrived to see the ambulance outside the house. Chris and Robert had come over to see what was going on.

"How's he doing?" Austin asked.

"I'm not sure. Cindy's in the room with the paramedics and John," Chris replied.

"I hope everything's okay." Robert said.

Cindy came out of the room, ran up and embraced Austin. The moment was not lost on Chris or Robert.

"How is he?" Austin asked.

"I don't know, they had a hard time getting him to breathe normally. It was like he was having a heart attack or something," Cindy replied.

Austin could see the concern on Cindy's face. "I'm sure he'll pull through this. He's a tough cuss."

"I know, you're right. I just promised Mom that I'd take care of him."

"I think your mom knows that you've done a great job of that."

The paramedics came out with John on the stretcher; he was conscious.

"We're going to take him to the hospital to run some tests; everything appears to be normal at the moment, but we just want to be sure," the one paramedic said.

"Okay, we'll be there shortly," Cindy replied.

As the stretcher passed, John looked up and grabbed Austin's hand. The paramedics stopped. "You take care of her," he whispered.

Austin held onto John's hands. "I will, but you're coming back here to tell me the rest of the story."

"Look for the fifth," John struggled to say as the paramedics started rolling him out to the ambulance. "Look for the fifth," he repeated.

The fifth, mumbled Austin. *What's he talking about?*

Cindy took Austin's hand. "I need to go to the hospital to be with him. Will you take me?"

"Sure."

Cindy left to gather a few things and returned. "Thank you for being here," she said.

"I'll always be here for you," Austin replied.

Chris and Robert glanced at each other and smiled.

94

"We'll take care of things here; you two go and check on John," Chris said as Austin and Cindy headed out the front door.

"Cute couple," Robert said.

"It's about time she found someone," Chris replied.

CHAPTER

24

The drive to the hospital only took a few minutes; it was just a few miles from the house. Not much was said as they hurried into the driveway of the emergency room.

"I'm worried about him," Cindy said.

"He's lived through a lot. I'm sure he'll battle this just like he did with everything he's gone through," Austin said in a comforting and reassuring tone.

Austin pulled up to the entrance of the ER. Cindy got out and rushed in. He parked and walked into the emergency room waiting area to see Cindy standing there. She waved for him to come with her. She walked to a draped area and pulled back the curtains. John was laying there with oxygen tubes in his nose. He was unconscious and looked gray. Austin was concerned about his condition but didn't want to give that impression to Cindy.

"Hello, my name is Doctor Ballinger," said the ER doctor as she entered where they were standing. "All his vitals look good. We just want to run a few tests to make sure that everything is working right. We'll keep him here tonight and if everything checks out, we'll release him in the morning."

"Do you know what happened to him?" Cindy asked.

"We don't really know but at his age it could be anything. He's a strong man to have lived this long. He must have lived a special life."

Cindy smiled and held John's hand. "He sure has. Can I stay here with him tonight?"

"Unfortunately, we can't have anyone stay overnight in the ER. Ms. Davis, we'll take really good care of him. We'll call you if there's any change."

Austin put his arm around Cindy. "Thank you for all you've done for him doctor."

Cindy wanted to stay but she knew there was nothing more that she could do. She looked down at her grandfather, kissed him on the forehead and then she and Austin left for home.

It wasn't long before they arrived back at the house. Chris and Robert walked over when they saw Austin pull into the driveway.

Chris's face spoke to concern. "How's he doing?"

"He's doing better but he just looked so weak and frail laying there," Cindy replied in a quiet voice.

"He's a tough son of a bitch," Robert said.

Chris looked at Robert and slapped him on the arm. "Really?"

Austin looked over to Cindy. "When John was on the stretcher, he said something about looking for the fifth. Do you have any idea what he was talking about?" Austin asked.

"No, I don't. Why, is it important?" she replied.

"I don't know. He made it sound like it meant something – who knows, maybe it's nothing."

Austin walked to the bookshelf and started looking at the books that were neatly organized. He turned his head sideways to get a good look at the titles. He was rubbing his fingers across the binders when he noticed a book titled, *The Artifacts of the Emperor.* It didn't particularly stand out for any reason except for a red bookmarker sticking out at the top. He pulled the book from the shelf and opened it to the section that had been marked. He didn't notice anything significant, just that a page had a red book marker stuck to it. Austin started reading but didn't take note of anything.

So why this? Austin mumbled.

"What did you say?" Robert asked.

"Oh nothing, I just came across a book that had a bookmarker on a page. There's nothing noted so not sure if it's anything material," Austin replied.

"Really? I don't think John does anything without some thought to it. What's on the page that's marked?"

"Well, there's a lot referencing Japanese history and antiquities but other than that, I don't see anything in particular."

"Interesting, wonder why that page was flagged?" Chris asked.

"Papa John was always researching things about the history of Japan," Cindy said. "He loved looking that stuff up."

"Any particular reason why this would be noted?" Austin asked.

"Not really," she replied.

"Do you mind if I take this with me?"

"I'm sure Papa John wouldn't mind."

"Interesting. I think there's got to be more to that than meets the eye," Robert said.

"You're always thinking there's more to everything," laughed Chris.

Robert looked at Austin. "Well, isn't the Emperor's Palace in the Chiyoda District and didn't the map that was in Papa John's journal have the Chiyoda District noted?"

"Yeah?" Austin replied.

"Well, maybe there's a connection."

'I guess there could be, who knows."

Cindy had ducked into the kitchen and popped her head out a few minutes later. "Austin? Would you like to have dinner here tonight?"

"I'd love to."

"I make a mean meatloaf."

"I can attest to the meatloaf; it's awesome," Robert said.

Chris looked at Robert and pointed to the door. "I think that we should exit now. If you kids need anything, just give us a call. We're only a few steps away."

Robert looked back at Austin. "I don't think that Papa John would have flagged that particular section unless there's something to it. I think you're the one that'll have to put the pieces together."

CHAPTER

25

Before the dinner, Cindy called the hospital to check on her grandfather. She was told that he was doing much better and would likely be able to come home the next day. Cooking was Cindy's way of relieving stress, and she was stressed. She had prepared her famous meatloaf dinner and served it up to a very hungry guest.

"Wow, you were right; you make a mean meatloaf," Austin said.

Cindy smiled as she wiped her lips with a napkin. "I'm glad you liked it."

Austin pushed his chair from the table. "Man, I could get used to this."

Cindy smiled again and got up to start clearing the dishes.

"Here, let me help." Austin grabbed a few glasses and utensils.

"Do you think there's anything to the book you found?" she said, as she stood holding some of the plates.

"I don't know but I think that Robert's right. There must be some connection between the map and that book. It's odd that it was the only book that I noticed that had a marker sticking out of it."

"Are you sure that was the only one?"

"I don't know but I have a week to find something."

Cindy stood frozen. "A week, what are you talking about?"

Austin felt a pit in his stomach. "Well, I gave Anthony a draft of what we've found so far, and he thought it was interesting but he needs me to get things wrapped up here so I can get back to Vermont."

"When were you going to tell me this?"

"I'm sorry, I was going to tell you…"

Cindy interrupted. "When?" She put the dishes down and retreated to the living room. Austin followed.

"You knew that I was going to have to go back to Middlebury at some point," he said.

"I know, I know, but I guess I was hoping that you'd stay longer," she replied.

"I want to, but… you know, I have to get back to my life in Vermont." Austin winced. "I mean, I have to return to Middlebury… "

Cindy cut him off, "I thought that maybe your life would be here now." She hesitated. "So, all that stuff you told me on the porch, was that real?"

"Yes, I really meant what I said."

"What about Papa John? Were you just going to abandon him after you finished your story."

"Well, things got complicated. I didn't think things would end up this way when I came down here."

"Complicated! Is that what you call it?"

"No, I don't mean it in a bad way, actually it's a good complicated." Austin knew he was grasping for straws.

Cindy turned and looked at him. "I love you, Austin!" she blurted. She walked into her bedroom leaving Austin standing there stunned. He knew it was time to leave.

Austin drove back to the hotel thinking along the way that he had blown the best thing going for him. He pulled in the parking lot and put the car in park. His mind was on Cindy's final words before she left him standing there.

He wished he had found the strength to tell her that he felt the same; now he had missed that opportunity. He slowly got out of the car and decided that he'd make a stop before retiring for the night.

"Hey, how's it going?" yelled Cal, as Austin walked into Bruno's.

"Fine," Austin replied, but his disposition spoke differently. He grabbed a chair at the bar.

Cal finished a conversation he was having with a customer and strolled up next to Austin. "You don't look fine," he said.

"Well, just wanted to come in one last time."

"One last time? You leaving?"

"Yeah, I've been told that I have to get back to Middlebury."

"Oh man, sorry to see you go,'" Cal said. "What about John and Cindy?"

Austin raised his eyebrows and shrugged.

Cal shook his head. "Oh… I'm guessing that it probably didn't go over well, did it?"

Austin pointed to a glass and nodded to the back of the bar with shelves filled with a variety of liquor. Cal hesitated but grabbed a bourbon bottle and a glass, poured a drink, and left for the kitchen.

Austin stared at the glass then reached for his cell phone and called Cindy; it went to voice mail. *I need this,* he justified to himself spun the glass on the bar.

Suddenly the phone rang. "Cindy?"

"Austin, this is Anthony," came the reply. "Listen, I know that I gave you a week, but I need you up here now. This investigation that we're doing is talking off and I need you to do some digging; this is right up your alley."

"But Anthony, I haven't finished John's story down here. I need the week; I think there is much more and…"

Anthony cut him off. "Yeah, yeah, I get it, but that OSS bit may not turn into anything and I'm not sure we should publish something that may not be accurate. You can make the changes and the finishing touches up here and we'll get it to print. It's just a character story anyway and, as I said before, I don't think people really care about World War two vets anymore."

Austin face twisted as he took in Anthony's words. "But…"

Anthony interrupted. "Hey buddy, pack your bags!"

"Okay," Austin got it; there was no debating. He picked up the glass and twirled the liquor inside, then looked over to the table where he and Gladys had dinner. He put the glass down and walked out.

CHAPTER

26

Austin returned to the hotel and started packing. He called Cindy again hoping that she'd answer, she didn't. "Hey, I just wanted to call and apologize. I really need to talk with you." He hesitated before he broke the news. "I also wanted to let you know that Anthony called and he needs me back in Middlebury sooner than we thought so I'm heading back there in the morning. Please, call me so I can explain everything." He held the phone to his ear for a few seconds before hanging up. He tossed the phone on the bed, turned, and saw the lonely bourbon bottle sitting on the table. He slowly strolled over and picked it up. Then he walked to the front door and set it outside.

The flight back to Vermont felt like an eternity. Austin had Cindy and John on his mind the entire time. All he could see out the window was the gray sky as the plane taxied to the gate. When he left baggage claim and walked out the front door to the awaiting taxi, a burst of cold air hit him.

"Welcome to Middlebury," said the cheery driver.

"Thanks," Austin grunted and then gave him directions home.

Austin looked out at the snow and bare trees as the driver left the airport. He paid no attention to the drive back to his place as the thought about the warm Florida weather, Cindy and John.

"We're here," said the driver, as he pulled up in front of Shamrock's.

Austin got out of the car, grabbed his bags, and walked into the Pub.

"Hey Austin, man, it's great to see you. Welcome home!" said an enthusiastic Shannon from the back of the bar.

"Thanks," Austin mumbled.

"Can I get you anything?"

Austin looked at his watch. It was 10:00 in the morning. In the past, it didn't matter what time it was before he had his first drink, but things were different now.

"No, but thanks. I'm just dropping my stuff off and heading to the office."

"No problem, I'll have one waiting for you when you return."

Austin didn't say anything and headed upstairs, dropped his bags, and immediately headed to work.

Austin walked into his office, sat at his computer, and just stared at it.

"Hey buddy, glad to see you made it back. Looks like you got some sun down there," Anthony said, as he walked over and shook his hand. "Man, we missed you here. Things have been heating up and we need your help in getting this investigation done."

"Well, I still have the story on John to finish up," Austin replied.

"Yeah, yeah, we'll get to that, but this is more important."

Austin turned his chair around and looked out the window at the dreary day. He knew he would miss everyone in Fort Myers; he just didn't realize how much.

The day seemed like it went on forever as Austin finally shut down his computer and grabbed his coat. He hadn't had to wear one for a while and could understand why people in Florida were so happy all the time. *Shorts and sandals in the middle of winter,* he mumbled to himself.

"What?" Anthony said, as he walked by his office.

"Nothing," Austin replied.

"Listen, thanks again for coming back. I know I dumped this story on you, but we really need to get this thing going and you're the one to do it."

"I know but I still want to finish the John story. If we don't get it done, somebody else will and we'll lose out."

"Listen, the draft you gave me about John was good. You know, I think you really found yourself down there."

You have no idea, Austin whispered.

"Go ahead and clean up your 'John' story but I'll need you to focus on this investigation. This could be big."

"Thanks, I appreciate it." He turned around again to look out the window.

Austin finished up a few things at the office and headed out for his drive back to Shamrock's. He entered to see the bar humming with people. Afterall, there wasn't much to do in the winter in Middlebury except drink, complain about the cold and argue about whatever sport was on at the time.

"Hey, you want your bourbon?" Shannon yelled over the noise.

Austin waved him off and headed up to his apartment. When he entered, he was taken by how messy it looked. *Geez, I'm a slob.*

He looked down at his phone hoping that there was a message or text from Cindy; there was nothing. He also wondered how John was doing. He wanted to reach out to Cindy again, but he had already left several messages with no return call. He sat down at the small kitchen table and took out the book that he had taken from John's shelf. He opened the section that had the bookmarker and started reading. He still had no clue why John would have flagged this particular page. *What's so important about this?* he whispered to himself.

He suddenly saw something lightly written in pencil on the side of the page that he had missed before. He turned the book sideways to get a better look at it; there it was, May 25, 1945. He grabbed his briefcase, pulled out the journals and map. He unfolded the map and there written on the side, May 25, 1945. Austin couldn't believe it.

A map of Chiyoda City, a special OSS operations team. Shit John, what were you involved with?

He went back to the fourth journal to see what it would tell him.

CHAPTER

27

C indy looked in on John; he was asleep but noticeably having a difficult time breathing. She walked back into the living room, sat on the sofa, and looked at the bookshelf where she imagined Austin standing looking through the books. It had been a week since he had left, and she missed having him around. She looked down at her phone, she wanted to return his calls but didn't know what to say; he was back home and perhaps that's where he needed to be.

"Cindy?" called John.

She got up and went to his bedside.

"Where's Austin?" he asked.

"He's not here right now," she replied.

"When's he coming back?"

"I'm not sure but I'll check."

She didn't want to tell him that Austin had left. She wanted him to focus on getting stronger. He looked frail and hadn't improved since returning from the hospital. Each day he looked weaker and weaker.

Cindy heard a knock at the front door. She left John and walked over and opened it. "Hey, Chris."

"How's John doing today?"

"He's really weak and he's sleeping at lot more. I'm starting to get worried."

"Well, he'll pull through this; he's always been a fighter."

"I know, you're right, I just don't know if he still wants to fight anymore."

"You have to stay strong for him. By the way, how are you holding up?"

Cindy didn't say anything. They both walked into the living room and sat down on the sofa.

Chris picked up on Cindy's mood. "You know, Austin hasn't been gone that long. Have you two talked?"

"No, he's left me messages, but I haven't returned any of his calls."

"Why not?"

"I don't know, I figured that he's happy back in Vermont."

"But you don't know that for sure, do you?"

"No, but…"

Chris interjected. "But what?"

Cindy didn't say anything. "I guess I probably overreacted when Austin said he was going back home," she said.

Chris didn't respond.

She looked down and quietly reflected. "I knew that he had to go back but after our evening together I thought he might change his mind."

Chris's eyebrows raised. "Evening?"

Cindy smiled, "Never mind."

He chuckled.

"I don't know, I guess I should've understood that Austin has a job to do and been more sympathetic about that."

"Uh huh," Chris uttered.

Cindy shook her head. "I guess I haven't been seeing things clearly lately, especially with Papa John's health. I know he misses Austin as much as I do. He keeps asking where he is."

Chris nodded. "We all miss him."

"I probably made him feel worse when I told him that I loved him just before he left."

"You said what!"

"Yeah, probably not a good thing to blurt out especially when he has one foot out the door."

"Well, do you?"

Cindy nodded affirmatively, "I do but I am not sure he feels the same. He said that he has feelings for me, but I don't know what that really means to him."

"Wow, I really think you've missed all the signs."

"What signs?"

Chris shook his head and chuckled a bit. "The guys crazy about you."

"What? How do you know that?"

"Listen, Austin's been part of my family for a long time. He's lost a lot, then he started drinking and basically gave up on life."

"Yeah, he told me about his daughter and your sister; it's so sad."

"So he told you about that." Chris said. "Well, that's good; so now you understand. He's blamed himself for what happened with Mandy. When he and Teresa split, he moved into a one-bedroom apartment over a bar in Middlebury and shut people out. My brother's been there for him but even he has had hard time getting Austin focused on anything. The guy used to be one hell of a reporter."

Cindy looked down and closed her eyes.

"I could tell when he met you that something clicked. Austin's pretty articulate but he was tongue-tied when he first saw you."

She looked up a smiled.

"We knew you guys had something when Robert and I saw you on the front porch."

She laughed and punched Chris on the arm. "So, you guys were watching us?"

"Well, we didn't mean too, we were just......well, it doesn't matter. Listen, I know Austin and he doesn't show emotion, but he has with you. I think you owe him a call. At least you'll know if it's meant to be. Right now, you're guessing. Girl, you just need to call him."

Cindy smiled again and grabbed Chris's hands.

"So let me know how it goes." He got up, hugged her, and left.

She walked into the other room picked up the phone. Her heart started pounding as she looked at Austin's number.

CHAPTER

28

The morning was gloomy and cold. For that matter every morning seemed like Groundhog Day in Middlebury. *How do people live in this,* Austin thought, as he left for the office. His perspective had changed having had the warm Florida winter to compare it against. But this particular morning he had a mission: John's journal entries, the map and date pointed to something much more compelling than being the last living veteran of a war. This was big and he knew it, he just needed to convince Anthony.

"Wow, I don't recall seeing you in here this early before," Anthony said, as Austin stopped by his office.

"Well, I was going through one of John's books last night and found something that I think may be big."

Anthony leaned back in his chair. "Come on Austin, we've been through this already. I get it but just write John's story and move on. I need you on this governor's investigation."

"Just listen to me, this could be a bigger story!"

Anthony was taken by Austin's insistence. He hadn't seen him this fixated on anything since his early investigation on the government contracts. He also picked up on Austin's appearance, he was noticeably not under the influence.

"Wait, let me show you something." Austin went to his office and collected the map, book, and journals. He plopped everything on Anthony's desk. "See look at this." He pointed to the corresponding dates on the map and book.

"So, the dates are the same, so what?" Anthony said, in an incredulous tone.

"I went through John's last journal, and it references that he was involved in a special operation in Japan near the end of the war, I'm sure that's the *Operation Sundown* that's noted here." Austin pointed to the corresponding references.

Austin grabbed the journal and started reading out loud: *Captain Burton ordered us to prepare for a mission in a place near Tokyo on the 23rd. All we know is that we're the only team for this mission. We've been told this will be big and that the Ticonderoga will get us there. They also said that she's been fitted specifically for this mission. I'm praying that I'll make it; I'm really nervous about this. I've heard what the Japanese do to prisoners. I hope I make it home to Evy.*

"Okay, sounds interesting but I'm not sure where you're going with this," Anthony said.

"The *Ticonderoga* is an aircraft carrier. They typically travel with a fleet for protection, like submarines, destroyers. I looked up the ship on Google to get some details of how it got to the Japanese coast on the date John noted in his journal. What I found out was that it wasn't in the Pacific at that time. It was in Pearl Harbor. I can only imagine that had to be modified in some way for this particular mission." Austin said.

"So?"

"This means that the ship was really somewhere near the Japanese coast for a special mission and the government rewrote history."

"Again, I don't get it."

"Well, I read the entire journal and it ends with John and his group preparing for some kind of mission; it has to be *Operation Sundown*. I don't know why that's the last of his entries. I'm not sure what specifically happened next but there's got to be something to all of this."

Anthony looked at the map and then to the book. "So what's the significance of the date and this Chiyoda district reference?" he asked.

Austin nodded his head, "Yeah, I looked up May twenty-fifth, nineteen forty-five and it appears that we bombed the hell out of Tokyo. From what I read it was rather brutal, and the Chiyoda District, well that's where the emperor's palace sits," Austin replied. "That has to be why the *Ticonderoga* was off the coast! So they could send in a aircraft to bomb the city and maybe the emperor!"

"Okay, so we bombed the place. Again, I don't see anything significant here."

"Jesus Christ Anthony! John was part of an OSS team, there's this raid on Tokyo, there's a map of where the emperor lived. It all points to something really big!"

Anthony looked down at the map and the journals again, shook his head from side to side. "I don't know, I'm not sure about this. It seems pretty farfetched that after all these years nothing has ever come up about any of this."

"I get it, but so much time has passed, it's probably been forgotten. Listen, this is something that I've gotta finish. Just let me go and see what I can find out. If it ends up just being a ghost hunt, then I'll come back and dedicate all my time to your investigation story."

"Well, I don't have anyone up here as good as you to do this kind of work."

Austin grinned. "Yes, you do.

Anthony chuckled; he knew what Austin was inferring. "Okay, I'll do what I can, but you better be right about this. Go ahead and finish with John. Also, let me know where you're staying. Hey, maybe Chris and Robert can take you in. You know we have a budget and I think you've overspent it on this story."

"Thanks Anthony, I really appreciate it." Austin gathered the journals, book and map and started back to his office.

"Austin?"

"Yeah?"

"I'll give you a few weeks to find something or we just go with the last living veteran story."

Austin nodded and gave Anthony a 'thumbs-up'. He was excited to get back to Fort Myers and finish the story and to see Cindy, that is, if she still wanted to see him again.

CHAPTER

29

Austin finished his day and walked into Shamrock's; Shannon waved him over. He'd been in-and-out of the bar since his return from Florida and hadn't spent any time with Shannon - and he hadn't had anything to drink.

"Man, I haven't seen you these past few weeks," Shannon said.

Austin sat at the bar, "Yeah, I'm sorry but I've been really tied up with this piece that I'm doing on a veteran in Florida."

"How's that going?" Shannon turned, grabbed a bottle of bourbon from the shelf, poured a shot in a glass and slid it in front of Austin.

"Okay I guess, there's a lot more to it than I thought."

"So how are you doing?"

"I'm fine, why do you ask?"

"Well, it's good to see that I'm not pouring you a drink first thing in the morning. I guess you prefer that crappy coffee at your office now," chuckled Shannon.

"Well, things kind of changed a bit when I was down there. I figured that it was probably time to get my act together," Austin replied.

Shannon smiled and nodded. "So, who is she?"

Austin scowled and cocked his head to the side. "What are you talking about?"

"Listen my friend, I've been behind this bar for a long time, and I've gotten pretty good at reading people. Now, I may have read you wrong but you're different. Granted, you're a bit tanner than the rest of us, which I'm jealous of by the way, but you're different."

"Really?"

"Yep, you're not drinking. Typically, I'd be upset cuz you're killing my sales but it's good to see that you're focused on something other than Mandy and Teresa."

What's with these bartenders, thought Austin as he sat there looking up a Shannon. *Do they all read people's minds?*

"So, who is she?"

Austin smiled, "Cindy Davis. She's the granddaughter of the guy that I'm doing a story on."

"Cindy Davis…she pretty?"

"Are you serious?"

Shannon didn't say anything, just smiled.

"Yeah, she's pretty," Austin said.

"She sexy?"

Austin laughed. "Seriously, will you quit it?"

Shannon smiled. "Did ya do her?"

Austin laughed again. "Geez, you know, you're really sick!"

"So, how did you leave it with her when you came up here?"

Austin's expression changed; it was clear to Shannon that he'd hit a sore spot.

Austin reached for the shot glass and slowly twirled it around in his hands. "I don't know, I'm not sure. I've left her messages, but she hasn't returned my calls."

"So, what caused the issue?"

"Things got a bit more complicated than we both thought. I imagine she had certain expectations and when I left earlier than expected, well... let's just say that it didn't go well."

"Hum, complicated?"

"Yeah, complicated."

"So, you did her," Shannon said with a wink.

Austin looked up, he wanted to laugh but didn't. He also kept glancing at the drink. "And to add to it, I'm going back down there again to do more work on the story,"

"Yep, I can see your dilemma, but I don't get it."

"What don't you get?" Austin asked.

"Does she like you?" Shannon responded.

"Well, it's interesting you ask that. The last thing she said to me was that she loved me."

"Wow, that's a big bomb to drop. What did you say?"

"Nothing"

"Shit, seriously, nothing, and you're wondering why she hasn't returned your calls."

"I guess that wasn't the smartest move on my part."

"Well, how do you feel about her?"

"I feel like we haven't been together that long but...."

Shannon cut him off. "Shit man, just tell me how you feel!"

"I love her," blurted Austin. There was silence.

Shannon smiled, grabbed the bourbon drink from Austin's hands and chugged it. "Welcome to the real world my friend. Now go down there and tell her that."

Austin sat there looking up as Shannon winced after he guzzled the drink. He finally knew what he had to do. He got up and started to his apartment upstairs, he was excited and nervous at the same time. He thought about calling Cindy again to let her know that he was coming back down, but wasn't certain how she'd respond.

CHAPTER

30

John looked around the room as if he were somewhere else. It took him a few minutes before he realized where he was. He felt weaker than normal and had difficulty moving around in his bed. He knew what all this meant and perhaps having been told that he was the last living survivor of the great war impacted how he felt.

The last living bastard of that war. The stories will end with me, he thought. He pulled himself up and propped against the pillows.

"Cindy?" He tried to yell but it came out a whisper. "Cindy!"

She didn't hear John at first, but the second request was discernable.

Cindy entered the room in a panic. "Is everything okay?"

"Where's Austin, I haven't seen him in a while."

She knew that she couldn't dodge the question anymore. "He went back to Vermont," she said in a sad voice.

"Back to Vermont? Is that where he lives?"

"Yes, that's where he lives." She could see her grandfather digesting the news. A few minutes passed.

"I thought he lived here."

"No, he lives up north." She knew her grandfather's memory was fading which caused him to be confused at times.

"When's he coming back?"

"I'm not sure if he is."

"Why?"

Cindy didn't say anything; actually, she didn't know what to say.

"I need to talk with him, it's important," John said in a serious and forceful tone.

"What about?" she asked.

"I just need to talk with him," he insisted.

"Okay, let me call him," she said, as she started to get up.

"You two are meant to be." She looked back at him and sat back down. "I could tell when you were both together, you were meant to be," he said.

She started to sniffle. "I don't think that's going to happen."

"Why do you say that?"

Cindy sat there with her eyes cast down. "I don't know, I just don't think that we're meant to be."

"Well, you're wrong!" he said in a tone that contradicted his weakness.

She looked up with her mouth open. She hadn't heard that voice in a long time.

"Now listen to me, when I met your grandmother, we knew that we were going to be together. You kids today have to go through all this thinking to determine whether you want to be together, it's not that hard to figure out."

"Yeah, but he's up there and I'm here."

"And I was on the other side of the world but that didn't stop us." John coughed a few times. Cindy could see that whatever energy he had gathered had been spent.

"Cindy, you need Austin and Austin needs you."

She was struck by how sincere his statement was. She got up and kissed him on his forehead. "I love you, Papa John."

Austin was throwing his clothes into his suitcase for his return trip and looked down at his phone. He was questioning whether he should contact Cindy. She never returned his calls which he felt sent a message.

Why would she simply ignore me? I thought what we had was special, why the cold shoulder? I just don't get it, not even an up-yours call, just nothing. The emptiness he had from not hearing from her turned to anger. He could feel his temperature rising and started to feel justified for having to return to Middlebury. *I'm just going down there to finish the story and then I'm done,* he said to himself as he looked into the mirror. *Yep, that's what I'm going to do.*

He felt secure about his decision. He kept tossing his clothes into his suitcase as he continued the juvenile self-talk, then his cell phone rang, his heart started pounding. It was Cindy.

"Hi," Austin said in a soft voice, contrary to the tone he had just a few minutes earlier.

"Austin, how are you doing?"

"Fine, I mean, I'm doing okay, well fine I guess," He stammered much like he had when they first met. There was something about her that seemed to throw him off track. "How's Papa John doing?

"He's not doing well. He's been weak since he came back from the hospital."

"I'm sorry to hear that. I'm sure he'll get stronger soon."

No one said anything further, but each could sense the other.

"Papa John misses you; he's been asking for you and......I miss you too," she said.

Austin paused, he had already forgotten about his self-absorbed, self-talk and was happy to hear Cindy's voice. "I miss you too," he finally confided.

"I'm so sorry for the way I acted and especially not calling you back. I don't know what I was thinking.... I'm just so sorry," she said.

"Cindy, I'm sorry too. I guess that I should've been more intuitive. We both knew that my time was limited down there but when I told you how much you meant to me; I don't know, guess I should have been more understanding and clearer when I left. I just wasn't thinking."

"You don't owe me an apology Austin. I simply over-read our relationship and put too much on you. I shouldn't have said what I did to you when I last saw you."

"You didn't over-read anything," he replied.

Cindy didn't say anything, she was trying to figure out where Austin was going.

"You didn't over-read anything," Austin repeated figuring that Cindy needed to hear it again.

Cindy's heart was pounding. *He said it twice, that must mean he's serious,* she thought.

"But I thought...." she started.

"You thought wrong."

"Oh...I did?"

Austin laughed. "Listen, I am going to straighten this all out."

"You are?" Cindy's heart started racing so hard she could feel it.

"Yep, I'm on my way back down. I told Anthony that I had to finish this story on John. I still believe that there's a lot more that he hasn't told us. He agreed with me so I'm coming back to finish the story."

"Austin, I don't know what to say. I know Papa John will be happy to hear that you're coming back."

"And you?" Austin asked.

Cindy giggled, "Me too."

"Well, this time I'll communicate better," laughed Austin.

"And I promise not to scare you away," Cindy replied.

"I'll be there tomorrow. Anthony is calling Chris to see if I can stay with him given that I apparently have been on a budget that I didn't know about."

"I have an extra bedroom if you need a place to stay." Cindy said it so quickly and without any thought that she shook her head in disbelief. *I just promised not to scare him away and I told him he could stay here.*

Austin didn't think twice. "Well, that'd be wonderful. I accept. Do you think Papa John will be okay with it?"

Cindy reflected on what Papa John had said to her just moments before. "I think he'll be fine with it."

"Cindy, I can't wait to see you again. I really missed you."

"Ditto," laughed Cindy.

"Touché" laughed Austin. "I deserve that!"

They both hung up. Cindy held the phone looking down at it as if she could see Austin's face. She smiled got up and did a twirl. She wasn't sure why she did it, but it felt like the right thing to do.

Austin smiled, tossed the phone on the bed, and looked over at the mirror to see if the hard-headed, bull-minded guy was still standing there, he wasn't. *Life's getting good old man,* he whispered to himself.

He turned and pulled out all the clothes that he had haphazardly tossed in his suitcase and started to refold things.

CHAPTER

31

The fireball was bright and the heat intense. The mud and shrapnel pounded the ground as large chunks of metal flew through the air. The flash of the explosions was blinding and the screams frightening.

"Get down, we're too close!" came the order.

"This wasn't supposed to happen, what the hell are they doing!" came a yell.

"They have the coordinates wrong; I'm trying to tell them they have the wrong coordinates!" came a panicked voice.

"I'm hit, I'm hit!"

"I'm coming, I'm coming!!"

"Papa John, Papa John," Cindy said. She heard him yell *I'm coming,* so loud that it alarmed her. He was startled after Cindy shook him a few times and woke him from his nap. He was sweating and he could feel his heart racing.

"Are you okay? You must've had a bad dream," she said, as she wiped the sweat from his forehead with a towel that was on the bedside.

John didn't say anything and looked around the room to see where he was. His dream was so vivid that he thought he was back in the war.

"You just had a bad dream," Cindy said in a reassuring voice. She could see the expression on Papa John's face. It was fear.

"I haven't had a dream like that since I came back from the war," he said.

"Do you want to talk about it?"

John shook his head from side-to-side. "No, I'm fine. I want to go sit in my chair," he said, as he struggled to get out of the bed.

Cindy grabbed the walker and aided in getting him up. "Here, let me help you; we need to do this slowly. You haven't gained all your strength yet."

"Nonsense, I'm fine," he said then waved her off.

"Let me help you up." Cindy noticed that he wasn't as strong as he thought he was. They struggled for a few minutes until he was stable and then they slowly walked into the living room.

"Well, I have some good news for you."

"What!" exclaimed John, as he struggled to walk.

"Austin will be returning to finish up the story on you."

John plopped down in his chair; Cindy sat next to him. "Austin will be staying with us, and he'll be finishing up your story."

"What?"

Cindy slowed her conversation to ensure that he was absorbing the information. "I said Austin will be coming back and staying with us so he can finish your story."

"Good…. that's good," he replied.

"Can I get you anything?"

"Coffee." John coughed a few times. Cindy was concerned, it was clear that just walking a few steps took a lot out of him. She got up and patted him on the hand. She noticed that he seemed to be somewhere else.

"I'm glad that Austin will be staying here," John said.

"Me too," she replied.

John sat staring ahead, reliving the dream he just had. He wondered how he could explain his role and if anyone would believe that he acted honorably. *I was just following orders.*

He'd been thinking this same thing for years. Whether it was learning that he was the last veteran or his conversations with Austin, or both; all he knew is that he had a burden that he needed to unload, and perhaps the time had come to tell someone what he had done.

CHAPTER

32

Austin finished packing his suitcase with clothes that he hadn't used since last summer. He had taken some of them when he first went to Florida not sure of the winter weather, but having been there, he knew that all he really needed were shorts, T-shirts, and sandals; the latter he didn't have. He was whistling Margaritaville by Jimmy Buffet; he wasn't sure why that popped into his head, but it was fitting.

"So, you're going back down there to finish off your tan," Shannon said, as Austin came down the stairs lugging his bags.

"Yeah, gotta get some rays," chuckled Austin.

"We're going to miss you around here."

"Well, I'll be back."

"I'm not so sure," said Shannon as he walked Austin to the front door. "You know what to do when you get down there, right?"

"Yeah, thanks," Austin said.

They both looked at each other for a moment as if it was going to be the last time they would see each other.

"I'll miss you, but you've found another life down there and you need to follow that path. You need to remember what you had here, but you can't live in the past anymore. You have something now and to give that up would be a damn shame. Go with your heart my friend, you deserve it."

Austin didn't say anything, he felt a lump in his chest. He knew that Shannon was right but hadn't thought that this could be the last time he would see his friend.

"Thanks," Austin struggled to say.

They hugged one another like brothers who were going their separate ways. Austin turned, walked out the front door and got into the cab.

The ride was much different to the airport than it had been when he arrived. The day was cold, but the sun was shining. Austin chuckled as he thought the weather was trying to entice him to stay.

"What a beautiful morning," said the driver as he peered out the front window and looked to the sky. "I haven't seen a day like this in a long time."

"Yeah, nice day," Austin replied.

The driver was right, this was the nicest day since he came back, but the memory of the Florida winter was all that Austin was thinking about. *The first thing I'm going to do is buy a pair of sandals, well, maybe the second thing*, he thought.

The driver pulled up to the airport departure gate. "Have a nice flight," he said, as he gathered the luggage from the trunk and placed them on the curb.

"Thanks, you have a great day too," Austin replied. He knew that he was headed to a much better place, at least in his mind.

The flight seemed shorter than he remembered when he first went to Florida. He decided that he wasn't going to drink on the plane, a good plan but a difficult one to execute, but he did it. He figured the sobriety had something to do with his perception of time. The flight attendant gave her usual landing instructions as they got closer to the Fort Myers airport. He looked outside the window to see the lakes and beaches come into view as they prepared to land. He looked around the cabin hoping that he would see Gladys. He smiled when he thought about what he was doing. Austin exited the plane and headed down to the baggage area. Along the way, he noticed the pictures of the beaches and the palm trees. *Good to be back.* He arrived at the luggage carousel and noticed Chris standing there. "What are you doing here?"

"Well, Anthony called me and said that you were headed back down here. I guess he had your flight info and asked that I pick you up. He said something about staying with us which would be great," Chris said.

"Well, um, yeah, Anthony had my flight stuff but I kind of made some lodging arrangements," Austin replied.

"You did?"

"Yeah, um, Cindy invited me to stay at her place."

"She did!"

"Yeah, I hope that doesn't mess up anything for you and Robert."

"You kiddin', not at all, I'm happy for you."

"You are?"

"Sure, you're just across the street. I'm sure that John will be glad to see you."

"I'm looking forward to seeing him as well."

"And I bet Cindy will be happy too, I'm sure," Chris said. He smiled and patted Austin on the back. Chris noticed Austin's overall appearance and demeanor; he looked good, but nervous.

While Austin loaded the luggage in the trunk, Chris called Cindy to let her know that they would be arriving soon.

CHAPTER

33

J ohn looked over to the bookshelf and noticed where the journals had been. He felt compelled to walk over and look at things. As he got closer, he could see that there was a gap where the book he had documented some information that was missing. He wasn't upset but was concerned. It was the book that he never thought anyone would find but Austin was an investigative reporter, and apparently a good one. He also knew that Austin was starting to put things together but was missing the one thing that would finish the story. The dream had shaken him, and he knew that he needed to make amends after all these years. He strolled back to his chair and waited; it was time to make things right.

Cindy hung up her cell phone. "Papa John, Austin will be here soon," she said.

She walked into the extra bedroom that she had prepared, to ensure that everything was in place. She paced around the house to the amusement of John until she heard the car drive up and then out the door she went.

Austin opened the car door to see Cindy on the porch. Chris smiled as he noticed the expressions on their faces. It was clear that each had patched up whatever differences they had and were excited to see one another. Cindy came bolting down the stairs as Austin approached, they both embraced.

Well that certainly didn't take long, Chris muttered under his breath. He pulled Austin's luggage from the trunk and walked to the porch, smiling as he passed them both.

"Hey, do you want me to take these to your room, Mr. Paige," yelled Chris.

"I'm so sorry," Cindy replied. She let Austin go, turned, and started toward the porch.

Chris laughed. "Just tryin' to see if I was going to be able to get a tip."

"You can run my bath," Austin replied.

"Yeah, I think I'll pass on that," Chris said as he walked back to the car. "Hey Austin?"

"Yeah?"

"Good to have you back."

"It's good to be back."

Cindy grabbed one of Austin's bags and started to carry it through the front door.

"Hey, let me get that." He bolted up the stairs.

"What do you have in here? It doesn't even feel like you brought anything."

"Well, not much, just some shorts and shirts. All I'm missing are some sandals."

Austin picked up the bags and carried them through the front door and put them down when he saw John in his chair.

"John, I'm glad to see you doing better."

John just nodded.

"I was able to talk to my editor and he's giving me some more time to complete the story on you."

"That's good," John said. He coughed a few times, but this time he couldn't stop, and he bent over as he tried to catch his breath.

Cindy went over and bent down. "Papa John, are you okay?"

"I'm fine," John gasped.

"John, you sure you're, okay?" asked Austin.

John waved them both off. "I'm fine."

Austin and Cindy took the cue and grabbed the bags and took them into the bedroom.

Cindy started scurrying around and nervously pointing. "I hope everything is okay. The bathroom's around the corner. I put fresh towels out and......"

Austin chuckled. "Everything's fine."

"I just want everything to be perfect."

"Everything's absolutely perfect." He took and kissed Cindy's hands.

"Oh, um, I guess I should make you lunch or something.... are you hungry?" She started to pick up Austin's luggage and put it on the bed.

"Cindy, the room is perfect, the house is perfect, you're perfect," he said. "Are you okay with me being here? I could move over to Chris and Roberts'."

"No, I'm fine It's just that I've never done this before, and I want to make things comfortable for you." She gave a nervous laugh. "I guess there's been a lot of things I've never done before."

Austin reached out and took her hands. "You're something." They both stood staring at one another, then he quickly shook his head. "I guess, I should chat a little with Papa John; don't you think?"

"Oh, yes, um, sure, you should do that." Cindy turned and walked out to the kitchen.

Austin smiled, *man, she looks good,* he thought as he picked up his briefcase and followed her.

John was sitting in his chair with his eyes closed.

"John?" Austin gently touched him on his shoulder. John slowly opened his eyes, he looked weak, and in the moment, Austin started to think that he had better finish the story before the storyteller was gone.

"John, I wanted to follow-up on some information that I discovered and thought that you could shed some light on a few things. Would it be okay to ask you a few questions?"

"Okay," he mumbled.

Austin could see that John didn't appear to have the energy to do much talking and thought it better to wait before he launched into inquiring about the information that he uncovered.

"You know, on second thought, why don't we have a talk a little bit later when you're up to it," Austin said.

"Okay," John replied. He seemed to be answering the question without fully comprehending what was being said.

Cindy came into the room after doing some things in the kitchen. Austin got up and whispered that she should probably take John back to his room to rest.

Cindy helped get John up, and with Austin's assistance, got him set with his walker. Despite being weak, he seemed to be able to navigate his way back to his room without any further help.

"You two kids enjoy yourself," he said.

John slipped into his bed and pulled up the covers. He looked up at the ceiling and closed his eyes. He could see Smitty, Ghost, Jaws and Captain Burton gathered together slapping one another on the back. They were all making jokes as they prepared for their mission. Their faces were so young and vibrant, and their entire lives laid ahead of them. They were making fun of him when he bragged about his Evy, and laughed when they told him that she was way above his paygrade. The moment was a mixture of past and present thoughts. He saw Cindy and Austin together and was happy for his granddaughter. He opened his eyes to see where he was and looked around the room. He closed his eyes again and whispered, *I love you Sunshine*, and with that, the last of the greatest generation joined his team.

CHAPTER

34

Cindy and Austin found themselves on the front porch sitting at the table where they talked when they were first together. He remembered how beautiful she looked when the wind blew through her hair. The early afternoon was not much different than it was then, only this time Austin had to set things right.

Cindy looked around. "The day is certainly wonderful."

Austin remembered Shannon's advice and took Cindy's hand. "I know that things sort of got off track when I left here, and I wanted to clear some things up."

Cindy gripped Austin's hand. "Okay?"

"I really didn't tell you the full truth when I saw you last." He felt the grip tighten on his hands.

"What I really mean is that when I told you that I had strong feelings for you, well, I really didn't tell you everything."

"What do you mean?"

The grip got stronger. He thought he had better tell her soon or she'd stop the blood from pumping in his hand.

"Well, I never thought I'd ever say this again to anyone, but the moment I met you my world changed. It took me some time to realize just how much but it was clear when I was back home that I couldn't go on the way I had in the past."

Cindy sat there staring into his eyes and hanging on every word.

"A friend of mine told me that I should go with my heart and remember the past but stop living in it. He was right, and perhaps it was good that I went home when I did because now everything makes sense to me."

Cindy's eyes started to well, she hoped that he would say what she's been feeling about him.

"I just can't think of my life anymore without you. I've loved you since I met you but thought that it was all perhaps infatuation and........."

Cindy didn't wait to hear the rest or didn't care; she jumped up and hugged him. And likewise, he embraced her. They looked at each other and kissed. The moment felt like it lasted forever. They both sat down, and Cindy wiped the tears with her sleeve.

"I'm so sorry about how things went down when I left. I just had a tough time processing everything and I guess was too scared to say anything. And when you told me how you felt, I was a bit stunned. I know it sounds stupid, but I guess I never thought anyone would say those words to me again," Austin said.

Cindy sniffed a few times. "I'm sorry to have put you in such an awkward position. I just didn't know what to do and it just came out."

"Well, it gave me something to think about when I was home, so, I guess that in the end it was pretty cool what you said."

Cindy smiled and wiped more tears from her eyes. "So, who's your friend that gave you the advice?"

"His name's Shannon. He's sort of my landlord. He runs a bar in Middlebury, and I rent a room above it."

"I remember Chris saying that you lived above a bar."

"Yeah, not very romantic."

"Must be hard to live in that environment."

Austin knew what she was inferring. "It was actually convenient. I could always get what I wanted whenever I wanted it. But, since I met you and everyone down here, it's been more of an annoyance. I haven't had anything to drink since I returned and admittedly, it's been a tough thing for me." Austin chuckled. "Actually, I think it was tougher on Shannon because his bar revenue significantly dropped."

Cindy laughed. "I like him already."

"Well, I hope you get to meet him. I know he'd love you."

"You know we have to quit doing this," Robert said, as he and Chris were looking out the front window.

"What! I'm just curious," Chris said.

"It's creepy!" Robert said, then looked back out the window at Cindy and Austin.

"Well, I just had to see if things would finally work out between the two of them."

"You know if they saw us, they'd think we're nosy neighbors."

"We're looking at them, so I think we're nosy neighbors."

"They're a cute couple," Robert said, still mesmerized by what was going on across the street.

"Yep, they sure are," Chris replied.

They both continued to look across the street when they noticed Austin and Cindy hug again and start walking into the house. Suddenly, and without even turning his head, Austin waved toward Chris and Robert's house.

Robert ducked assuming that they'd been caught. "Shit, did he see us?"

Chris ducked too. "I don't know."

They both laughed as they realized how childish they both were behaving.

"Who are you waving at?" Cindy asked.

"Oh, just a hunch, but I think our fan club was curious as to how the show was going to unfold."

Cindy laughed. "Well, I think we gave them an award-winning presentation."

"I concur," Austin said.

"Are you hungry for some lunch?"

"I'm starving. You wouldn't have any meatloaf around, would you?"

Cindy chuckled. "No, but I am sure I can put something together for you."

"Tell you what, why don't you go check on Papa John and I'll put something together for us."

"Well, well, Mr. Paige. I'd love to see what you can do."

They both walked into the kitchen. Austin put on an apron that was hanging by the door. They kissed as Cindy gave him a little wave and a smile as she left for John's bedroom.

Austin opened the refrigerator door wondering what he was going to do. It was a nice idea but not one that he fully thought out. He grabbed a few things and started putting them on the counter. *Man, I have no idea what I am doing,* he chuckled.

"Austin!" yelled Cindy. It was a tone that sent shivers down his back.

CHAPTER

35

The morning was cold and so much like Vermont that it was hard to make the distinction, but Buffalo was known for its long blustery winters. Even though the season was coming to an end, at least by what the calendar indicated, it felt like the winter still had time to give. There was a small crowd gathered at the cemetery site, mainly people who were old friends of John and his daughter, Rebecca. They were happy to see Cindy and talked about her when she was very young and would come to Buffalo to visit from time to time. It was nice and fitting that John was being buried next to his wife.

"It's nice to see people gathered here," Austin said, as he held Cindy's hand.

Cindy didn't say anything but squeezed his hand.

The pastor who facilitated the ceremony was fitting. He was a Vietnam vet and spoke of the sacrifices that the World War II veterans made to make America safe. While the people appreciated the words, it would be hard for them to understand what true sacrifices John had made.

Austin looked around, *if they only knew.*

No one there had any idea that they were actually paying their respects to the last living World War II veteran. He didn't feel it was his place to tell anyone so he let the ceremony pass without the recognition John should have received. There was no fanfare, no military presence, no significance to his passing except a cold, damp grave.

A tear rolled down Cindy's cheek. "I hope he's happy now."

"He's with his Sunshine, I think he's very happy," Austin said.

Cindy pointed to the adjacent grave. "There's my grandma Evy. Over there are my great uncles and aunts."

Austin gazed around the cemetery. "Well, he's with a lot of family now."

"Yes, he is. I knew this day would come but I never thought it would be so hard." Austin reached for a tissue from his pocket and handed it to her.

The service ended and everyone walked by Cindy to give their final condolences. She and Austin were standing alone next to John's grave.

"I'll miss him," she said, as she stared at the freshly turned soil.

Austin put his arm around her. "He'll miss you too."

"I don't know what I'm going to do now," she said. "I took care of him for all these years, it was a job that I loved; now, I just don't know what I'm going to do. He was my life, and I'll miss taking care of him."

Austin could sense her loss of purpose. "You know, if it weren't for you, it's likely that John could have spent the last years of his life in a senior home. You gave him something few people his age would ever have had. You should be proud of what you did. I know he was proud of you."

Cindy looked up at Austin and smiled. Then they turned and walked to the car.

"I'm so sorry that you didn't get to spend more time talking with Papa John. I know he wanted to talk to you and missed not having you around," she said.

"I'm sorry too," Austin replied. He was thinking about his timing and the fact that he didn't have the opportunity to clear up some of the things that he had uncovered, and now, wasn't sure he could. He opened the passenger door, Cindy looked back at John's grave site, stopped, and blew a kiss. Austin's chest hardened when he saw it and a small tear rolled down his cheek.

The drive was quiet as they left the cemetery. There wasn't much to say. Austin reached over and stroked Cindy's hair. She reached up and rubbed his cheek. It was fitting that they were together. It was what John had wanted.

"You know, since we're up this way, what'd ya think of making a trip to Middlebury?" Austin asked trying to lighten the moment.

"Vermont?"

"Sure, why not, it's just a short flight. I could show you around the town, although it'd probably only take about an hour."

Cindy perked up. "Vermont, huh? I've never been that far north."

"It's beautiful up there, granted not as nice as Fort Myers, but it has its own charm."

"You know, it might be nice to see where you live."

"Well, about that, you might not find that very nice. But I do know a few people who'd love to meet you."

"You know, I think that would be a nice change from everything. I'd like that."

"Okay then, I'll make the arrangements."

Austin started thinking about what he was going to tell Anthony about John's story. Now that he was gone, it was going to be tough to find out whether the assumptions that he made about the OSS connection, *Operation Sundown* and the Chiyoda District were true. All he had were four journals and the fourth one ended without any details. He was concerned that Anthony would change his mind and just have him write the last living veteran article and move on. He needed to get back to Florida and see what he could find and perhaps having Anthony meet Cindy would help him with that. The fact was, he had nothing significant to offer and figured that John's story likely died with him.

CHAPTER

36

The early morning flight to Vermont was just over thirty minutes. By the time they took off, it was time to land. The winter weather hadn't changed much since they left Buffalo and looking out the window of the plane as it taxied to the terminal solidified Austin's resolve to get back to Florida.

This sucks, he thought.

"Wow, I didn't realize how close we were," Cindy said.

"Pretty close for sure. You know, it can be cold up here. I have some stuff at my place you can use if you need it,'" Austin said.

"Well, I packed for Buffalo so I think I'm set. Besides, I've got my sweaters that I wear in Florida. I hope we don't get a warm spell." Cindy replied.

"Funny. Yeah, we're expecting a warm front up here. Maybe we'll get above freezing."

Cindy grinned. "Well, I'm looking forward to seeing Middlebury."

The plane came to a stop at the gate. As people exited, Cindy started feeling the anticipation.

Austin picked up on Cindy's expression. "Are you okay with this?"

"Yeah, I just didn't think things would happen this way. I'm just a bit nervous about it. I guess that coming here was a good idea at the moment," she said. "What if your friends and Anthony don't like me?"

"You're not serious, are you?"

"Yeah, I'm serious. I'm the girlfriend coming into the town where you and your wife lived. Your family's up here."

Girlfriend. It was the first time there was a definition put to their relationship. Austin smiled. "They'll love you," he said in a reassuring tone.

The cab ride to Shamrocks was a short trip and one that Austin didn't pay much attention to; instead, he was pointing out places to Cindy along the drive. He was doing his best to narrate a tour but there wasn't much to show so he took some liberties with the landmarks.

"It's very nice up here," Cindy said.

"Well, it's nice but it doesn't have the palm trees and beaches," Austin replied.

"It's still nice."

The car pulled up to Shamrocks; Cindy exited looking up at the sign and entrance way. "Interesting."

"I told you, it's not much, but it's home, at least for now."

Cindy smiled as she grabbed Austin's arm. She knew this was going to be something new for her and despite being nervous, she was exhilarated to be out of Fort Myers and doing something different. The moment took her thoughts away from the funeral and her loss. Austin reached for the front door and opened it.

"Shit, what are you doing back here!" came a yell from the back of the room as Austin entered the bar. "I wasn't expecting you or I would have cleaned up the place."

"Well, some things changed, and I thought I'd come up here and introduce you to someone," Austin said, as Shannon came around from the bar wiping his hands with a towel.

Cindy was timid as Shannon approached but relaxed as she saw a big warm smile on his face. He was a big burly guy wearing an apron that looked like he'd been wearing for some time, as indicated by the stains.

"Shannon, this is Cindy. Cindy this is Shannon," Austin said. Shannon reached out and grabbed Cindy and gave her a big hug.

"So, you're the gal that this guy's been drooling over," Shannon said, as he winked at Austin.

She looked back at Austin. "Drooling?"

Shannon laughed, "Yeah, his head hasn't been the same since he came back from Florida, and he's been killing my liquor business since he's apparently stopped drinking!"

She smiled.

"I'm very pleased to meet you Cindy," Shannon said. "I don't know if you knew this, but this guy has been walking around in a daze since he met you. I'm happy to finally get to meet the person that has made Austin Paige a new guy."

Austin felt his face warming and wondered if it was obvious that he was blushing. "Okay, enough big guy."

Shannon laughed. "Cindy if there is anything that I can do for you, please let me know. And, again, it's great to finally meet you."

"It's wonderful to meet you too. And, by the way, thanks for giving Austin the advice that you did."

"My pleasure." Shannon smiled and walked back to the bar.

Austin grabbed the bags and walked Cindy up the stairs to his apartment. He hadn't factored on anyone seeing the place, especially her, and wondered in what condition he left it. He slowly opened the door and winced when he noticed that he hadn't picked up the clothes that he had thrown around when he packed for Florida.

Cindy looked around and didn't want Austin to feel uncomfortable. "This is nice."

"Well, I don't think I'd say that, but it's home. I guess I'm not a tidy as I should be, but I was in a hurry when I found out I was going back to Florida."

Austin quickly walked around picking things up and placing them on the kitchen table. Cindy smiled as she walked around and helped him.

They both turned and looked at one another. There wasn't anything said but each could feel the intense energy. Austin picked her up and took her to his room.

Shannon shook his head and smiled as he wiped down the bar and heard muffled noises coming from upstairs. Ordinarily he can't hear a thing when the bar is full, but for the moment, it was empty. The morning led to afternoon and neither came out from the bedroom.

The cell phone rang. "Hello?" Austin said, as he tried to clear the fog from his head.

"Austin, buddy, I hear that you're back in town!" came the response from the other end of the phone.

"What, um, yeah, who is this?" Austin hadn't looked at the phone number and didn't immediately recognize the voice.

"Anthony!" came the reply.

"Shit, I'm sorry, yeah, I made a quick trip back here. I guess news travels fast around here," Austin said, as he suddenly gathered his faculties.

"Man, what are you doing back so soon? Did you wrap everything up with the old man down there?" Anthony asked.

"Well, not exactly. He passed away," Austin replied.

"Shit, I'm sorry. I didn't know, man, I feel like an idiot. Geez, I'm sorry to hear that."

"No problem, I should have told you. The service was in Buffalo, and I thought I'd bring Cindy up here for a quick trip to get her mind off things."

"Cindy?"

"Yeah, John's granddaughter."

"Cindy! John's granddaughter, that's right. Wow, she's here?"

"Yeah, she's here."

"Well, I'd love to meet her. Tell ya what, I know it's last minute, but bring her over here and we'll do some cocktails and dinner."

"Dinner.... now?" Austin reached for his watch on the bedside table. It was six o'clock.

"Yeah, no time like the present."

"Well, let me check and see." Austin covered the phone and looked over at Cindy who was starting to wake up.

"Cindy?" He slowly reached over and touched her arm.

"Yeah?" she said half with it, half out of it.

"Anthony wants us to come over tonight for cocktails and dinner."

"What? What time is it?"

"Six O'clock."

"Tonight?" she said, now more with it.

"Yeah," Austin said. He hoped that she'd be too tired to go.

"Sure, whatever would work for you," she replied. It wasn't the answer Austin was hoping for.

He uncovered the phone. "Yeah, sure we'll be over there in a bit. We'll need to freshen up."

"Great, see you two soon."

Austin clicked off the call. "Damn." He laid his head back down on the pillow. All he wanted to do was cuddle with Cindy and enjoy the evening in bed.

CHAPTER

37

Austin and Cindy were leaving his apartment for Anthony's when, for some reason, he went back inside and grabbed his briefcase. He wasn't sure why but just felt compelled to have it close by. They came down the stairs as the crowd was filling the bar.

Shannon saw them and waved. "Where are you guys headed?" he said over the noise of the crowd.

"Going to dinner at Anthony's," Austin replied.

"I thought you guys would be too tired to head out now," Shannon smiled and looked to the wooden ceiling.

Austin frowned and looked up. The ceiling was made of old wooden planks that had been there for years. He got the inference; apparently the wooden ceiling, or in his case, the floor, gave away the secrets of the passion that had occurred earlier. He never took note of it before for a variety of reasons; first, he never had anyone in his room and second, most of the time he was drunk and passed out in bed. Austin shook his head and smiled as he looked back. Shannon didn't say anything but grinned and gave him a thumbs up.

"What did he say?" Cindy asked, as she smiled and waved at Shannon.

"Nothing," chuckle Austin.

Austin turned the corner toward the back of the bar and pulled a cover off a car.

Cindy looked at the car, she was impressed. "Is this yours?"

"Yeah, it's the only thing that I got out of my divorce. I keep it covered when I'm out of town."

"Wow, I've never rode in one of these before."

It was his White 1965 Mustang. "Yeah, it's nice. Fortunately, the car runs like a dream and the heater works," Austin said, as he turned the key, silently praying that the engine would turn; it did.

They drove for a few minutes as Cindy looked at the passing buildings.

"Are you sure that this will be okay?" she said.

"What do you mean?" Austin asked.

"Well, I mean, we're going to see your brother-in-law. Don't you think it's a bit awkward to bring me to his place given, you know, having been married to his sister."

"Anthony will be fine with it. At first when Teresa and I split he had a hard time with it, but over time I think he came to terms with what happened. He's been more than a brother-in-law and we were friends long before I married his sister. Don't worry, it'll be okay."

"I guess I understand, just didn't know how I should deal with everything."

"Just be you. He'll love getting to know you."

"Well…. now that we're on the subject," came a curious tone.

Austin knew where the conversation was going. "Yeah, about my ex-wife. We had a place in Franklin, North Carolina that was our little retreat. She had a bunch of her friends down there so when we divorced, I signed over the house to her. She moved down there not long after we split. It worked out the best for the both of us."

"I didn't mean to pry. I was just curious as to the situation."

"No, it's a fair question. I guess we've got a lot to talk about. Kind-of funny that we're starting to get to know each other this way. It's nice to be able to talk to someone about my past and not feel guilty."

"You can always talk to me," Cindy said as she rubbed Austin's arm. "I didn't even ask, is Anthony married. Does he have any kids?"

"No, he's been kind of a player in these parts. He was engaged once but that didn't work out. He stays busy with the paper up here and, quite honestly, likes being in charge which doesn't bode well with his relationships."

Cindy grinned. "And you?"

"Not me, I like having someone to partner with."

"Good answer Mr. Paige." Cindy leaned over and kissed Austin on the cheek.

The drive took about a half an hour. They pulled into to the driveway of a house that was up a hill. It had a very large wrap-around porch with big floor-to-ceiling windows. You could see that the interior of the house looked masculine and if you didn't know it was a residence, you would think it was a hunting lodge.

Cindy got out of the car and looked up at the house. "Wow, this is nice."

"Well, yeah, considering my place," said Austin, in a defensive tone.

"Well, I mean…"

Austin laughed, "Just kidding; you're right, it's pretty nice."

Cindy cautiously navigated the hill hoping that she didn't slide on any ice as Austin held her hand. She wondered why anyone up north would have a house on a hill when you have snow and ice most of the year.

Anthony was already at the door when Austin rang the bell. "Get in here you old nut." He grabbed and hugged him.

Austin freed himself from the embrace and pointed to Cindy. "Hey, this is Cindy Davis."

Anthony grabbed her and gave her a strong hug. "So nice to meet you," he said.

"Nice to meet you too," she replied.

"Please, come on in and get comfortable."

Cindy looked around the house, the interior matched the outside. It was masculine with a few deer heads peppered around the room for good measure. A robust fire was burning in a huge stone fireplace that heated the entire living area. "This is beautiful," she said.

Anthony gave a quick glance around the room. "Well, it's just a place to live."

She smiled at his attempt to be humble.

"Cindy, I want to give you my sincerest condolences on your loss. I was so sorry to hear of your grandfather's passing."

"Thank you, Anthony. Well, I was at least glad that Austin was there to see him one last time."

Anthony looked over to Austin. "Yeah, well, you know, at least you all were together and I'm sure that meant a lot."

Anthony motioned to Cindy and Austin. "Hey, please make yourselves comfortable." He headed over to a large oak bar which looked like a mini version of Shannon's place complete with about every kind of liquor one could imagine lining the back wall. "Cindy, what can I get for you?"

"A Cabernet would be fine, thank you."

Anthony came back holding a glass of wine in one hand and with his finger and thumb of the other hand, held two glasses of bourbon. He handed out the drinks, held up the glass. "Here's to John," he said, as he took a sip.

Cindy and Austin lifted their glasses.

"Here's to a wonderful man and even more wonderful grandfather," Cindy said.

"And to the last of the greatest generation," Austin said.

Cindy took a sip of her wine. She used her peripheral vision to look at Austin as he lifted the glass and stared at it. He held if for a few seconds then slowly put it down on the table.

Anthony took another sip from his glass and looked at Austin. "So, my bourbon not good enough for you?"

"No, actually I kind-of decided to slow it down a bit."

"Really, no bourbon or anything?"

"Yeah, figured it might be a good time to focus on other things for now." But everything in him wanted the drink.

Anthony looked over at Cindy and winked then looked back at Austin. "Happy to see you change your focus. Proud of you, my brother." He looked back at Cindy, tipped his glass, and smiled again. He picked up Austin's glass and chugged it down.

"Well, listen, I've grilled some unbelievable steaks while you guys were on your way. I hope you both like'm because these babies are awesome."

"I love steak," Cindy said. She was being polite; she wasn't much of a meat eater.

"Well, let's enjoy." Anthony directed everyone to the long rustic dining table that had a large chandelier made of deer antlers hanging above it. The continued lodge theme wasn't lost on Cindy.

The evening dinner was pleasant. The conversation was casual with much of the talk centered on Anthony and Austin's relationship in their college years. Anthony joked with Austin about who was the better writer, but after a few jabs, admitted that Austin was by far the best. Austin smiled and appreciated Anthony's self-deprivation.

Cindy also liked that Anthony kept her in the conversation and didn't talk around her as if she wasn't there. *He's really nice*, she thought.

Austin folded his napkin and neatly placed it on the table. "I think you topped yourself with dinner tonight."

"Yes, this was wonderful," Cindy said.

Anthony picked up on the cue that dinner was over and pointed. "Well, let's retire to the living room." He walked over and stoked the fire to get it to burn stronger.

Cindy wiggled herself into an over-sized leather sofa. "I can't thank you enough for having us over."

"You're more than welcome," Anthony replied. He turned and sat at the other end of the sofa opposite Austin. "So, I know that everything was sudden and I'm sure things have changed, but where are you with the story about John?"

Austin knew this topic would come up and he truly didn't have anything new to add except his assumptions, which by now were nothing more than that. "Well, unfortunately, I wasn't able to get any closure on some of the things that I found but I feel that there is a much bigger story than when we first started."

Anthony shook his head indicating that he understood. "Yeah, but as I understand, there aren't any facts to back up your assumptions, right?"

"True, but I like I said before, everything seems to point to something that's much bigger, I just have to dig a little more, but I know that I'll find it."

"Listen, I get it but, in the end, you have a pretty good story as it is. Geez, the last living veteran of World War two. I think that's pretty impressive, don't you?"

"Yeah, but if you remember, there were a lot of things that, if they have legs to it, could be huge. Think about it, what if John was actually tied to the *Operation Sundown* thing and to something to do with the emperor, well, I think people would be very interested."

"I don't disagree, but at this point there isn't anything that could substantiate anything, so it'd be complete conjecture on our part."

"Yeah, but the map, the date, the positioning of the *Ticonderoga*, the special operations, it's all pointing to something. This just can't be coincidental."

Anthony rubbed his chin. He looked over to Cindy, sensitive to the fact that she just lost her grandfather. "I don't know. I just don't see anything here that points to something significant, some documents and a map. Is there anything you think you could find that could put all of this together?"

Austin looked down and shook his head; he knew that he was in a losing argument. "I guess nothing except the four journals and the last one doesn't really say anything."

Austin put his hands to his head. He knew that Anthony was right and just had to accept the fact that there was nothing more he could do or say.

Cindy had stayed out of the conversation; she really couldn't see anything that she could add. Her heart sank as she noticed Austin's disappointment. The room was quiet; Anthony didn't say anything further, he had made his point.

Austin was still looking down with his hands covering his face when he looked up as if someone had prodded him with an electric probe. "Wait a minute!" He looked at Cindy. "Do you remember when John was taken to the hospital; you know that day that he was out of it, and you called the ambulance?"

"Yeah, I remember it," she replied.

"He reached out to me as he passed."

"Yeah?"

Anthony glanced at them both as they exchanged conversation.

Austin's tone got excited and became animated. "He mumbled to me, look for the fifth… look for the fifth! There must be a fifth!"

Cindy's expression changed as well and for a similar reason.

"Do you have the journals here!" she asked with as much excitement as Austin.

"Yeah, why?"

"I remember when we were together that one evening, I looked through them the next morning. There was something that I didn't understand but I think it may help."

Anthony looked at them both and smiled, *the next morning, huh.*

Austin bolted down the stairs and was back within seconds carrying his briefcase that had all the journals in them. *Geez, I knew there was a reason that I brought these,* he mumbled.

He grabbed the journals and gave them to Cindy. She opened the first one and looked in the same area that she noticed the letters and numbers that morning. Then she opened the second one and the letters and numbers were a little different, she did the same with the third. She now knew what they meant. She looked at Anthony and Austin and gave a big smile and handed the open journals to Austin and pointed to what she found.

Austin couldn't contain his excitement. "What!?"

"Look in the upper corners," she said.

There it was, clear as day. "Shit! How did I miss this!"

Anthony's expression turned to curiosity. "What?"

Austin pointed to the upper corner of the first journal, written in the corner was J 1 – 5. He showed Anthony the second, J 2 – 5 and so on until he got to the last journal J 4 – 5.

Anthony rubbed his forehead. "What does it mean?"

"There's a reason that I haven't found the conclusion of the story!" Austin replied.

Anthony looked at him trying to figure out what he was trying to convey. Cindy smiled and could see Austin's expression.

"Because there's a fifth journal," she said.

Anthony looked at Austin with a puzzled expression.

"Don't you see? John wrapped up these journals but for some reason didn't include the last one. He only gave me four of them. There's still one missing and I bet that's where all the answers are!" Austin looked at Cindy and winked.

Anthony paused for a moment trying to take it all in. "So, what you're saying is that you've drawn some assumptions based on what you've found in the journals up to this point and you think that the last one will reveal all the secrets."

Austin pointed to the journals. "Well, think about what I've found so far; the map with the same date that's in the book that I found in John's library. The historical reference to the emperor. The contradiction on where the *Ticonderoga* was during that time of the war. John's OSS connection. Yeah, I think that there are some secrets here and I know that the last journal ties it together."

Anthony looked at Austin and then to Cindy. He sat back in the sofa and looked down at the stack of journals and then back at them both. "Well, it looks to me that you two better get back down there and finish the story."

Austin smiled, looked at Cindy and mouthed, *thank you.*

CHAPTER

38

The next morning was full of excitement. Austin felt like he had found a new lease on life. He and Cindy had uncovered the mystery and now they were on a mission. Now it was time to finish the work.

"I can't thank you enough for coming with me last night," Austin said.

Cindy came out of the shower with a towel wrapped around her hair. "What?"

"Last night. I can't thank you enough for your help."

She came over and kissed him. "You did all the work; I just happen to provide a gentle nudge."

"Gentle nudge? I don't think so, you found the clue that I totally missed. I think you're a better reporter than me."

"No Mr. Paige, you're the investigative reporter not me." She looked over to the bed.

Austin grinned. "You know these floors talk."

Cindy frowned, "What?" There was a pause as she put two-and-two together and laughed. "Seriously?"

"Well according to Shannon."

Cindy blushed and started to put on her clothes.

Austin's tone got serious. "You know, I'd like to introduce you to someone."

"What? Another friend?"

"Yeah, someone who I think would like to know you."

"Sure, I like meeting your friends."

"Actually, we can do it on the way to the airport. I made the arrangements to go back later this afternoon."

"Okay." She finished getting dressed.

Austin paused for a moment and opened the drawer next to the bed. He looked down and smiled when he saw what he was looking for. He grabbed it and put it in his pocket. It had been a long time since he had thought about it, but it always meant a lot to him. He arranged for a driver to take them to the airport but had given directions for a detour before they headed out. The weather had turned unseasonably warm and sunny, at least by Vermont standards. Versus the layering of sweaters, which was the only winter wear Cindy had, she only needed one this particular morning.

"Where are we going?" Cindy asked.

"Just a little ride up the road," Austin replied.

It wasn't long before the stop revealed itself and Cindy's behavior became somber.

"Truthfully, I haven't been back here for some time. I feel a bit embarrassed to admit to that, but I've never been able to deal with it, at least sober."

The walk took about 10 minutes, but Austin knew where he was going.

Cindy held onto his arm as they finally approached their destination. She wasn't sure she should be there but felt it important to be with him, especially now.

"Mandy, this is Cindy," Austin said, as he looked down on her gravestone. "I thought I should stop by and make an introduction." He started choking up and looked up to the sky to try and compose himself. "I know it's been a while since I've been here, but I wanted to make sure you knew that I'm finally happy." Cindy hung onto his arm. Her nose started to run as tears welt up in her eyes.

"I'm so sorry, sweet pea, for everything." He struggled to get the words out. Tears started down his cheeks and he rubbed them away with the sleeve of his jacket.

"I miss you a lot." He bent over and brushed off what remaining frost was on the gravestone. "I'm better now."

They both stood in silence.

"It is very nice to meet you," Cindy said.

Austin turned and smiled. He took a deep breath and wiped the remaining tears from his eyes. They both turned and started back to the car. After taking a few steps, he turned back around one more time. "I love you sweet pea."

Suddenly a gust of wind blew and what remaining leaves had hung on to the trees through the winter began to fall. *I love you daddy, be happy,* came a whisper, at least in Austin's mind. The guilt left him as the breeze died down. It was closure that he never thought he'd have. He put his arms around Cindy, smiled, and walked back to the car.

CHAPTER

39

The plane landed and taxied to the terminal. Austin pulled the carry-on out of the bin and then helped Cindy up. They held hands as they walked to baggage claim. The trip had been short and emotional on several levels. It was good to be back in Fort Myers and Austin was feeling like it was more home than Middlebury. He called an Uber to take them back to Cindy's house. When they arrived and walked in it was eerily quiet. Perhaps it was just their imagination, but everything appeared to be staged, almost as if they had never been there before.

"This is so weird," Cindy said.

"I know, things feel different," Austin replied.

Cindy started to take her bags into her room and Austin to his. "Where are you going?"

Austin didn't say anything and just pointed to his room. He looked at Cindy, raised his eyebrows and then pointed to her room.

"Well, you shared your bedroom, I guess I can share mine," she said, with a smile. "And, by the way, my floors don't squeak."

Austin grabbed his bags and quickly took them into her room. They both laughed, which lightened the mood.

They had just laid their bags on the bed when the doorbell rang.

Austin chuckled. "I'll give you three guesses as to who that would be and the first two don't count."

Cindy laughed and walked to the door. He was right, of course.

"Hey, how is everything?" Chris asked; Robert was standing next to him.

"Hey guys, come on in," she said.

"How are you two doing?" Robert asked. He nudged Chris; they glanced at one another when they realized that Austin was coming from Cindy's bedroom.

Austin chuckled. "You know you two don't do a good job of concealing things."

Robert laughed. "Guilty!"

"Seriously, how is everything? How was John's funeral?" Chris asked.

"It was small and sad, needless to say, but pleasant; not a lot of fanfare for someone who was the last of his generation," Cindy replied.

"We're so sorry to hear that. He was such a wonderful person. We'll miss him," Robert said.

"Thank you. Can I get you two anything?"

"Sure, your sweet tea if you have any," Chris replied.

"Same for me," echoed Robert.

Robert saddled next to Austin. "So, how are things going?"

Cindy and Austin looked at one another and smiled.

"Really good," Austin replied.

"And how long are you staying?"

"I guess until we can get the final story done." Austin pointed to Cindy. "Thanks to my cute cracker jack reporter over there, who uncovered a mystery, we have some work to do."

Cindy came back in the room with a tray of glasses filled with tea. "I don't think I uncovered anything."

"Well, she figured out that the journals we have aren't the complete set. There's one more that we're missing and perhaps the most important one; it must be here somewhere," Austin said.

Robert looked around the room. "Oh my, seriously?"

Austin picked up one of the glasses. "Yep, there's a fifth journal. We don't know why it wasn't with the four that Papa John gave me, but we figured he planned on giving it to us."

"It's just so sad that he couldn't tell us everything," Chris said.

Cindy looked at John's chair. "I don't know, I kind of believe he's still here to help us."

Chris reached over and patted Cindy on the hand. "You know, I think you're right."

"Well, we certainly can help. I would think that it's probably with all the books that are over there," Robert said, as he pointed to the shelves.

"You're probably right but it's been a couple of emotional days, so we'll probably start doing some digging tomorrow."

Chris nudged Robert. "I think we should leave these two alone and let them unpack."

Austin looked at Cindy and winked.

"Hey, if there is anything we can do to help, please let us know. You know that we love doing research on things," Robert said.

"Will do," Austin replied.

Cindy walked them both to the door. She came back into the room and burst out laughing. She didn't know why but something with Chris and Robert was just funny. Austin was thinking the same thing and started laughing as well. It was a release for both; it had been a hard, few days and it felt good to let loose.

"Well, what next Mr. Paige?"

"Well, what do you mean Ms. Davis?"

"I'm hungry and I don't have a thing in the refrigerator."

"What? No meatloaf?"

"No meatloaf."

"What about Bruno's?"

"What is it about that place? You seem to be stuck on it. You know there's more places to eat than just Bruno's."

"Okay, I'm open; where do you want to go?" Austin asked.

Cindy looked at him with a sheepish grin. "Bruno's?"

"I approve of your decision," he said, with a laugh.

Austin grabbed Cindy and gave her a hug. She went to the bathroom to freshen up. Austin looked around at the bookshelf and then to John's chair. He felt a sense of sadness come over him, realizing that any story told would happen without John knowing how it turned out. He at least felt better knowing that he got to see him one last time. He walked over to the bookshelf thinking that the fifth journal would simply pop out.

There were hundreds of books, but he felt confident that it was just misplaced among the many.

This shouldn't be that difficult, he thought. At least, he was hoping it would be that simple.

CHAPTER

40

T he morning sun peered through the curtains. It looked to be a beautiful start to another Florida morning. Perhaps it was the wonderful dinner at Bruno's followed by another passionate evening with Cindy. Austin rubbed his eyes and groaned as he got out of bed. *Geez, I'm getting old* he mumbled. He slowly shuffled to the kitchen and started making the morning coffee.

It wasn't long before Cindy came around the corner. "Good morning."

Austin grabbed a cup from the cabinet. "Morning…. I didn't want to wake you."

"I smelled the coffee, so I figured you were up. By the way, last night was really something." She huddled up to him.

"Ditto."

"There you go again," she elbowed him in the stomach. "So, what's on the agenda today."

"Well, we need to start going through the library and see if we can find that last journal."

"We?" she asked.

"Yep, your part of the investigative team now," he replied.

Austin was impressed with how many books John had accumulated over the years and wondered if he read them all. As he pulled each one from the shelf, he looked at the titles and flipped the pages to see if anything might fall out. He had been lucky to find the book that had the marker in it and was hoping that he would find another one, perhaps with more clues. The collection was larger than he had thought and hadn't considered how many there were until he started to go through them one by one.

Cindy was sitting on the floor looking through the books on the bottom shelf and occasionally sipping her coffee. "There sure are a lot of these. You know, I've seen these books for years, but they just became a fixture in the room; kind-of like a picture on the wall that you don't see after a while."

Austin was on the step ladder pulling books from the top shelf. "I know, it's something that your grandfather kept these. They must've meant something to him."

The books were very well organized and in great shape considering some of them had been on the shelf for many years.

"Hmm, look at this?" Cindy said.

"Did you find it!" Austin quickly came down the steps of the ladder.

"No, I'm sorry. It's just a book about the *Ticonderoga* with a bunch of pictures in it."

Austin sat next to Cindy as she flipped the pages. The book had several photos with sections set apart that showed the departments and the men that ran the massive ship. It was as if they were looking at a high school yearbook complete with candid black-and-white pictures of the crew on holidays and in action. There were even pictures of the damage to the ship after it was hit by the kamikaze pilots.

"The ship looks impressive," Cindy said.

Austin looked at the pages as she quickly flipped through them. "Well, those aircraft carriers could carry over three thousand men."

"Seriously, that's as big as some towns."

"I know."

"Do you think Papa John is in here?" Cindy asked.

"Let's see," Austin replied.

She handed the book to Austin who went to the index to see if he could find John's name. "It should be easy to find, they typically list names in alphabetical order."

Austin scrolled through the list and found the name John Anderson with a series of page numbers next to it. "See, here he is," pointing to the name in the list.

He flipped to a page that had several sailors stacked in rows looking at the camera, some were smiling, some grinning and some showed no emotion. It was hard to pick out a perfect face, but the names corresponded to the position they had in the picture.

"Let's see, I think if I count correctly, this should be your grandfather." Austin pointed to a picture of a young sailor smiling from ear to ear. "Wait, I must have done this wrong." Austin went back and counted again to ensure that he coordinated the name with the picture.

"What is it?" Cindy asked.

Austin had a confused look. He counted again, verified the name with the position of the sailor in the photograph. He was correct, but something wasn't right.

"Did you find him?"

Austin didn't say anything and flipped to another page corresponding the name to a picture and looked at the photo.

"Did you find him?"

Austin looked at Cindy with a puzzled expression. "Well, I certainly found John Anderson but not sure it matches."

"What do you mean?"

Austin flipped the book over and pointed to the picture.

"What! Who's that?"

"Well, according to the book, it's John Anderson."

Cindy looked up with a confused expression and chuckled. "Well, they must've made a mistake. Is there another John Anderson in the book?"

Austin flipped to another page and found a photo. "Well, it's the same picture of a sailor as the last one. And there's only one John Anderson listed in the appendix."

"I don't get it," Cindy said.

"I don't either but clearly your grandfather wasn't Black," Austin replied.

Austin leaned back against the base of John's chair and rubbed his head. "Man, I'm not sure what's going on, but things are getting crazy."

"What are you telling me? That my grandfather wasn't in the Navy? That he wasn't on that ship?"

"No, no, I'm sure he was. I'm not sure why his picture isn't here or at least not as John Anderson."

"So, what do you think happened?"

Austin shook his head. "I don't know, it doesn't add up."

Cindy sat there looking at Austin hoping that he had an answer. "Well?"

He looked at Cindy. "I think the water just got muddier."

"What?"

"We know that your grandfather was part of the OSS, right?"

"That's that secret agency you were talking about, correct?"

"Yeah. I think that your grandfather may of had an alias when he was on the ship."

"An alias, why?"

"Because no one was to find out who he really was."

"What!"

"I bet his mission wasn't intended to be known by anyone."

"You mean that my grandfather's name isn't John Anderson?" she asked.

"No, I'm not saying that. It's just that things aren't adding up like I thought," Austin replied.

Cindy sat there wondering what was going on; Austin wasn't too far behind. He thought that he was on track to figure things out, but now his assumptions were clouded. It made it even more imperative that he find that fifth journal.

Austin got up from the floor. "We need to keep looking. I know it has to be here somewhere."

Cindy closed the book and put it back on the shelf. She hadn't expected to find out that her grandfather wasn't who he said he was, or maybe he was. She was so confused.

CHAPTER

41

The afternoon progressed without much headway into finding the fifth journal. What Austin thought would be an easy search was ending up being a bit more daunting. He appreciated the vast number of volumes that John had accumulated but hadn't expected to have to go through the shelves to find one particular book.

Austin was pulling books from the shelf. "You know, I thought this was going to be easy."

"I know, I did too," replied Cindy.

"I figured that the fifth journal would have the same cover as the first four, so just looking at the binders would have been the simplest way to go."

"Do you think that he may have changed the journal?"

"I beginning to think that could be a possibility. Granted, I just quickly went through the shelves to see if it would stick out, but it doesn't look like it's going to be that simple. We may have to resort to looking at each book to see if it's the one."

"Each book?" Cindy looked up at the shelves from the floor. "Wow, that's a lot of books."

"I guess we have no other alternative unless we get lucky."

It was early in the evening when they decided to take a break and stretch. They had been at it all day.

"I don't think we even made a dent in it," Cindy said.

Austin looked back at the shelves where he had tagged the last book he had gone through. "I know."

"What if it's not here?"

It has to be here, Austin said under his breath.

They both stood in front of the shelf staring at it when Austin's cell phone rang.

"Hey, how are things going?" Anthony asked.

"Well, we're still looking through the library to see if we can come upon the last journal but it's becoming more of a task than we thought."

"Well, we have a problem," Anthony said.

"What?" Austin replied.

"It appears that someone at John's funeral said something to a friend who is a reporter at the Buffalo newspaper. They're looking to write a story about John given that he seems to be a local celebrity now."

"A local celebrity?"

"Well, maybe I overstated it a bit, but the fact remains that they want to do a story and may be reaching out to Cindy."

"We can't have them doing a story and possibly finding out what we have."

"I get it, but we need to get something published so that we can be ahead of the game. Can you get me anything that I can get printed and sent out to the major news agencies? If we do that, then I think the Buffalo paper will do a pass."

"Yeah, I'll put something together and send it to you. Do you think it will be newsworthy enough at this stage?" Austin asked.

"Well, if what you told me when you both were up here has any legs to it, it will certainly be a lot more interesting to the masses. You know, people love mysteries even if it ends up being nothing," Anthony replied.

Austin chuckled. "Well, I hope it's more than that."

"How are you and Cindy doing?"

"Very good, thanks for asking."

"You know, I like her a lot. I think you did well."

"Thanks."

"Okay, just get me something that I can print tomorrow."

"Shit, tomorrow!"

"You're a reporter, you know how this works. I need something that I can get out."

"Okay," said Austin. He clicked off the call and shook his head. He figured that he'd be burning the midnight oil.

"Is everything okay?" Cindy asked.

"Yeah, apparently, there is someone up in Buffalo that wants to do a story about your grandfather. They may try and reach out to you. You'll need to pay attention to who is calling now as it could be someone from the Buffalo paper."

"Okay, what do I say if they call?"

"Just say, no comment."

Austin penned the article and sent it up to Anthony the next morning to review and edit. He looked it over one more time and then reached for the phone. It buzzed a few times then Anthony picked up. "So, what'd you think?"

"I think it's good, but do we want to divulge this much on the speculation that you have regarding a special operations mission in Tokyo? After all that's just a guess at this point. And, what's this about him not being identified on the *Ticonderoga*. I thought you said he served on that ship," Anthony asked.

"Well, we were going through a type of yearbook they did for the crew that served on the ship and it turns out when we looked him up, the picture wasn't John," Austin replied.

"You mean he wasn't on the ship?"

"I am certain he was but apparently not as the John Anderson we know."

"Austin, this is getting crazier by the moment."

"I know but that's what we've uncovered. We figured, based on the journal and John's statement, that he was part of the OSS so who knows what his total role was at the time."

"So how do we publish assumptions. I can't risk printing something that's complete fiction and pawn it off as real."

"Well, so far, we've concluded that he was part of a special mission that went into Tokyo, we just won't mention it as *Operation Sundown* for now. We also can reference that the *Ticonderoga* was not where everyone thought it was on May twenty-fifth, so we can go with that. And John was the last veteran, so we have that. We can keep out the fact that he wasn't on the *Ticonderoga's* records for now, and the OSS part, but the rest should be good enough for print. Think about it Anthony, this may have bigger implications, and, at minimum, it'll keep people tuned in for more. You know how everyone loves a good mystery."

"Not sure I agree with you, but I've gone out on a limb before, and you were on point. I'm going to trust you on this. I just hope you're right or our little paper up here will be the laughingstock of the media industry."

"Thanks Anthony."

Austin clicked off the call and crossed his fingers. He knew he was reaching with the story but felt confident that he was right. Then he crossed his fingers on his other hand for good measure.

CHAPTER

42

I t was noon in Washington, D.C. Captain Clavender Hughes was going through a file of papers on a picnic table in the courtyard of the Pentagon. Tall, muscular with a slight limp, Clavendar or Clay as he was known by his friends and colleagues, was captain of the Senior Intelligence Oversight Department, which included the little-known Military Antiquities Division which was part of the Department of Defense.

"Hey Captain, how are things going?" said Lieutenant Matthew Broadmeyer, as he plopped down at the picnic table. Medium height, slim with a noticeable restriction in the use of his right hand, Lieutenant Broadmeyer was Clay's second in command. Matthew had a wicked sense of humor that often felt flat with his boss.

Clay looked up and didn't say anything.

"Hey, congratulations on 25 years of service," Matthew said.

"Thanks," Clay grunted.

"Twenty-five years is impressive given the circumstances."

"Guess so."

"Come on Cap, you have to at least be thankful that the Army kept us disabled guys engaged in something. They could 've cut us both loose after our injuries in that damn Afghan war, but they didn 't."

Clay looked up again and nodded.

"Well, you, of course, you got all that West Point education in military history, so no wonder they kept you." Matthew reached in his lunch bag and grabbed a sandwich. "Never, could figure why they kept me though."

Clay looked back up from the file he was reading. "Because I needed a good administration person." He put the file down and opened a plastic bowl of salad.

"Shit Cap, I can't believe you keep eating that stuff."

Clay shook his head and picked up the file again as he ate from the container.

"Is that the file the major wants us to review?" Matthew asked.

"Yep," Clay replied.

"Is that the one regarding the special operations unit assigned to the Iraq infiltration?"

"Yeah, mundane stuff in the end but that's what the Major wants. And you know…"

Matthew nodded. "Yep, whatever the Major wants, the Major gets."

Clay grinned. He knew that his team's role was simply to follow orders regardless of how insignificant they thought it was.

Matthew took a bite out of his sandwich. "Cap, you've been doing this work for a long time, have you ever decided to just hang it up and retire?" he muttered with his mouth full.

"And do what," Clay replied.

"I don't know, maybe go down to Florida and fish."

"Yeah, I'll do that when the birds fly south."

Matthew frowned and shook his head. "What?"

"Never mind."

"I know that doing this kind of work isn't what you had in mind when you started with the army, hell, it wasn't mine either but you, man, you could still command an active unit. Not sure why they would keep your ass here instead of in the field."

Clay heard all of this before and simply shrugged. "Those are my orders and that's it." He closed the folder and started to flip through the news feeds on his phone.

"I know, I just think you could do something more dramatic than filing reports that have no value in the end."

"That's what the army wants us to do lieutenant and that's what we'll continue to do, regardless of what impact it may have on us."

Matthew gave a half-ass salute. "Yes sir." Suddenly he noticed Clay adjust himself in the seat as if something had sparked his interest. "What's up Cap?"

Clay didn't say anything; he continued to scroll through something on his phone. Matthew saw Clay's expression change.

"Interesting," Clay said.

Matthew leaned in. "What is?"

"There's an article here about the last living World War two veteran who recently died. It says that he was part of a special operations team that went into Tokyo in May of Nineteen forty-five. It also says that a team was shuttled to Japan via the *USS Ticonderoga*. It says that more will follow."

"Well, it's an interesting story and I hate to be a buzz killer on this, but who cares. I mean, the last living World War two veteran is cool but other than that, I don't think anyone today would really care about it."

"You're probably right but my grandfather served on the *Ticonderoga* although no one in our family knew much about what he did. He died during the war. My mom doesn't really know much about what happened to him. His life's been kind-of a mystery for us."

"Wow, I didn't know that."

"I guess that's why I always had interest in that ship. I did a lot of research on the *Ticonderoga;* I suppose it was a way to get closer to my grandfather. The one thing I do know is the ship wasn't off the coast of Tokyo during the time this guy reports. Also, as far as I know, we never had any military troops in

Tokyo until after the war ended. That's when the *Ticonderoga* was sent back to Japan. I'm not sure where this guy's getting his information."

"Do ya think it really matters? Afterall, it's been years since anyone even talked about that war."

"Well, at minimum, it'd be interesting to see if there's anything to this guy's story… that's if it goes anywhere," Clay said, as he saved the article to his phone file.

"Who's the guy writing the story?"

Clay looked back down at the phone and scrolled for a few moments. "Some guy named Austin Paige. I'm sure I'm probably making more of this than it needs to be."

Matthew shrugged and took a bite out of his sandwich.

Clay stared at this phone. *Ticonderoga, I haven't heard that name in a long time,* he mumbled.

CHAPTER

43

The morning stretched to late afternoon as Austin and Cindy were pulling book-after- book from the shelf. The excitement of finding the last journal was beginning to wane as they continued their search.

"I'm not sure it's here," Cindy said, as she closed another book and returned it to its place.

"It's here somewhere," Austin said.

Cindy got up and sat in John's chair. "I don't know Austin; I'm beginning to think that perhaps we're chasing a ghost."

"I'd probably agree with you if John didn't tell me to look for the fifth, and the fact that you figured out that there's another journal. We'll find it."

Cindy looked over at Austin who was pulling another book from the shelf. "I sure do love you."

Austin turned and smiled. "I'd say ditto, but I'd probably get punched."

"Yes, you would."

"Well, then, I love you too Ms. Davis. You wanna take a break?"

Cindy glanced at the bedroom. "You do say."

Then the doorbell rang.

"Are you kidding!" Austin exclaimed, shaking his head realizing the lost opportunity. Cindy smiled and headed to the front door.

"Hey, how are ya all doin'? We thought we'd drop these off for you guys?" Robert said, as he held out a plate of cookies.

Chris was standing next to Robert. "We knew you were probably working hard and thought we'd bring over some treats for you."

Cindy walked into the living room with Robert and Chris in tow. She looked at Austin with the look that he picked up on... *Well, we tried.*

"So how is the search going?" Chris asked.

"It's getting a bit frustrating; they're more books here than we imagined. We've been looking through each one, but anything could be the last journal at this point."

"Wow, that's a lot of work. Are you sure that it's not somewhere else?" Robert asked.

Austin closed the last book and put it back on the shelf. "Well, we initially thought it would be where the other four journals were, but I guess that would have been too easy. Now we're starting to think that it may be a totally different book altogether."

Chris walked over to the bookcase and brushed his hands across the binders. "Do you think he actually read all of these?"

"He always had one near him," Cindy said. "He'd open one from time-to-time and look through them. It was kind-of sad in a way; these were the only things that he had to remind him of his time in the war."

"Maybe whatever's in the last journal wasn't meant for anyone to read," Chris said.

Austin shrugged. "I don't know, you might be right, but I think that John wouldn't have made reference to it if he didn't want someone to read it."

Robert looked over to the bookshelf. "Well, I think he wanted you to be the one to read it."

"What?" Austin replied.

"I don't know but I think that John figured that his past would go with him. You showed an interest that he must've picked up on. You're the one that started to poke around and found something that he likely didn't think would be discovered. After a while he must've felt comfortable with you. I'm sure he was going to tell you about it but ran out of time." Robert looked over to Cindy hoping that he didn't come off as insensitive.

"I'm sure he wanted you to write his final chapter. It's a big responsibility but one that he must've felt you could handle," Chris said.

Austin felt a lump in his chest as he took in Chris's words. "Wow, I never thought about it in that way. I'm just a reporter doing a story. I guess it was just about the facts."

"I'm sure it was from your perspective, but it's John's legacy that you're going to ultimately write about. I'm not sure, but I think you're going to find something that will change history," Chris said.

Austin shook his head. "Well, I wouldn't go that far."

"Hey, I'm not kidding. I think that John was a hell of a lot more than anyone could have imagined. You already know that now. It's time that everyone else knew it."

Austin was a bit taken by the sensationalism Chris was trying to make of things, but he wasn't too far off. What he had found out up to this point was much more than he could have imagined, he just wasn't sure if anyone else would find it as interesting.

"Well, I can tell you that we're certainly going to work until we find that last journal," Austin said, with a bit of new-found enthusiasm.

Chris smiled, nodded at Austin, and then waved to Robert. "Let's let these two investigative journalists get back to work."

"Hey, I want to thank you both for all your support and help. Don't think that you haven't been an integral part of this work, because you have. If you hadn't done your due diligence to begin with, this story would have died a quiet death," Austin said.

"Well, let's get it right for John," Chris replied.

Cindy walked Chris and Robert to the front door. "Thank you so much." She gave them both a big hug. "I love you guys."

Chris and Robert walked out and across the street. Cindy stood at the door as she watched them walk into their house.

Austin was standing looking at the shelves of books. *We're going to find it,* he mumbled to himself. Cindy snuck up from behind and put her hands around him.

"That was kinda heavy," he said.

"He's right. You're the one that Papa John had been waiting for, just like me."

Austin turned around, looked at Cindy and then kissed her.

CHAPTER

44

C lay sat back in his office chair and scrolled through the Austin Paige article he had saved to his phone. He wasn't sure why it stuck with him. The interest in the *Ticonderoga* and his grandfather had laid dormant for many years and now his curiosity was piqued.

Clay was immersed on the computer and didn't notice Matthew standing at the door. "Cap?"

Clay was startled. "Sorry, Matthew, I was lost looking up some information."

"Something about that ship and your grandfather?"

"Yeah, I guess that article got me thinking about him."

"Find anything?"

"Yeah, well, the ship was attacked by Kamikazes and had some significant damage done to it in January of nineteen forty-five and was routed to Pearl Harbor for repairs. Not sure how she could have managed to be off the coast of Japan in May. I don't understand where this guy's getting his information."

"Maybe he's just trying to get some notoriety or something. You know these types of people, they're only as good as their last piece so they do stories to make them relevant again."

"You're probably right."

"Do you want me to do anything?"

"No, thanks, if I need you, I'll let you know," Clay replied.

"Okay Cap." Matthew turned and walked down to his office.

Clay wasn't sure why he was becoming so engrossed in the article. It was as if something was drawing him to dig deeper. Clay stared at his computer and the picture of the *Ticonderoga* in harbor and read and re-read the caption. It read: *USS Ticonderoga in Pearl Harbor after it was hit by Kamikazes in the Pacific, January 1945.*

There's no way this ship could be off the Tokyo coast in May, mumbled Clay to himself. He continued staring at the ship on the screen as if he was looking for something; he shook his head, *I've got to get over this.*

Then he looked closer and squinted his eyes. He wasn't sure what he was looking for at first but continued to get closer to the screen. Then he expanded the picture. There, very faded, and almost indistinguishable, was the ship's name, *USS Yorktown.* Clay shot straight up, shook his head, and looked back at the picture and description: *Ticonderoga in Pearl Harbor after it was hit by Kamikazes in the Pacific, January 1945.*

Then he looked again at the picture to confirm what he had seen and there it was, *USS Yorktown.*

Clay shook his head. *I'll be damned. This isn't the Ticonderoga. There's gotta be a simple explanation. Why in the world would this picture be wrong, and why hasn't anyone made the same discovery?*

Clay hit a button on his phone.

"Yes sir," came the voice from the other end.

"Lieutenant, get in here, I need you for a minute."

"Yes sir, be right down."

A few minutes passed as Clay enlarged the picture even more to see if the ship's name would be more prominent. The name was so faded and unless someone were really looking for it, no one would have ever noticed it.

Within minutes, Matthew was at Clay's door. "What's up Cap?"

"Look at this," Clay said, as he put the picture back to its normal size and swung his computer around for Matthew to see.

"Okay, it's a picture of a ship."

"Yeah, yeah, you're right but do you see anything weird?"

Matthew stared at the picture. "Uh, no, sorry Cap it's just a picture of the *Ticonderoga* in port. Just like the caption reads."

"Look closer," Clay said.

Matthew bent down and got closer to the screen but didn't notice anything different. "Sorry Cap, nothin' there."

Then Clay enlarged the picture and centered the aft of the ship with the name on it. "See anything now?"

Matthew looked at Clay wondering what had gotten into him. Then looked back down. "Wait a minute, *USS Yorktown*. What the hell!"

Clay smiled. "Interesting, isn't it?"

"Why in the world would the picture be of another ship. It doesn't make any sense. Maybe it's simply a mistake," Matthew said.

"That's what I thought too. And maybe it was a mistake but why after all these years would someone not have noticed that."

"Well, Cap, first, you can't see the name and until you expanded the picture, I didn't even notice it."

"Right, and think about it, during the war, all they had were black-and-white photos that they'd put in newspapers. The quality was so bad that no one would have even noticed the name."

"Okay, but why do this, it doesn't make sense?" Matthew asked.

Clay grinned. "Well, maybe it was to keep it secret as to where the *Ticonderoga* really was."

"Cap, you're not believing what that reporter wrote, are you?"

Clay shrugged. "Well, maybe not, but something's off, don't you think?"

"Could be, but again, why get involved? It's old history."

"I don't know lieutenant, but I wonder...."

Matthew saw the expression in Clay's face, he'd seen it before. "Cap don't tell me. You're not going to get involved with this are you?"

"Gotta find out why this picture is wrong and where the reporter is getting his information," Clay replied.

"I don't know if this is our call. The Major won't take it fondly that we're chasing down a story that has no relevance to anything."

"If this reporter is right and we had something to do with some operation deep in Tokyo during the war, don't you think that it'd be important to find out what it was?"

"Respectfully, Cap, I don't think it's a big deal." Matthew could see that Clay was starting to grasp onto something that he wasn't going to let go. "I just don't think that we should spend any resources on this."

"We're not," Clay said.

Matthew shook his head. "Sorry Cap, but I don't believe you. Once you get something in your head, you see it to the end."

"No Lieutenant, this isn't anything that you have to be concerned with." Clay turned the computer around and straightened himself in his office chair.

Matthew stood there for a moment, then smiled. "So, Cap, where do we begin?"

Clay smiled back, "We go to the Dungeon."

CHAPTER

45

I t had already been several days, and it was getting late into the evening. Austin and Cindy had looked through almost every book on the shelf and had begun to stack them throughout the house to ensure that they weren't looking through the same ones twice; the stacks looked like a maze.

Austin pulled the book from his briefcase that he had earlier taken from the shelf. He stared at it; he hadn't found anything further save the date that would tie it to anything material. And with the exception of the red marker that was stuck to the page, thought its relevance was moot. The fatigue of looking through so many books clouded his judgement and, in a decision he would later regret, he placed the book back on one of the stacks.

"Austin, I don't know. Perhaps we weren't meant to find the last journal. Heavens, maybe we were wrong about this whole thing," Cindy said, as she looked around the room.

Austin's expression showed the frustration. "We just can't give up. It's here somewhere!"

"We've looked at all of these, it's just not here," Cindy said, with a sigh of resignation.

Austin plopped down in John's chair. "Man, I could use a drink.,"

"Seriously?!" Cindy said.

Austin waved it off. "Sorry, I guess I'm just getting tired."

The tension of getting the story finished weighed on him. He had published a teaser article and had committed to another. He also knew that he had sold Anthony on John's special operations mission and short of the few things he had found in the first four journals, he was worried that Anthony may be right; there wasn't anything to it. When under pressure, the best thing to do was to decompress and bourbon was his medicine.

Austin rubbed his head. "Shit, I don't know. We're down to the last few rows of books and nothing's popping out"

"We need to take a break," Cindy said.

"Yeah, I guess you're right."

"Look outside."

"What's outside?"

"The moon's out."

Austin peered through the windows and could see the tree leaves luminated by the glow of the moonlight.

"Fresh air would be good right now," Austin said.

"What?" Cindy replied.

Actually, a good stiff drink would be better, he mumbled under his breath.

"I heard that."

"Did I say that out loud?"

"Yep."

Cindy got a blanket from the closet and took Austin's hand. "We're going down to the river."

They walked to the bench where they had been before. They sat in silence and gazed out at the water. The last time they were there, they had talked about their lives and what they hoped they could become. Now each wondered where they would be going together. The water was tranquil, and the moon made the waves look like they had floating diamonds.

"I'm sorry," Austin said, as he broke the silence.

"What?" Cindy replied.

"I thought I had a handle on the stress, but clearly I was wrong."

"We all handle stress differently."

"I know but to quickly jump to wanting a drink isn't a smart thing to say, especially given my history."

"Well, it was just a comment, you didn't do anything."

"Yeah, but you're here. I don't know if I would have been that strong otherwise."

Cindy rubbed Austin's arm. "Yes you would. You're not the same person you were before."

Austin reached over and started rubbing her hand. "I don't know. I think I'm the same person, I just have you here to keep me straight."

Cindy smiled, reached up and gave Austin a kiss on the cheek.

The days had started to warm but the breeze from the water made the evening temperatures a bit cooler. Austin wrapped the blanket around their legs and pulled it up to their waist and just took in the beauty of the dancing glitter across the water. Cindy was right, he needed to get away from things and relax. He closed his eyes; his mind started to wander. He saw Mandy's gravestone and remembered feeling her presence.

Cindy laid her head on his shoulders.

"You know, you're the best thing that's ever happened to me." Austin turned and stared into her eyes. "I really don't know how things would have turned out if you hadn't come into my life."

Cindy wrapped her hands around his arm. "Well, you mean a lot to me Mr. Paige."

He hesitated, his heart started pounding; then he took the moment. "Well, you mean a lot to me too, Mrs. Paige."

Cindy sat up in the bench looking at Austin wondering if she heard correctly. "What did you say!"

He looked down and smiled. "I know this is completely unexpected, but I feel a connection that I never thought I'd ever feel again. And I figure that this is pretty sudden for you, and I understand if you have your doubts, but I know it's right for me."

Cindy froze, her heart pounded so hard that she could feel it.

He stammered for a moment. "Uh, what I'm trying to say is, would you be Mrs. Paige?"

"Um, I... I... I," she stuttered.

"Well, I really wasn't adequately prepared. I mean, I guess I should've gotten down on my knee and had a formal ring, but I guess that can come later."

Cindy sat there in shock.

"I know I should have done a better job of this." Austin paused a moment, "But would you be my wife?"

Tears started running down her face. "Yes... yes, I would love to be your wife."

Cindy jumped up and into Austin's arms; they both kissed. "I love you so much," she said.

"I love you more than you'll know," he replied. He really wanted to say *ditto* but thought that he may have overused that phrase for now.

They started back to the house arm-in-arm. Austin was surprised at himself; frankly, he'd planned for things to happen a bit differently. The decision to ask her wasn't in question but he just thought he'd do it in a more romantic way and perhaps have given their relationship more time. But the moon was dancing off the water and he knew she was 'the one'. And besides, they were together on a beautiful night.

Well, nothing could have been more romantic than that, he thought.

CHAPTER

46

Cindy and Austin walked into the house after their visit to the waterfront. He knew that he had proposed in a way that she hadn't been prepared, but thought, *who's really prepared for a question like that.* She hadn't said anything on their walk back and he started wondering if she was having any second thoughts.

"Are you okay?" he asked.

"Yeah, just in a state of shock," she replied.

"I'm sorry that I popped it on you like that."

"No, I'm so excited, I…. I…I just don't know what to say."

"Well, I got a yes, so I'm happy."

They walked inside. Cindy sat in John's chair, looked up at Austin and smiled. He smiled back. No one said anything, then Austin's cell phone rang.

"How are things going down there?" Anthony asked.

Austin looked over at Cindy who was in a daze. "Going well."

"Well, your story seems to have gotten some traction."

"It has?"

"Yeah, it has. I guess I hadn't consciously thought about it, but we put it out on Memorial Day, so it got some hits as a result."

"Hits, what are you talking about."

"Well, in addition to putting it in the paper up here, we put it on our Facebook page and, well, you wouldn't believe it, but the things gone viral. We're getting comments from everywhere; people are reading it!" Anthony said.

"Everywhere?" Austin inquired.

"Yep, we have people as far as Japan reading it. I guess you were right, people are captivated by the fact that we had the last living US veteran and even more interested to learn what John was up to during the war. Geez Austin, you nailed it with your premise that people would have interest in this kind of thing. It's certainly beyond me."

"Wow, I wouldn't have expected that kind of response."

"Well, I'm glad that you talked me into releasing the story; I had my doubts, but you were on target with this. We need to do a follow-up. How are things going with the last journal?"

"We're still looking but we'll find it."

"Still looking? Austin, we need to get something out and take advantage of the notoriety we're getting from this. It's not like our little paper up here gets much notice, but your story seems to have resonated in some way. When can I get something?"

Austin looked at the stacks of books. "I'll get something to you soon."

"Okay but let's not let too much time go by or we'll lose the momentum."

"Will do."

"Tell Cindy I said hi. I'm looking forward to reading what you have coming next."

"Okay, thanks. Talk to you soon." Austin clicked off his phone.

Cindy looked at him, she didn't need a recap of things; she knew what was being said and could see the expression on Austin's face – he was worried.

"We'll find it," she said.

"I hope so, or I'm toast," he replied.

CHAPTER

47

Austin walked around the room weaving between the stacks of books that they had scattered throughout the room. *Come on, come on, where are you?* he mumbled as he approached the last two shelves of unopen books.

Cindy could see how anxious Austin was becoming and decided he needed time alone. Besides, she was still reeling over his proposal. She got up and decided to go into Papa John's bedroom. She hadn't been in his room since she returned from his funeral. She wasn't sure why, but it just didn't feel right at the time. She looked at the pictures on his dresser that she had seen so many times before, but, for some reason, it felt like it was the first time she'd seen them. There was a collection of family photos in old, dusty frames. She picked up a picture of John and Evy which looked to be when they first moved to Florida. Both had big smiles which probably was a result of moving from Buffalo to sunny Fort Myers. There were photos of her parents and her when she was a small child. She smiled as she thought of how her grandfather loved his family. She walked around the room, opened the closet, and brushed her hand across the pants and shirts that were hanging there. The clothes were old and wrinkled, just the way he liked it. She shook her head and smiled thinking of the numerous arguments they had when she would try to get him to upgrade his wardrobe. Then she walked over and sat on the side of his bed. *I really miss you Papa John; you wouldn't believe what just happened,* she said in a whisper.

Cindy sat there for a while and, for some unexplained reason, reached over and opened the bedside table drawer. It was full of clutter that John had collected over the years. She pulled out a folded newspaper clipping that was on the top of everything. She remembered seeing John read this several times and then fold it neatly and put it back in the drawer. The paper had yellowed over the years and the folded seams were taped together to keep it intact. She slowly opened it; it was a photo of her young grandfather in his army uniform. He was posed with his foot on, what looked like a footlocker, while holding a box that looked to be military issue. It was a small newsclip that the Buffalo paper wrote about him when he returned from the war. He had a serious, almost sad expression. It read:

> *We, in Buffalo, are proud to have one of our own return to Robert and Emily Anderson. John served with distinction on the aircraft carrier, USS Ticonderoga. It was due to his bravery and sacrifice that resulted in so many lives being saved when the Japanese Kamikazes attacked the ship in January 1945. John Anderson is a hometown hero. Welcome Home!*

Cindy started to wonder why John looked so sad and noticed on the margin something written in pencil, and by the look of it, was written when he cut the article from the paper. It said: *Bullshit!*

She sat there for a moment staring at the picture trying to figure out why he had written that and for what reason. She was surprised; in her mind, her grandfather was a hero, but apparently, he didn't think so. He had served admirably and, from what he and Austin had uncovered, was more than just a sailor; he was a special operations person on a secret mission.

Well, you're a hero in my eyes. Why are you so sad, she whispered.

She started to fold the paper back up but took one more look at the photo. Something stuck out. *Wait a minute; I remember that.*

She folded the article and put it back in the drawer, got up and went to the closet. She looked on the top shelf that was cluttered with shoes, hats, and assorted clothing. She pushed aside some dusty sweaters that had been up there for years. There it was the box that John had been holding in the picture. Her heart started to pound again, almost as much as it had when Austin asked her to marry him.

The box wasn't heavy but certainly dusty. She put it on the bed, brushed the dust from the lid and lifted the latch that secured it. She slowly opened the box and started flipping through the contents. It was full of papers, military ribbons, Purple Hearts and what looked like dog tags.

I never knew he got a Purple Heart, she mumbled.

She held one of them and wondered how many more secrets John kept from everyone. She put it back in the box and started shuffling through the documents that were bound together with rubber bands. She flipped a few more things and noticed something at the bottom of the box.

"Austin!" she screamed.

CHAPTER

48

There was a reason they refer to the area as the Dungeon. It's the basement of the Pentagon which is filled with rooms and rooms of boxes of written records and historical military documents dating from as far back as the Revolutionary War. The area is tightly monitored, environmentally maintained, and has a high-level security system; very few people have clearance to this area. Fortunately, as the senior officer for the Antiquities Division, Clay has access, but he seldom ventured down.

Clay and Matthew walked down the hallway that looked to have no end.

REDRUM, mumbled Matthew.

"What?!" Clay said.

"You know sir, the scene from the movie The Shining, when the boy writes REDRUM on the door." Matthew could see Clay's eyes roll. "Uh, never mind."

"Seriously lieutenant!"

"Sorry sir. Just got a bit weirded out about being down here."

They turned a corner where there was a door with a plaque; Room 00467A-WWII-Pacific, and a numerical pad. Clay punched in a few numbers and the door clicked open. The lights automatically turned on. The room was a comfortable 72 degrees, as the thermometer beside the light switch indicated, and it was very, very large.

"Are you serious Cap. You think we'll find anything in here?"

"One thing I can say Lieutenant, is that the military is very well organized."

"Organized! Did you see the way we left Afghanistan? Not sure about that Cap."

"Listen, we need to focus on finding something on the *Ticonderoga*. This room is set up to warehouse all the World War two records for the Pacific theatre so it's gotta be in here somewhere."

"Shit, where do we start?" Matthew asked.

Clay didn't say anything and instead started down the main aisle that had rows and rows of file cabinets and shelves full of boxes.

Matthew followed Clay. "I feel like I'm in the warehouse at the end of the Indiana Jones movie. You know, the one that had the Arc that was boxed and stored. There were thousands of boxes piled up for as far as the eye could see."

Clay didn't say anything and continued walking down the aisle looking at the side of the racks that had signs with naval engagements and dates.

Guess I'm just talking to myself, Matthew mumbled, as he threw his arms in the air.

"Just keep an eye out for 1945 and let me know when you find it," Clay said.

Yes sir, that'll be a miracle, mumbled Matthew.

A few hours had passed as Clay and Matthew split up to gain as much ground as they could. Matthew was impressed by some of the artifacts that had been stored down in the room. There was a framed battle worn Japanese Rising Sun flag that was taken when the US captured Okinawa. He stopped and looked at some photos of the troops as they landed on the beaches in the Philippines. He was really impressed when he saw a Naval Officer's hat that was in a glass encasement. The plaque read, *Admiral Nimitz.*

"Anything yet?" came a voice from the distance.

"No sir, not yet" Matthew replied, as he hurried to get back on track.

"Keep looking!"

Matthew shook his head; he felt the task of finding anything was just a prayer given the sheer size of the room. He walked down several aisles and started to wonder how he was going to find his way out. *Geez, they'd never find me in here,* he sighed.

He looked at his watch, wondering when his captain was going to call it quits when he looked up and saw, *Pacific Theatre, 1945, Aircraft Carrier Operations.*

"Cap!!" yelled Matthew.

It took several minutes before Clay got to where Matthew was standing. In the interim, Matthew started humming the Indiana Jones movie theme.

Matthew pointed as Clay turned the corner. "Here you go."

"Good Job," Clay said.

"Okay, what are we specifically looking for?"

Clay looked at the labels on the cabinets. "Anything that has a *USS Ticonderoga* or *USS Yorktown* tag."

A few more minutes passed when Matthew found a section of file cabinets that were labeled, *USS Ticonderoga, Operational Files*. A few cabinets down were the *USS Yorktown, Operational Files*. Each had about 10 cabinets dedicated to each ship.

"Got it!!" yelled Matthew."

"Which one?" came a voice from several aisles over.

"Both!"

It took only a few seconds for Clay to find Matthew. "Great job Lieutenant."

"Just call me Indiana Jones," Matthew said, hoping to elicit a laugh. He didn't get one.

"Okay, let's see what we can find here," Clay said.

"What are we looking for now?" Matthew asked.

"See if you can find anything labeled May 1945. Specifically, any operational status of the ship during that time. You look through the *Yorktown* files."

Clay opened the *Ticonderoga* cabinet starting from the last drawer. "Start from the back and move forward. May was near the end of the war so no sense starting at the beginning."

"Good idea," Matthew replied.

Clay started working up a sweat as he flipped through the files despite the cool temperature of the room.

"Anything yet?" he asked.

"Nothing." Several minutes passed. "Wait, I think I found something for May!" Matthew shouted.

"Okay pull that and let's take a look," Clay said.

Matthew walked over with the file and was flipping it back and forth in his hand.

Clay didn't pay any attention to it as he continued going through the *Ticonderoga* files.

Some time passed. "Lucky day, I just found the one for the *Ticonderoga*," Clay said. He pulled it out. "What, this isn't right."

"Not much in yours?" Matthew asked.

Clay opened the file. The only thing in it was a document noted, *Classified – Admiral's Eyes Only – Operation Sundown.*

Matthew opened his file, similarly as thin, and pulled out a document and showed it to Clay. It read: *Classified – Admiral's Eyes Only – Operation Sundown.*

"What we got here is a mystery," Matthew said.

"Shit, maybe there's something to that reporter's story," Clay said.

"Well Cap, I can tell you this. I don't think anyone was ever to find this stuff. And we're probably walking down a path we shouldn't."

Clay didn't say anything. He was thinking that Matthew was probably right, but now he was committed to find out what *Operation Sundown* was all about. The problem was, they just opened a door that was supposed to stay closed.

CHAPTER

49

C lay and Matthew had taken pictures of the *Ticonderoga* and *Yorktown* files with their cell phones before putting them back in their respective places. They started heading back to the entrance in a fast pace.

"What do ya think *Operation Sundown* is all about?" Matthew asked.

"I don't know but it's something that might be interesting to find out," Clay replied.

"Seriously Cap, that reporter was writing about an old man that served in the war. Granted he's found a few things out that may have been a secret back in the day, but it's surely not important today."

"I get it lieutenant, but I have to find out if this story has anything to it."

Matthew was puzzled as to why Clay felt there was such a need. "Cap, I don't know if we should be poking around something that had *Admiral Eyes Only*. I think we're going above our paygrade."

They got to the entrance, turned off the lights, secured the door and strode down the long hallway. The walk back to the office didn't seem as long as the walk to the Dungeon. Clay didn't say anything in the elevator as they headed up to his office.

"Okay Cap, what's next?"

"Now we start digging." Clay smiled, turned, and went into his office.

Matthew scratched his head. *Digging, shit, I thought that's what we just did.*

Clay was a driven officer. It served him well in Afghanistan when he was responsible for his team's missions. After returning to the States from his injury and being assigned to the Antiquities Division, he felt that he had lost his edge. Having a mystery, even if it happened decades ago, was something that gave him a sense of purpose.

"Cap, what do you want me to do now?"

"Nothing for now. I'm going to do some checking through the computer and see if anything pops up."

Matthew shook his head. "I don't know Cap, me thinketh that some things are just not meant to be found, just sayin'."

Clay didn't say anything and flipped open is laptop and started typing. Matthew got the message and walked back to his office.

Several minutes passed as Clay unsuccessfully checked the files on the *Ticonderoga* and *Yorktown*. Many of the files that he was able to access were some photos and reports that looked to be electronic copies of the files he and Matthew just went through. Given his security clearance, he felt comfortable pulling up data that isn't available to other military officers or to the public.

Clay was clicking away on the computer keyboard. *There must be something to this reporter's story.*

He pulled up the article from his phone and read through it again. The special operations reference had more significance then when he first read it, especially now given what he had found, but *Operation Sundown* was not mentioned in the reporter's piece.

Clay's fingers were dancing across the keyboard as if he was worried that someone might find out what he was up to. He pulled up information on both ships on and around May 1945. Nothing spectacular came up and he was starting to wonder if he had poorly hyped his curiosity.

I don't know, maybe I'm just too close to this, Clay mumbled.

He decided to type in *Operation Sundown* in the query section of the *Ticonderoga* file that he had open. Clay hit the last key and pushed enter. *Don't know why I didn't do this to begin with.*

The small search circle in the center of his screen started spinning and spinning. He leaned back in his chair waiting for something to pop-up. He shook his head as the circle continued spinning. *Come on, come on.* Suddenly, the screen went black.

Clay shook his head in puzzlement. *What the...*

He leaned forward and checked the power button; it was still on. He turned the computer off and on, but nothing seemed to get the screen to light up. He punched a button on his desk phone.

"Yes sir?"

"Matthew, does your computer work?"

"Sure does, workin' fine," Matthew replied. "What's up sir?"

"My screen just went dark. Maybe it's just something with the computer."

"I'll be right down." Matthew hung up and headed to Clay's office.

Clay checked the power cord to see if it was plugged in before Matthew came down. He didn't want the issue to be something that was an easy fix.

"Hey Cap, let me check it out." Matthew came around the desk. "Typically, it's something really basic." He checked the power cord in the wall and in the computer. "Well, that's good," he said.

Clay was relieved that he had at least done that. Matthew clicked several buttons on the computer.

"Shit Cap, I don't get it. There's really no reason that your computer should've died. I guess it just crapped out."

"Maybe, but it's a new computer so I am surprised it died like that."

"What was the last thing you had up before it went out?"

"I did a query on *Operation Sundown*. It was taking a while and the search circle was spinning for some time and then suddenly, the screen went black."

Matthew's expression emoted concerned. "Holy shit!"

"What?" Clay replied.

"Maybe you weren't supposed to pull up that file."

"Lieutenant, I'm the department head of the Antiquities Division. I can pull up any damn file I want to." The words had just come out of Clay's mouth when his office phone rang. He looked at Matthew; it was the Major's direct line.

"Yes ma'am. Yes ma'am." Clay went silent but Matthew could hear the garble from the handset. "Yes ma'am, I'll be right up." He slowly hung up the phone.

"What?!"

"The Major wants to see me."

"Shit, did she say why?" Matthew asked.

"No, and she didn't sound very happy." Clay responded.

CHAPTER

50

Austin was sitting on the floor pulling books from the last two shelves when he heard Cindy's scream. He was startled but it seemed more to be a sound of exhilaration. He popped up and ran to the bedroom. *Whatever it is, I hope it's good,* he thought.

He turned the corner to see her grinning from ear-to-ear and holding up a book. It had the same cover and the same look…it was the fifth journal.

"This is it!" Cindy said with notable excitement.

"Seriously!" Austin replied.

"Yep!"

"Where in the world was it?"

Cindy pointed to the closet. "It was in this box that Papa John had on the shelf up there." Austin glanced at the box and then to where she was pointing.

"I can't believe it. You're truly amazing. You just keep discovering things every time we're almost at wits end."

He hugged her and at the same time looked down at the journal she had placed on the bed. *I can't believe it, finally.* He was excited but mostly relieved.

Austin grabbed the book and headed to the living room. Cindy closed the box and put it back on the shelf. She didn't reveal anything else that she had found; she was simply too excited to have found the fifth journal.

Austin had the book in his hands and was flipping through the pages. He thought that perhaps something might fall out that would provide some additional information, like when the map fell from the earlier journal, but nothing came out.

Cindy came out of the bedroom and joined Austin. "I hope this tells us everything that we need to know," he said. "I wonder why he had this separated from the other four journals?"

"Maybe he just forgot to include it with the others," Cindy responded.

"Could be but it really doesn't matter now. We found it, well, you found it; I just pray it tells us something."

Austin held the book as if it was a precious one-of-a-kind heirloom. He looked around at the books that had been strategically stacked throughout the room. He was thinking that he wished Cindy had found the book earlier instead of having spent so much time sorting through everything.

He chuckled; *hindsight's always twenty-twenty.*

"So, what do you think it says?" Cindy asked.

"I'm nervous to read it now," replied Austin.

"Why?"

"Well, we've put so much emphasis on the assumption that this journal will reveal the final chapter that, well, now I'm worried that it won't tell us anything at all."

"You won't know unless you open it."

Austin rubbed the cover. It was almost as if he was rubbing the magic lantern hoping that it would reveal secrets. "You're right," he said.

"Listen, I'm going to make some of our favorite coffee. I think this is going to be a long night." Cindy got up and walked to the kitchen, dodging several stacks of books along the way.

Austin sat in John's chair. He wasn't sure what prompted him to do that, but he felt an eerie connection to him now. John told him to look for the fifth and now it was in his hands.

Okay Papa John, talk to me, he whispered.

CHAPTER

51

C lay hadn't talked with Major Beverly Whitestone in almost two years, but he knew her well - very well. She was a no-nonsense officer. Major Whitestone had risen through the ranks on sheer determination and persistence, which was the reason for her being so tough. She graduated with a master's in military statistical operations from West Point and had served principally in administration capacities throughout her career. At the Pentagon, she was responsible for Military Clandestine Operations, a unit that very few were aware of. The unit was responsible for controlling communications of past and present secret military operations. Many of these operational successes and failures were kept confidential and never saw the light of day. The Senior Intelligence Oversight Department, and Clay, reported to her.

Clay walked into the Major's administrator's office. "I understand Major Whitestone wants to see me," Clay said to the lieutenant sitting behind the desk.

"Yes sir," he replied. "I'll let her know that you are here. Please have a seat."

Clay looked around and found a chair. Several minutes passed when the lieutenant walked back from the Major's office. "Captain, the Major will see you." He opened her door.

The Major was very attractive, tall with black hair that was cut just below her ears. She was on the phone when Clay entered and was motioned to sit at the chair in front of her desk. He looked around the room at several photos with her and dignitaries from around the world. There were a few photos of the Major with the President of the United States and another with the Secretary of Defense. In short, she was well connected.

Major Whitestone finally finished the conversation and hung up her desk phone.

"Captain how are you doing?" she asked in a polite way.

"Doing very well ma'am," replied Clay.

"Captain, how are things going down in the Antiquities department?"

"Going very well, ma'am."

"I'm sure that your role down there doesn't get the recognition it deserves."

What is she getting to? Why the small talk, that's not like her.

"Well, I just want you to know that you've done a great job there. I haven't been down in some time and that's my fault; I should rectify that," the Major said.

"Thank you, ma'am. I have a great team." Clay stiffened in the chair. "Major, with all due respect. Why did you want to see me?"

Major Whitestone got up, walked around, and sat on the corner of her desk. "Captain, we have a section of our department that has the responsibility to keep an eye on code words that are unique to any military operations either past or present. We use a computer algorithm to flag anything that anything that corresponds to a set of key words, phrases, dates and then it provides us with the surrounding information and context."

"With all due respect, it sort of sounds like big brother to me," Clay said.

The Major chuckled. "Well maybe, but we're really trying to determine if anyone has compromised our operational plans and are communicating it within their networks."

"Still sounds a bit Orwellian."

"It's served us well over the years. We've been able to intercept communications that we've used to head off compromises in our strategic initiatives."

"Interruptions in our strategic initiatives?"

"Yeah, our secret operational plans."

You could have said that, thought Clay. He also figured that he had been had; *key words, key phrases, well that's what was on my computer when it went blank.* He let the Major continue.

"We typically have a lot of activity and, generally speaking, the information we get is benign; it's typically coincidental and harmless. But on occasion we get word combinations and phrases that raise eyebrows," she said.

"Is the public aware that we have this capability?" Clay asked.

"This has the approval from the White House and that's all we need."

So no, Clay thought. "Okay, I still don't understand why I'm here."

"Well, we had something come up that caught our attention. A few weeks ago, an article was published about an operation back in World War two that involved the *Ticonderoga*. It states that it was tied to a specific special operation back in May of nineteen forty-five."

"Yes ma'am, I read that as well. It was really about the last living veteran of the war. What's so interesting about it?"

The Major leaned forward. "That's what I'd like to know?"

"Excuse me?"

There was silence as the Major stared at Clay. "It seems a bit coincidental that we have this article pop up at the same time you tried to access operational files that are beyond your authority."

The Major got up and walked back behind her desk and sat down in her chair.

"I wasn't aware that I had restrictions to any archived information," Clay said.

"Typically, that's correct, but there are some things that are off limits," she responded.

Matthew was right, we went above our paygrade. Clay knew he'd been caught. "You must mean *Operation Sundown.*"

She didn't let on, that besides him, there had only been one other time that *Operation Sundown* had been queried. "Why were you pulling up that information?" she asked.

"I was curious about the *Ticonderoga* in May of nineteen forty-five. The article piqued some interest, so I went to the Dungeon and dug up the *Ticonderoga* file. The only thing I found from that time was a reference to *Operation Sundown.* I started to do some digging to see what that was all about."

"Why?"

He didn't want to reveal the details about what he had already discovered about the *USS Yorktown* picture and the similar *Sundown Operation* reference tied to that ship.

"I was curious and wanted to see what the connection was with the *Ticonderoga.* Is there a reason why that information is classified?" he asked.

"Didn't your grandfather serve on that carrier?" she responded.

"Yes ma'am, but you knew that already."

"Captain, that's a long-ago war. *Operation Sundown* was an old military operational plan that was scrapped during the latter part of the war."

"Major, if it was an old plan that was scrapped then why have the details remain restricted?"

"Captain, it's just not material anymore. Is that clear enough?"

"Yes ma'am, I'll stop poking around."

The Major sat staring at Clay for a moment, she wasn't certain if he was sincere or just giving her lip-service. She looked across, ran her finger through her hair, leaned forward and put her hands on her desk. She slowly shook her head back and forth and then leaned back in her chair.

"Shit. I shouldn't have you do this." There was a pause. "Captain, I need you to do something."

"Ma'am?"

"The article that came to our attention is from a reporter in Fort Myers, Florida." She opened a file on her desk. "His name is Austin Paige. I need you to go down there and find out what he knows."

"Do you think that the special operations mission that he mentioned in the article is really *Operation Sundown*?"

"That's our assumption."

"But he seems to have focused his attention on the last living veteran. The operational reference seems to be an ancillary note."

"I'm not sure that it is. If so, then fine, but if not then we need to know what he knows."

"Major, if there isn't anything to this, then why make something of it? Don't you think that he'll wonder why we're there?"

"Captain, we just need to figure out what this reporter knows and where he's getting his information. Figure out a story to tell him but you need to report back to me with what you find out and talk to no one, but me."

"I'd like to take Lieutenant Broadmeyer with me if I may."

"Not sure why you need him."

"He can be my second set of eyes. He can give me a different perspective on things. He may see something that I might miss."

She rubbed her temples. "Okay, go ahead but whatever you two find out needs to stay strictly confidential."

Clay was curious as to the contradictions he was getting. *Operation Sundown* is not important but whatever I find needs to be confidential.

"Major, I'm getting the impression that you aren't telling me everything. Is there something that I should know?" Clay asked.

"Captain, I only need you to determine where the reporter is getting his information and what he knows," she replied.

"Ma'am, I can't do my job with bits and pieces of things. What am I looking for?"

"Just report back to me with what you find out?" she said matter-of-factly.

Clay stood up and saluted; the Major returned the salute. Clay turned and started toward the door.

"Clay?" she said.

He turned around.

"It's good to see you again."

Clay smiled, "It's good to see you too, Bev."

CHAPTER

52

Austin was dozing in the chair with the journal next to him. He started reading it and had fallen asleep during the night. The search for the fifth journal had kept the adrenaline running but the exhaustion of worrying and then finally finding it had taken the toll on both.

Cindy woke up on the sofa having slept there all evening. *Austin?* she whispered. *Austin?* she whispered again.

He slowly woke up and started to churn in the chair. "Man, my body is killing me," he said as he stretched. He started arching his back and rubbing it with both hands. "I can't believe I fell asleep in this chair."

"What did you find out?" she asked.

Austin shook his head to clear the fog. "Very interesting," he said as he stretched and gave out a big yawn.

"Well?"

"I got through a few pages before I dozed off, but it appears from what I read that John's entries in this particular journal were after he returned from overseas. That may be the reason why it was separated from the rest. He was documenting things that he experienced in the latter part of the war and afterwards."

"What does it say about his time on the ship? Does it say anything about who he was?" She was still puzzled as to why he wasn't in any pictures in the book she found on the *Ticonderoga*.

"Nothing in particular yet, but from what I read so far it was about the men he served with, especially, Frank Balboa."

"Who was that?"

"You remember when John started to talk about the guys that he served with when he was with the OSS?"

"Yeah."

"Well Frank Balboa was Jaws, remember?"

"Oh, yeah, I remember. There were Smitty and Ghost, right?" she clarified.

"Correct. Well, it appears that Papa John and Frank became very close. He mentions him several times. Frank was from New York City so the fact that they both were from New York probably made their connection even tighter," he replied.

"Yeah, I can see how that would make sense."

"Actually, the group of them became a pretty solid team according to Papa John."

"What else?"

"They all had the utmost respect for Captain Burton. He apparently was like a father figure to all of them. When he said to jump, they all responded with how high."

Cindy laughed; she could see Papa John responding that way. "I still don't understand why he wasn't in the book," she said.

"Well, when you fell asleep last night, I went and found the *Ticonderoga* book again to see if I could find the others."

And?" she asked.

"None of them are pictured," he said. "I'm not sure yet but I think they weren't supposed to be identified for some reason."

"That doesn't make sense. They were all on the ship, weren't they?"

"Yes, but you gotta remember, the OSS was in its infancy. There wasn't a playbook at the time, so they were likely making things up along the way."

"Okay, I guess that makes sense."

Austin stretched again and stood up. "Man, I need a shower. I gotta wake up," he said. "Hey, I found this wedged in the first few pages."

Austin pulled a picture out and gave it to Cindy. It was a picture of John, Smitty, Ghost, Jaws, and Captain Burton. It was the first picture during that time that she had seen her grandfather smile, actually all of them were smiling. They were clearly oblivious to what was coming.

CHAPTER

53

The shower cleared Austin's head and it felt good having the hot water run over his body. He stood there wondering how he was going to write the next installment of John's story. He already made mention of him being the last World War II veteran and had planted the seed that he was also part of a special operations team on the *Ticonderoga*, but he didn't provide any details, which was by design. He hadn't expected the article to gain as much traction as it had, and honestly, was surprised by it all. Now, it was time to unravel the mystery and he felt confident the last journal would tell the final story. He reached to turn the water off when he noticed Cindy come into the bathroom. He wiped the fog from the shower door and realized that she wasn't wearing anything. The door slowly opened.

She entered the shower. "What would you like for breakfast?"

"I like my eggs over easy," Austin replied, as he wrapped his arms around her.

"Well, I'll get right to that," she said, then they kissed.

They lightly dried off and climbed into bed. The next hour was filled with passion that was not hindered by the damp sheets. When they finished, they just laid there looking at each other as he brushed her hair.

"That was the best breakfast in bed that I've ever had," Austin said.

She laughed and gave him a soft punch in his stomach.

"Whaaat? I'm looking forward to lunch," he chuckled.

"I'm sure you are. I think you have some work to do, Mr. Paige." She climbed out of bed and went into the bathroom.

Austin propped up and watched Cindy go into the bathroom and close the door. *I have to be the luckiest guy in the world.*

Austin laid back down when his cell phone rang, he knew who it was without looking. "Hey Anthony, how's it go'in?"

"I was just going to ask you that," came the reply.

Austin felt uneasy, he knew that Anthony wanted a finished product. "Well, we finally found the fifth journal; I started through it but unfortunately dozed off last night, so I'll be getting back into it this morning."

"Great to hear you found it. I want to get your next story published so I need something this evening that I can put in the paper tomorrow."

"I'll get you something but not sure how I'll frame it yet."

"What'd ya mean frame it? Isn't it pretty clear where you're going, given what you've learned so far?"

"Yeah, you're right, but I haven't gotten to all the details yet, beyond what I've gleaned from the other journals, but I should have more once I finish this one."

"When are you going to finish it?"

Cindy came out of the bathroom wearing nothing. She walked over to the closet, turned and smiled. Austin was captured by how beautiful she looked and forgot his train of thought.

"Austin! Did you hear what I said?"

"Oh sorry, I got distracted by something."

You're so bad, Cindy mouthed.

"I need you to get this next story written and then finish it up with the final one after that," Anthony said.

"Okay, I'll get this one done and get it off to you tonight," Austin responded.

"Alright. Tell Cindy I said hi. And I'm sorry for calling so early, I probably interrupted your breakfast."

"Nope, had an outstanding breakfast." Austin looked back at Cindy.

"Good. Talk to ya soon."

"Yep, talk soon."

Cindy laughed when Austin hung up the phone. "Outstanding breakfast, huh."

"Doesn't get any better," he chuckled.

Austin got dressed, walked into the living room, picked up the journal and started reading it. He had his yellow notepad next to him. *I've got to get this done*, he muttered. As he slowly read each page, he became even more engrossed.

Cindy had gone into the kitchen and started breakfast, this one included food.

"Are you kidding me!" Austin said, loud enough for Cindy to hear.

"What?" she asked, as she hurriedly came around the corner.

"*Operation Sundown* was some serious shit."

"What was it?"

"Well according to John, he and the team were going on a reconnaissance mission to pinpoint the coordinates for the emperor's palace."

"What were they doing that for?"

"They were doing it so they could bomb the palace."

"Why'd they want to do that?"

Austin took his finger across his neck. "Chop off the head of the snake, the snake dies."

"What?"

"If you kill the emperor, the empire falls."

"But weren't we winning the war anyway? Why do that if we were winning?"

"Well, we were winning, but we knew that we had to invade Japan to end the war.

According to what Papa John is saying here, the aim was to kill the emperor and save American lives."

"We dropped the atomic bombs so there was no invasion after we did that, right?" Cindy asked.

"Right, but no one knew about the atomic bomb at the time. Think about it. Someone had to conclude that if we killed the emperor, it was only one life that would be lost, and the war would likely have ended. They had to take into consideration that thousands of innocent Japanese lives would be wiped out when they dropped those bombs. It makes sense to take out one to save thousands. And that doesn't even include the American lives that would be lost in the invasion," Austin replied.

"So, Papa John and his team were going on a mission to take out the emperor of Japan?"

"That's what he's saying here."

"Wouldn't that be dangerous?"

"It was actually a suicide mission. What isn't said here was that it wasn't only one life that was going to be lost, it was likely going to be six. The emperor and John's whole team."

"What!"

"Seriously, they all had to know that the odds of returning were slim-to-none. Your grandfather signed up for a one-way mission to save millions of lives."

"I can't believe that!"

"I assumed from what I had found in the other journals that Papa John was connected to something having to do with the emperor and the palace; now this confirms it. Geez, your grandfather was really something."

"He sure was. Well, something had to happen because he came back from that mission."

"You're right, not sure why, I haven't gotten that far into the journal yet.

But can you imagine how big this is? To know that the US had a secret operation identified to kill the emperor of Japan! Man, this is something that the world never knew. I get it now; the reference to *Operation Sundown* makes sense. The Japanese Flag's emblem is the Rising Sun, *Operation Sundown* intention was to make the sun set."

"What?"

"End the war."

"I can't believe that no one knows about this."

"Oh, I think someone knows, the question is why hasn't it ever been revealed."

"Maybe it's not that important anymore," Cindy said.

"Could be, but something tells me that no one was to find out what this was all about. This is certainly going to add something more to the storyline of the Pacific War. This is news no matter how you stack it," Austin said.

At the Fort Myers airport the plane landed from Washington carrying Captain Clavender Hughes and First Lieutenant Matthew Broadmeyer. Little did they know what they were about to uncover would have a major impact on the relationship between the United States and Japan.

CHAPTER

54

The sun was baking down as Clay and Matthew walked out of the terminal to the car rental area. The Florida winter temperatures changes could be dramatic. In a single day, it wouldn't be unusual to be wearing a bathing suit in the late morning and a winter jacket in the evening.

"Holy shit; it's hot here," Matthew said, as he grabbed the collar of his uniform to stretch it out.

"It's the humidity that gets you more than the heat," Clay responded.

"Whatever it is, I'm already sweating my ass off!"

Clay was taken by the palm trees and tropical feel than he was with the heat. "You'll get used to it."

"I don't know Cap; I'd prefer the cooler temperatures of the north then this oppressive heat."

"We need to find out where we can find this Austin Paige."

"You mean we're not heading to the beach for a little umbrella cocktail drink?"

Clay looked at Matthew and shook his head. "This is a small town so it should be easy to find him."

Matthew shrugged, *Cap's all business.*

The rental car location was just a short walk from the terminal but to Matthew it felt like a mile. He had packed a carry-on bag that he pulled behind, but it seemed to get heavier the further he walked. He wiped his brow with his sleeve.

"Where are we staying, Cap?" Matthew asked.

Clay pulled out the itinerary that the Major's administrator had given him at the Pentagon office. "The Luminary," he said.

"Sounds like a quaint hotel," Matthew replied.

"I understand that it's the middle of the town so everything should be easy to get to."

Probably not much of a town, Matthew mumbled.

They threw their luggage in the trunk, got a cab, and started into town.

Matthew gazed out the car side window. "Looks like all they have are palm trees around here."

"Seems to be a quiet place," Clay said.

"You think we'll see alligators?" Matthew asked.

Clay gave a look which Matthew took as; *are you serious?*

The driver pulled up in front of the hotel. The hotel looked recently built and was right on the river. Clay looked around and noticed the boats in the adjacent marina. The people walked around in shorts and flip flops, just the antithesis of the starched shirts and pressed uniforms of the Pentagon. He smiled as he saw Matthew dragging his bags into the lobby. *Sometimes people lose sight of the simple life,* he thought.

They checked into the hotel and after going to their rooms, met in the lobby.

Matthew hit the bell that was on the hotel front desk. A host turned and smiled.

"Hey, where's the best place for lunch?" Matthew asked.

"Well, one of the best places is just around the corner, it's called Bruno's," said the front desk host.

"Cap, gotta get something, I'm starving. What about this Bruno's place?"

Clay nodded. "Sure, let's go there."

They walked out the front door and started for the restaurant.

"Shit, it's still hot, does it ever cool off here?" Matthew asked.

"I'm sure it will when the sun goes down. We're in Florida so suck it up," Clay replied.

"Yes sir, just feel like the wicked witch from The Wizard of Oz.... I'm melting, I'm melting," Matthew said, in a witch's shrill voice.

Clay rolled his eyes.

They entered Bruno's, pulled up a couple of stools, sat at the bar and looked over the menu. Cal came over carrying a couple glasses of water. "What can I get for you officers?"

"I'll take your salad platter," Clay replied.

Matthew tossed the menu on the counter tapped his fingers on the counter. "Burger for me."

Cal took their orders and walked back to the kitchen.

Matthew leaned back in the stool and looked around the restaurant. "Well, this is a nice place."

A few people stared back at the two of them. It wasn't often that two military officers in uniform were seen in town.

"Maybe we should have changed out of our uniforms, it doesn't appear that we fit in at the moment," Matthew said.

Clay looked around but didn't take notice of the stares. He had a job to do. "Doesn't matter, we just need to focus on getting the information to the Major."

"Listen Cap, I've been meaning to ask, how are you and the Major getting along. I mean, it's been years but is everything okay?"

"Everything's fine Lieutenant."

"Okay, just checking; I know it's not my place to ask."

A few minutes passed in silence. Clay put his hands around the water glass and stared at it and started to open up. "It was hard to go to her office. I knew eventually we'd have to meet but for some reason thought that when we did, I'd feel that what we had was passed," he said.

"I don't think that things like that pass. I think that feelings fade but memories stay rooted," Matthew responded.

"I guess, but it was an awkward moment. I mean, I was respectful of her rank, and everything was official. I was just a bit uncomfortable; just didn't expect that," Clay said.

"Well, I'm sure that you were the perfect gentleman."

Clay glared at Matthew.

"OOOkay, I hope my burger gets here soon," Matthew said, as he started fidgeting in his seat.

They were finishing up their meal when Cal came over to clean up some of the plates. "So, what brings you two to Fort Myers?"

"We're looking for someone," Matthew replied.

Clay turned to Matthew and gave him a look that Matthew knew was a signal to *shut up*.

"Sir, we're actually trying to find someone that we would like to talk to about some research that we're doing," Clay said.

I guess that was a better way of putting it, Matthew thought.

"Really, who is it?" Cal asked.

"A reporter named Austin Paige," Clay replied.

"Oh, Austin. Sure, he's been here doing a story on Papa John."

"Papa John?" Clay inquired.

"Yeah, he was a legend around here. He served in World War two, great man. He just passed recently. We'll miss him."

"Do you know where we might be able to connect with this Austin Paige?" Matthew asked.

"Sure, he's just down the road a bit. Staying with John's granddaughter." Cal gave them directions to Cindy's house.

Clay paid the tab and he and Matthew started out of the restaurant. Clay turned and waved to Cal. "Thanks for the information," he said.

Matthew looked back at Cal and then to Clay. "Wow, I guess being in a small town has its advantages. I didn't think it would be that easy."

"I think you're right."

"What?"

"We need to change out of these uniforms," Clay said.

Matthew sighed. "Thank God, I didn't know how long I was going to be able to take this heat."

Clay was more focused on how he was going to approach Austin and wondered what he knew, if anything, about *Operation Sundown.* He also needed to know where he was getting his information.

CHAPTER

55

The only noise heard was the ceiling fan that buzzed above Austin's head. He hadn't looked up from the journal for over an hour. Cindy had come and gone through the room trying not to be conspicuous but was curious as to what Austin was finding out. She was quietly putting the stacked books that were removed in the search for the journal back on the shelf. John wasn't around to correct her organizational skills, so the books went back in no particular order. "Honey, listen to this," Austin said.

Cindy smiled. Honey, that has a nice ring to it. "What did you find out?" she asked.

Austin had been feverishly writing on his yellow note pad and picked it up to read a few things he had jotted down.

"Papa John's notes are enlightening. First, he was proud to have been selected to be part of this team. His relationship with the men of this group was like family. He references them all as brothers, specifically Frank Balboa, you know, Jaws. Frank had a tough time making it through the physical aspect of the training and almost was booted out. I guess he was scared of heights that no one, including himself was aware of. The revelation came when they were training for the parachute jumps."

"Really, wasn't Frank from New York City? It has tall buildings. Wouldn't he have known about fearing heights?" Cindy asked.

"I guess but I suppose a tall building is different than an open door of an airplane at 15,000 feet," Austin said. "Anyway, John was the one that helped him get over it, actually, he pushed Frank out of the plane on the first jump."

Cindy laughed. "Seriously. He pushed him?"

"Yeah, and I guess it worked. They almost got into it when John landed but then they both laughed so hard that any fear of heights moving forward was replaced by the fear that John might push Frank out of the plane before he put on his parachute."

Cindy laughed again. "I guess that would do it I suppose."

"Anyway, from that point on it sounds like Papa John and Frank were inseparable and watched each other's backs. Not sure but from what I am interpreting, Frank was the first real friend your grandfather ever had."

"Well, what happened to Frank?"

"That's what I am about to find out. I've been purposely going slow through this journal to ensure that I don't miss anything."

"Is there anything in there about *Operation Sundown*?"

"Your grandfather kind of jumps a bit when writing. It looks like he wrote much of this when he came back from the war." Austin put his yellow pad down and picked up the journal. "But this is what I found so far." He started reading:

> *Captain Burton pulled us aside and told us about our operation that was code named, Operation Sundown. We were told that we were going to destroy the emperor's palace and him with it. He told us that we'd be shuttled close to the Japanese coast and then take a motorized raft to the peninsula named Chida. Wasn't sure where the hell that was but the captain seemed confident and that's all that mattered. From there we were to go to the Kashidoki bridge and work our way close enough to get the coordinates for the palace. We'd call it in, and they'd send artillery in from the Ticonderoga to level the place. After that they'd finish it up by sending aircraft in to level the city.*

Sounded easy, but we'd be smack in the middle of the enemy. This was a
bullshit mission, but we were too stupid to question it as the time…

"That sounds a bit like what you found earlier," Cindy said.

"I know, can you imagine what they all must've been thinking? Five GI's
sneaking around in Japan trying not to get caught," Austin replied.

"What else did he write?"

Austin continued.

…. Jaws and I thought we'd be lucky to make it back alive. Captain
Burton told us that if we got separated that we'd meet back at the rendezvous
point where we dropped off the raft and take it back to a meeting point. We
had the coordinates sewn in our jackets and we had two radios, one that we
took with us and another that we left in the raft. Smitty was our radio
operator… he was a good man. The guys from the ship would meet us and
take us back to the Ticonderoga. We were sick of the war and figured if we
were successful in this mission, I could come home to Evy. All I wanted was
to come home and marry Evy.

Cindy had moved from putting the books back on the shelves to sitting
next to Austin as he continued to read from the journal.

I told Jaws that if I didn't make it back that he was to tell Evy what
happened. I wanted her to hear it from him and not the Navy. I wasn't even
sure if the Navy even knew what we were about. We were told that we had
been assigned to the Ticonderoga and would be part of the crew, but our
identities wouldn't be made known to anyone outside the ship. We were
kind of ghosts; that's the OSS for you.

"I guess that's why their pictures weren't in that *Ticonderoga* book that I
found," Cindy said.

"Right, none of them were," Austin replied. He continued:

We made it to the Chiba peninsula. It took us awhile, we made the trip
late at night and given the distance from Ticonderoga to the shore, we had
to lay low all day and go the next evening to the bridge. Jaws and I played
cards and took turns with Smitty and Ghost on watch duty. Captain spent
most of his time looking at maps. I remember thinking that perhaps this
mission was going to work and started to figure out how I was going to
propose to Evy. Jaws agreed to be my best man.

"Wow, I didn't know that about Frank," Cindy said.

Austin chuckled. "I guess you push a guy out of a plane, you owe him something."

Cindy smiled. "I guess so."

Austin continued.

> *We made it to the bridge that next evening and quietly made it through a few villages undetected. There weren't many people around. We figured that most of the villagers had retreated to the hills given some of the allied bombings that were happening throughout the country. We were good at sneaking around, but it was late at night so there wasn't anyone on the streets. Everything was going as planned.*

Cindy looked at Austin who was clearly in his element. "This sounds like a movie," she said.

"I know, it does, doesn't it." He continued.

> *We were close to our target area when all shit happened...*

Austin looked at Cindy. He figured everything from now on would be intense.

Cindy noticed Austin's concerned expression. "Go on," she said.

He continued.

> *.... we ran into a column of Japanese infantry that were heading toward the palace. We thought that we were hidden but some villager started shouting and pointing...Captain Burton shot him. That's when hell came......*

Austin glanced at Cindy. She was riveted.

> *......the column came our way, yelling and screaming. It was scary as hell. We started shooting, many of them fell but they kept coming. We continued killing them, but they just kept coming. Captain Burton yelled to Smitty to call in a strike to at least give us a chance to retreat. We knew that the mission was over and now it was just a matter of getting our asses back to the raft and back to the ship. We kept shooting and they kept coming.*

Austin paused for a moment. *Man, I can't even imagine,* he said quietly.

Cindy didn't say anything; she clasped both her hands to her mouth and closed her eyes.

> *…....If there is a hell, then I was in it. As Jaws, Ghost and I kept shooting, the captain was yelling the coordinates at Smitty to have the ship send in artillery. All I could hear were screams and yelling from the enemy as they advanced to where we were. Then all I remember were the sounds of incoming and flashes of light….*

Austin paused, "Are you okay?"

Cindy still had her hands clasped together over her mouth resting her chin on her thumbs. The tears in her eyes were noticeable. She nodded affirmatively.

> *…. the Ticonderoga was off by a few clicks. But it was effective enough. I saw Jap parts flying all over the place, but the rounds were getting too close to us. I remember Captain Burton yelling and motioning Jaws, Ghost and I to retreat when a round fell close to him. I was yelling that the rounds were too close. I saw a flash and never saw the captain again. Smitty took a hit from and died on the spot.*

Austin paused again to take notice of Cindy then continued.

> *Ghost, Jaws and I, for reasons that I can only chalk up to stupid courage, started racing toward the remaining Japanese infantry that were coming toward us. I guess we scared the shit out of them as they started to retreat. The bombs kept dropping and we kept screaming and somehow were able to dodge the shells. The Japanese eventually stopped coming at us, they had disappeared. We didn't know what to do at the time and noticed bodies everywhere. Then things got really quiet. We were standing there wondering what we would do next when Ghost found a box that had some special writing on it. We thought it might have some importance, maybe maps with enemy positions. All we knew was that we needed to get back to our raft and back to the ship. Ghost picked up the box and that's when hell came back again.*

"You sure you want me to continue?" Austin asked.

"Yes," Cindy replied.

"Listen, you don't need to hear this. We can stop for a minute."

"No, please, I want to hear it."

Austin continued:

> …. *The Japanese military group didn't retreat, they just were waiting for us. Then they came from everywhere, screaming, yelling. We didn't have time to be scared anymore, we just wanted to get our asses out of there. We ran as fast as we could while turning to shoot at the same time. We dodged in and out of streets, through houses. We had managed to lose most of them that were following us. We sneaked through the streets but were spotted by a few of them. We took off but Ghost was hit; I went back to help but he told me to go, he couldn't walk anymore, and I knew there was nothing more that I could do. He yelled at me to go and turned and started shooting, he gave us time to retreat. I opened the box he was carrying and took out the contents that were wrapped up in a cloth, then Jaws and I took off running. I could hear Ghost scream. I figured they had killed him.*

Austin paused again. He didn't say anything and just looked at Cindy.

"He never told us any of this," she said, as a tear slowly traced down her cheek.

"This is hard enough for us to hear let alone having John reliving it again. I can understand why he didn't tell anyone," Austin said. He reached over and squeezed Cindy's hands and continued.

> *We were just about to the place where we stored the raft when we heard bullets race by us hitting the dirt. It was like rain coming from the sky, the dirt and ground kept popping with bullets. They had stopped chasing us and were on a hill shooting at us. I felt a cold sensation hit my leg and knew that I had been hit. I heard Jaws scream that he had been hit but we kept going. I got hit again in the arm but for some reason was able to keep my balance. I reached back and pulled Jaws up. We made it back to the raft. I dumped him in, jumped in, started the small engine, and made it out of the bay. We still had bullets flying around us, but we made it out of their range and headed back to the rendezvous point. I ripped the coordinates out of my jacket, set my compass and radioed the ship.*

Cindy looked up at Austin and shook her head. "Papa John was so sweet and gentle. The fact that he had gone through all of this as a young man is more than I can imagine," she said.

Austin kept reading:

> ……*I went over to Jaws to check on him. He had been shot in the back and was bleeding badly. I knew that it wouldn't be long before he died; he knew*

it too. I kept talking to him like we were going to be together forever. I told him about Evy and how jealous he was going to be when he met her. He grabbed my hand and smiled and told me how proud he was going to be being my best man. He died in my arms.

Cindy sniffled as she tried to hold back her tears, she couldn't. Austin wanted to stop but he figured that Cindy wanted to hear this through and kept reading.

…. I made it back to the Ticonderoga with Jaws body. I saw him one last time before they buried him at sea. He looked tranquil like he was asleep. I told him how proud I was to have served with him. I apologized for pushing him out of the plane window and laughed when I told him about the expression on his face when I saw him on the ground. I reached down and pulled his dog tags off him and put them in my pocket. It would be the last time I'd see Jaws again, but his face has been with me every day of my life since. He was a great man. They all were great men. I didn't deserve to come home alive. I live every day for those men. I hope they know that.

Austin cleared his throat. He hadn't read the last part prior to reading it to Cindy and became a bit emotional when he finished. Cindy got up and walked to the kitchen, she leaned against the sink and started to cry. Austin could hear her from the living room but felt that she needed to be alone. He thought it was time to take a break when the doorbell rang.

CHAPTER

56

C indy composed herself and straightened her dress. She figured that Robert and Chris were making their ill-timed visit when she opened the door to see two men standing there. "Can I help you?"

"Ma'am, I am Captain Clavender, and this is Lieutenant Broadmeyer."

"Are you police officers?"

"No ma'am, I'm sorry." Clay pulled out his identification card. "We're from the Pentagon, we work for the SIOD, Senior Intelligence Oversight Department."

The puzzled expression on Cindy's face gave notice to Clay. Austin had heard the voices and came to the door.

"We're here to follow-up on a lead that was given to us regarding some reporting that was done on the last living veteran," Clay said. He looked at Austin. "I presume you're Austin Paige?" He reached out to shake his hand.

Austin reached back out and shook his hand. "How did you guys find out about John?" he asked. *And how do they know who I am.*

"May we come in?" Clay asked.

"I'm sorry, please come in," Cindy said.

Clay pointed to Matthew. "This is Lieutenant Broadmeyer."

Austin reached out to Matthew. "Nice to meet you."

"Nice place you have here," Matthew said, as he looked around the house and then at the books stacked around the room.

"Thanks," Cindy replied.

"How did you hear about John?" Austin asked.

"Well, we actually read the online article you wrote and wanted to find out more about the last veteran, uh, I guess that's John, right?" Clay said.

Cindy nodded. "Yes, his name was John Anderson."

"Ma'am, we're also very sorry for your loss, we understand that he recently passed," Clay said.

"Yes, he did… thank you."

Austin was puzzled by what Clay already knew.

"Yes, well, we had read about him and wanted to find out more. The military wants to recognize him for his service," Clay said.

Very smooth Cap, thought Matthew.

"We didn't think anyone would have taken notice of him. I'm happy that the Pentagon's interested," Cindy said.

Austin's investigative background instinctively kicked in. "So, the Pentagon sent you two down here to find out more about a veteran? Why didn't you just call or something?"

"Well, we thought that given significance to his status, I mean being the last living World War two veteran; that it was only appropriate that we talk with you in person," Clay said.

Wow, Cap's really good at this, thought Matthew.

"Can I get you anything?" Cindy asked. "Tea, water?"

"I'd love some tea," Matthew replied.

Clay shook his head. "I am fine, thank you."

Cindy disappeared into the kitchen leaving Austin to do his inquiry.

"I've never heard of the SIOD. What is that?" Austin asked.

"Well, part of the Senior Intelligence Oversight Department is the Antiquities Division, that's where we reside. It's a special department within the Pentagon that researches and collects historical information, past and present, to include military personnel that provide service to the United States," Matthew said. He purposely left out any reference to operational missions, past or present.

"Interesting, never heard of it before," Austin replied.

"Not many people have," Matthew said. Cindy walked in and gave Matthew a glass of tea, he sipped it. "Wow, this is really good."

"It's southern sweet tea," she said.

Matthew smiled and took another sip.

"Mr. Paige, we're interested in getting as much information as we can about Mr. Anderson so that we can determine how to recognize him for his service," Clay said.

"You can call me Austin; also, you can refer to Mr. Anderson as John. I'm still not sure what I can tell you. Wouldn't you be able to find him in your records? After all, you have information from past veterans, don't you?"

Clay picked up on Austin's suspicions. *This was going to be a bit more complicated.*

"Yes sir, we do have information, but we thought that given your article and connection, talking to you directly would be the best," Clay responded.

Clay looked at Cindy. "I also understand that you're his granddaughter."

"Please call me Cindy."

Another bit of information this guy knows, thought Austin.

"Cindy, we'd love to recognize you and your grandfather in some way."

"Thank you that would be very nice. I am sure he would have appreciated that."

"This is really good tea. I love how sweet it tastes," interrupted Matthew. He could sense the tension building between Clay and Austin.

"Captain, I appreciate the fact that you read my online article, I didn't think that many people would have had interest in it, but it appears that it's raised some eyebrows."

"Please call me Clay. And yes, it did raise some eyebrows but for sincere reasons. John was the last of his generation and it's important that we get as much information as we can, so that we can give him what he honorably deserves."

Bullshit, something's not right, thought Austin.

"I know that we sprung this on you rather quickly and we'd like to be able to talk more, perhaps tomorrow. We'd like to get some info on John to give to our superiors," Clay said.

"Sure, tomorrow will be fine, how about five o'clock?" Cindy said.

Clay turned and smiled, "Thank you Cindy. We really do appreciate this; five o'clock would be perfect."

Clay and Matthew got up and shook Austin's and Cindy's hands.

"Thank you again for the tea," Matthew said.

Cindy took the glass from Matthew. "Anytime."

Clay and Matthew walked out the door and to their car.

"They seem nice. It's wonderful that they want to recognize Papa John," Cindy said.

Austin stood and walked around the room. "That's not why they're here."

"What.... then why are they here?" Cindy asked.

"You don't send two officers here to find out about a veteran even if he's the last one. The article that I wrote had to have triggered something to have Pentagon military brass fly people down here." Austin started pacing back and forth. "A Captain, you don't send someone of that rank for a simple administrative task."

"Austin, you're too paranoid. They seem like nice men and just want to do something nice for Papa John."

"Maybe, but we'll see how they react when we print the next article."

Cindy shook her head and walked into the kitchen to put the glass in the dishwasher. Austin walked to the window and peered through the blinds as

Clay and Matthew pulled out of the driveway.

"Well, I think that went as well as could be expected," Matthew said.

"He knows why we're here," Clay replied.

"How do you know that?"

"He's a reporter. They have a sense of suspicion about everyone and everything."

"What?"

"Austin's good. I did a little research on him before we came down. He's been recognized for some serious investigative reporting that has some government people doing time."

"Really!"

"Yeah, he's right too. Why would the Pentagon send two military personnel down here to do a story about a veteran if we could already get information on him."

"Well, I thought you did a great job of directing the conversation, Cap."

"Not good enough. Also did you pick up on the room?"

"You mean the books stacked everywhere? Yeah, interesting but I just thought they were doing some spring cleaning."

"No, they were looking for something."

"Come on Cap, what are you talking about?"

"They were looking for something and I think they found it."

"What do you mean, they found it? Not sure I'm following you."

"When we sat down and started asking questions, I noticed that Austin closed a book that looked old and tattered."

"So?"

"When Cindy came in with the tea, you and I were distracted but out of the corner of my eye, I saw him tuck the book in the side of his chair. I think I know where he's getting his information."

"A book! Seriously Cap, what would he have that would be that significant."

"A first-hand account of what *Operation Sundown* was all about."

"Shit Cap, we don't even know what it's about!"

"Exactly, and that's what I'm about to find out."

Matthew stared at Clay and didn't say anything. He saw that look in Clay's eyes. It was the same look he had when he first learned of the *Ticonderoga* contradiction.

CHAPTER

57

A ustin remained skeptical of why the Pentagon had sent officers down to Florida and knew there was more to their visit then they had shared. He also figured that his next article would cause Clay and Matthew to 'show their hand'. It would solidify his assumptions that Washington was more interested in something other than John being the last living veteran. He pulled the journal from the chair and went to the dining room table to write the article that he owed Anthony.

"What are you going to say about what you learned from the journal?" Cindy asked.

"Well, for one, I think that *Operation Sundown* is an important story to tell. I don't think anyone realized the extent to which the US went to end the war. And the men that were with John gave their lives and no one knows who they were. We owe them something," Austin said. He reached down and pulled the computer from his briefcase.

"Do you think that Clay and Matthew are really here so that Papa John could be recognized?"

"I have a suspicion that they're really here to find out about the special operation even though they didn't come out and specifically ask." He wanted to believe Clay and Matthew's story, but he knew they had an ulterior motive.

"Well, I hope that's why they're here. It'd be terrible for them to tell us that they want to do something special and then not do anything."

"I agree." Austin started typing.

Cindy walked to the kitchen and returned with a glass of tea. "Do you think that Clay and Matthew know anything about *Operation Sundown*?" she asked.

Austin looked up from the computer. "I don't think they know anything. All they know is that John was on a special operation. They got that from the article. I think they want to find out what we know. Like I said, something's fishy about this whole thing."

"I don't understand what the big deal is. This happened so long ago. I can't see that anyone would find it that important anymore. Papa John was part of a special operation that involved killing the emperor, but we were at war. I don't think people today are going to be that interested," Cindy said.

"In the end, you may be right," Austin replied.

"After all, what do we know that Japan doesn't already know. It's not like we have any secrets that they don't know about anyway."

Austin paused and looked at Cindy. "What did you say?"

"What?"

"What did you just say?"

Cindy froze. "What do you mean, what did I just say?"

Austin looked up at her. "You said 'it's not like we have any secrets that they don't know about." He grabbed the journal and started flipping the pages.

Cindy came next to him trying to figure out what she had said that got him so excited.

Austin stopped flipping the pages, took his finger and scrolled down. "Jesus Christ!"

"What!" Cindy said in an excited voice.

Austin got up from the chair and gave Cindy a strong hug. He looked at her with a huge smile and kissed her. "You're unbelievable!"

"What did I do?!"

"It's right here!"

Austin started reading.... *We took off but Ghost was hit; I went back to help but he told me to go, he couldn't walk anymore, and I knew there was nothing more that I could do. He yelled at me to go and turned and started shooting, he gave us time to retreat.*

Then Austin pointed to the sentence. *I opened the box he was carrying and took out the contents that were wrapped up in a cloth, then Jaws and I took off running....*

Cindy had a puzzled look on her face. She had said something that triggered a reaction in Austin. Then it hit her. "You mean that whatever Papa John took from that box is something that's important?" she asked.

"It must be really important. Think about it, I bet that when I put something in the paper about John, the special mission, the *Ticonderoga,* and May nineteen forty-five, that something must have been triggered at the Pentagon. Why else would two military officers have been sent down here."

"Do you think that Clay and Matthew know about this?"

"I don't think they have a clue, but someone at the Pentagon knows about *Operation Sundown* and they've kept it under wraps for all these years, until now," Austin said.

"What do you think Papa John took?"

"That's a great question."

Austin went back to the computer and erased what he had written and started typing.

"I hope that we haven't opened up a can of worms," Cindy said.

Austin turned and looked at her. "I hope you're right."

CHAPTER

58

The drive back to the hotel was quiet. Clay was concerned about Austin's suspicions and how he was going to get the information he needed without having Austin close up and refuse to share anything. He needed to make a connection in some way but was struggling to figure out how to do that.

Matthew decided to break the silence. "So, what'd you think'n' Cap?"

Clay snapped out of his thought. "What?"

"You think that Austin knows what *Operation Sundown* is all about?"

"I think he has more information on it than we do."

Clay pulled into the parking lot of the hotel and they both went to the lobby bar.

Matthew flagged down the waitress. "Can I get two beers? Anything is fine, surprise me." In just a few minutes she placed a couple of cold filled beer glasses in front of them. *Wow, she looks nice,* he thought to himself as she headed back to the bar.

Matthew took a swig. "This is pretty good but I kinda like Cindy's sweet tea."

Clay chuckled and then took a sip of his beer. "Not bad."

Matthew leaned in. "Well Cap, we both know that something's not adding up. The *Ticonderoga* and *Yorktown* May nineteen forty-five files were empty, and the only reference was *Operation Sundown*. You also found out that the *Ticonderoga* was not in port that May. Austin's article points that out as well. You were blocked from getting any intel on *Operation Sundown* so I'm concluding that's the special mission Austin referenced. So, I guess the real questions are why was the ship where it was, what was *Operation Sundown* and what was John's mission?"

Clay took another sip of beer and stared at Matthew.

"You know we dropped the bomb not long after this so-called mission took place so what's the relevance of it all in the end," Matthew said.

"That's what's interesting. Why such a secret and why send an aircraft carrier so close to the Japanese coast. If it were some sort of surveillance or extraction, they'd have been better off sending a destroyer or something that has more speed and maneuverability," Clay said. "Furthermore, an aircraft carrier doesn't have defensive capabilities. That's why they travel with support ships."

Matthew took another sip of his beer. "Man, this is good." He looked back at the waitress. "Hey, what beer is this?" he yelled.

"Cigar City; it's a Florida brew," came the reply.

"Wow, I could get used to this."

Clay stared at his glass. "The only reason you send a carrier anywhere is to deploy aircraft."

"Guess that's right," Matthew said. He finished off what beer was left in his glass.

"So why send in an aircraft carrier with no escort?" Clay mumbled.

Matthew let Clay continue. It was clear that he wasn't asking him a question.

"Either to drop off a special ops team or drop some bombs, or both," Clay continued.

Matthew looked down at his empty glass of beer and mumbled. "Well, maybe the *Ticonderoga* was fitted with some long guns so that it could support a land offensive and have defensive capabilities at the same time."

Clay pointed at Matthew. "You know, you're right; that has to be it. Where did Austin say the special operations team landed?"

"Somewhere outside the Chiyoda District," Matthew replied.

Clay sat in silence. "That's where the emperor's palace is, right?"

Matthew didn't answer, he knew it was a rhetorical question. Clay started nodding his head up and down and combined with a grin, Matthew knew the wheels were turning.

Clay smiled; he started talking out his assumption. "So, we send in a special operations team into Japan near the emperor's palace with an aircraft carrier sitting off the coast that now has offensive guns that could send in artillery shells. They find out the specific details of the emperor's palace coordinates and call in a bombing strike. The emperor's killed and the war's over. It makes sense. That must be the special mission that Anderson was on."

Matthew shook his head and frowned. "Yeah, but I would think that we'd already be able to pinpoint the palace, send in a bomber and drop a bomb or two. We wouldn't need to send anyone in to give the coordinates."

"But what if they were sent in to verify the kill and if necessary, call in aircraft to finish it off."

"Maybe, but what's the point? We didn't kill the emperor; we didn't bomb the palace and we dropped the big ones a few months later and ended the war. So, why the mystery?"

"That's the part that I don't get," Clay replied.

"Hey, can we get this beer up north?" Matthew yelled back to the waitress.

"I don't know; maybe," came the reply from a distance.

"So, what next?" Matthew asked.

Clay pushed his glass to the center of the table. "Time to call the Major."

"What are you going to tell her?"

"What we found out?"

"We didn't find anything out."

"She doesn't know that."

Matthew shook his head. "I don't get it."

Clay grinned.

"Cap, you're not going in with your assumptions, are you? That's crazy, we're just guessing."

"Are we?"

Matthew leaned back in his chair. "Sir, with all due respect. I don't think that's a good idea."

Clay got up from the table. "Enjoy your evening, Lieutenant. I'll see you in the morning."

CHAPTER

59

C lay decided that he'd walk over to Bruno's again. He was familiar
with the place and needed to be alone to craft his call to the Major.
Having a beer from time-to-time was okay but he was a martini
drinker and needed one to steady his nerves. He knew he was going out on a
limb with his story. He left Matthew at the hotel bar, it appeared that he had
found his new favorite beer and chatting with the pretty waitress was more
fun than being with him.

"What can I get you?" asked the bartender.

Clay saw Cal in the background and waved. Cal waved back.

"I'll have a dry Russian Standard vodka martini, lemon twist, lightly
stirred."

Clay turned and looked around the restaurant taking more notice of his
surroundings. He hadn't done that when he first stepped in the place.

"Here you go," said the bartender, who gently placed his martini in front
of him.

"Thanks." Clay turned back around and sipped his drink as he looked around.

The Washington grind and military politics had taken a toll on Clay over the years. He had been thinking of retiring but had not known anything other than the army. He also had not given any consideration on where to go, but he liked what he saw in Fort Myers and enjoyed the weather despite Matthew's continual concern that he'd melt.

Cal came from the kitchen and leaned on the bar. "So how are things going," he asked.

Clay turned and smiled when he saw Cal. "Going great, thanks for asking."

"Did you get anything from Austin and Cindy?"

"Well, we just met so it was pretty much just an introduction. We have an appointment tomorrow afternoon, so we'll pick up our research then."

"Well, you'll find them to be very accommodating. Cindy's been taking care of her grandfather for several years. Austin's been here doing his reporting on John. Guess he'll be hanging around here a bit more though," Cal said, with a smile.

"Why? I thought he was a reporter from up north," Clay asked.

"Well, let's just say, when you come down here you find beauty everywhere. I think Austin found his."

Clay understood the inference. "I guess that's not hard to do." Clay lifted his glass in a salute.

Cal grinned. "Welcome to our little bit of paradise." He turned and grabbed a few things from the bar.

Clay remembered what he said when Matthew asked him about retiring, *when the birds fly south.* Clay thought about it for a moment, *Well, maybe it's time.*

He was sipping his martini when a lady came up to the bar and ordered some waters for her table.

"Hi, are you new in town?" she asked.

"Yes, I'm here for a short visit," Clay replied.

"Well, welcome. My name is Gladys. We love to see new people stop by and visit our little town. Just be careful, you may find yourself staying here," she laughed.

"I guess anything's possible," Clay said.

He watched her walk back carrying the glasses of water. She sat down and passed them to the people at the table.

"Is everybody so welcoming here?" Clay asked.

Cal laughed. "Yep, welcome to the south."

"Can I get you anything for dinner?" Cal asked.

"Tell you what, surprise me," Clay replied. He figured it worked with Matthew when he ordered a beer, so why not.

Cal winked. "I have just the thing."

"Hey, can you tell me anymore about Austin? I'm interested in partnering with him on my research and I'd like to know who I'm working with."

"Well, I can't tell you much. He and Cindy have come in here several times. I guess I'd say that he's a genuine person and very thorough. You know he's a reporter and a good one. I guess, like any reporter, they're all about building trust. You get that and you've got a good relationship. It certainly worked with Cindy and John. Well, with Cindy, it doesn't hurt to be so sweet and pretty," Cal chuckled.

Clay smiled. "Guess you're right." He sipped his martini. *Build the trust, work with him, not against him.*

It had been several hours; Clay was immersed in the atmosphere and his meal.

"This dinner was outstanding," Clay said as Cal passed by.

"Glad you liked it."

Maybe there's something to this surprise me thing, mumbled Clay.

Clay glanced down at his watch; he hadn't realized how much time had passed. It was late and he owed the Major a call. *Well, she's probably not at the office*, he thought.

He sat at the bar for a few minutes trying to figure his next move. Then he paid his bill, left the restaurant, and decided to walk down to the river.

The few martinis clouded his judgement, but he needed to get some information and figure out if his assumptions had any merit. He sat on a bench and pulled out his cell phone. He hadn't called the number in years and didn't know if he should again or if it still worked.

He punched in the numbers. The phone rang a few times.

"Clay?!"

"Bev, I'm sorry to call you this late."

"Just a minute," He heard a muffled conversation and picked up that he had interrupted something.

"Geez, why are you calling me on this line? I'm at a defense department event."

"I'm sorry to call so late, I know that you wanted me to let you know if I found anything out regarding *Operation Sundown*."

"Yeah, but I figured that it was too soon. Did you really get information this fast?"

"Well, we have another meeting with them tomorrow afternoon, but I wanted to verify some things that we uncovered." He knew that he was treading on thin ice but if he could get some solid information before he met with Austin again, he thought he'd be able to pull out more details.

"Okay, not sure what you have, but go ahead."

"We're pretty sure that the special operation that Paige wrote about was likely *Operation Sundown*. He has, what looks like a diary or journal of some sort, which belonged to John Anderson, one of the members of the special ops team. That's where he's getting his information."

From there Clay launched into the assumptions that he had made about the *Ticonderoga* and the operation. He described it in clear detail hoping that it would sound believable.

"So, you got this from Paige?"

Clay didn't say anything and let a few seconds tick by.

The Major sighed then lowered her voice as to ensure no one on her end was listening. "Okay, yes, *Operation Sundown* was intended to take out the emperor. President Truman gave the order for the operation to take place. He had hoped that it would end the war sooner, but the mission failed. It was the last effort before we dropped the bombs on Hiroshima and Nagasaki. All but one member of the team were KIA and we knew that John Anderson was the one that had survived. The *Ticonderoga* was ordered back to the States after the mission."

"So why am I here? If you have all of this, then what's so important that you flew us down here to question Paige?" Clay asked.

"Japan never knew about the operation. We didn't drop the bomb on Tokyo because we ultimately determined that the emperor needed to be the one to tell the Japanese army to surrender. We figured that after the botched mission it would be best to try and work with the emperor rather than take him out. We've never divulged *Operation Sundown* because we knew it would be an embarrassment if Japan knew what we had tried to do.

"I still don't get it. There was a war going on. Whatever was done back then had motives that had to be understood by the Japanese government. Things are different now. Geez, Bev, none of this is making any sense to me."

There was a pause on the other end of the phone. Clay could sense that she was holding something back.

"Major......Bev, if want me to find something, you need to tell me what I'm looking for."

The major put her hand over the phone, Clay could hear her tell someone that she'd be right with them.

"Okay, listen, this is confidential, and I need you to use prudent judgement when talking with Paige," she said.

"Okay," Clay responded.

"Despite the decades of close working relationship between the US and Japan, there's been an underlying issue going on. They've always had their suspicion that we tried to do something to the emperor and then there's this claim, and we have no proof that it's true, that the U.S. is in possession of something that's important to the Japanese Empire. We've denied it for all these years, but the feud continues. We're not sure whether that special operation team came into possession of something or not. Since the Japanese government wasn't giving us any details, we simply let the issue die a quiet death, but when Paige wrote his story it went viral in Japan. Now things have resurfaced again."

"So why do we think that after all these years that Anderson has anything to do with this?"

"We're not sure if he is connected, but he was on that mission and maybe there's some information that can put some closure to this?"

"Why didn't someone simply ask him when he returned from Japan."

"You're a Captain. What if your entire team was wiped out on a suicide mission? Would you be willing to hand over whatever it was that we were looking for or would you hold judgement against us for what we did to them?" the Major questioned.

"Okay, I get it. It's been years, I'm sure time heals all wounds," Clay replied.

"First, we have no idea what we're looking for. And whatever it is, could be priceless. We wouldn't want it to disappear."

"I've met Paige and Cindy, John Anderson's granddaughter. They aren't those type of people."

"Okay, I get it, but again, we have no idea what we're searching for. We can't let Paige find something and then publish it before we have an opportunity to do damage control. We need all of this handled diplomatically. Clay, just find out what he knows and whether he has found anything. And for god's sake keep this information confidential. I don't want Paige tipped off and blabbing it all over the media."

"Yes ma'am... and Bev, thanks for taking the call and thanks for being honest with me."

Maybe it was the martinis or hearing her voice again, but Clay felt at ease talking with her. "Bev, I'm sorry about what happened. I.... I hope you can understand."

There was a long silence on the phone.

"Captain, just find out what you can and call me."

The phone went silent.

Clay sat on the bench for a while and then headed back to the hotel. He had played his cards right and got the real story he needed, now he had to figure out how he was going to create a bond with Austin.

CHAPTER

60

It was early in the morning when Anthony walked from his kitchen to his breakfast table with his cup of coffee. He sat down, yawned, and opened his computer to start reading the article that Austin had forwarded that evening. He sipped his coffee as he continued scrolling through the remaining contents. He put the cup down and was focused on the article. *Are you shitting me?* he mumbled to himself the reached for the phone.

Austin woke up after a late night of writing and editing. He rubbed his eyes and rolled over to cuddle with Cindy. He heard her moan. She rolled over and gave him a kiss.

"So how did it go last night?" she asked.

"Well, I got it to Anthony late, but I think it's pretty good."

"Why of course it's good. You're good."

Austin smiled and gave Cindy another kiss. He got up and started toward the bathroom to take a hot shower.

"So, do you think you'll get a Pulitzer Prize for this?" Cindy asked, as she rolled out of bed and put on her robe and slippers.

"Oh, I think they'll be some recognition, not sure it will be a Pulitzer, but someone's going to be interested for sure."

Cindy got up and went to the kitchen and made their morning brew. A few minutes passed when she heard Austin's cell phone ring, she shuffled back to the bedroom while sipping her coffee.

She picked up the phone and noticed Anthony's name. "Hello Anthony."

"Cindy, how are you doing, is Austin around?"

"I'm doing fine. Austin's in the shower at the moment. I can have him call you after he gets out."

"That'd be fine, thanks. Tell him that I need to talk with him ASAP. I want to get his article put online first thing this morning."

"Okay, will do. Is the article alright?" she asked.

"Alright; I think it's great, but I'm worried how it's going to be interpreted. If what Austin's saying rings true, this could be a shit storm for the Japanese and US governments."

"I know, it's pretty remarkable isn't it." Cindy didn't know how much Austin had revealed but she knew enough to encourage Anthony's excitement.

"It sure is. If the final story is as good as the set up in this article, then I think we'll have some significant interest in our little paper."

Austin had just gotten out of the shower and was rubbing his head with a towel.

Cindy cradled the phone and shouted. "It's Anthony."

Austin came over and took the phone. "Hey buddy, what'd ya think?"

"It certainly piques your interest. Are you sure the connection with the team assigned to the *Operation Sundown* is really tied to killing the emperor?" Anthony asked.

"That's what I've learned from Papa John's journal. I have no reason not to believe it, but I have a feeling that I'll get the justification I need as soon as the story goes public," Austin replied.

"What do you mean, justification?"

"Let's just say that I recently have had some sources pop up."

"Sources, what sources?"

"Legit sources, let's just leave it there for the moment."

"Okay. Listen, I'm going to get this out as soon as I get to the office. I'll need you to get started on the final piece. I think we're going to have some interest in this. I just hope that we don't get the government breathing down our necks."

Too late, thought Austin. "No problem, I'll start formulating the outline," he said.

Austin didn't reveal what he and Cindy uncovered about the package that John had taken. He simply didn't have enough to determine if their assumptions had merit, nor did he have any idea what it could be or whether anything still existed. He figured that once the article was published that he'd get some information to validate their speculation.

"Man, you're on a roll my friend. I think Cindy and that Florida weather have made you a new man," Anthony said.

Austin smiled as he looked at Cindy in her robe and slippers. "I'd say that you're right about that. Talk soon." Austin hung up.

"So, he thinks it's good, huh?" Cindy asked.

"Yes he does. Come here my beautiful assistant reporter," Austin responded.

"Assistant reporter! If it wasn't for me, you'd still be trying to find that fifth journal."

Austin grabbed Cindy and started kissing her.

"Why Mr. Paige, you shouldn't." Cindy put down her coffee.

CHAPTER

61

The article hit the wires mid-morning. Major Whitestone was at her kitchen table finishing up her cup of tea and looking through her emails on her phone. She was pinged by the captain of the special department keeping an eye on what stories were hitting the mainstream.

You need to look at the Operation Sundown article, came the message.

She put down the tea and phone and opened her computer. She Googled the name and up came Austin's article.

"Shit!" she said out loud after reading a few paragraphs.

Austin had clearly laid out the operation and its intention. He had it almost perfectly articulated and spent a lot of time setting up the operational team and the reason for the *Ticonderoga* being where it was in May of 1945. He did not, however, mention the names of the team or anything else.

She noticed that Austin had noted that the remaining story would soon follow.

He must know something more, she mumbled. She reached for the phone.

Matthew strolled down to the breakfast table that Clay had occupied for the last hour.

"I guess your military time clock is off this morning," Clay said.

"Well, just a little, sorry Cap. I was doing some research on Fort Myers last night," Matthew replied.

"Research?"

"Yes sir." No sooner had Matthew said that, when Clay noticed the disheveled female bartender trying to sneak out of the lobby.

Clay looked at Matthew. "Research, huh."

Matthew figured the smartest move was not to say anything. He played it well.

Clay shook his head from side-to-side wondering whether bringing Matthew was a good idea after all.

"So how did your conversation go with the Major last night?" Matthew asked.

"Well, I gave her the story that we had cobbled together," Clay said.

"And?"

"We were right. Virtually everything we had guessed fell in place. She's validated the *Operation Sundown* scenario and is worried that the Japanese government will be a bit ticked off about the revelation that we tried to take out the emperor."

"Again, what's the big surprise that'll send the Japanese government into a tailspin? We've been working with them since the end of the war. It's been decades, we're allies now, so let bygones be bygones and let's grow some…..."

Clay interrupted. "I get it, but we need to find out how much more there was with *Operation Sundown* and what Austin knows. The Major wants to head off any future embarrassment that may come from whatever Austin publishes," Clay said.

"But…" Matthew started when Clay's phone rang.

Clay looked at the number, it was from the Major's private line. "Yes ma'am."

Matthew got up and walked over to the buffet to get a breakfast and coffee.

"Did you read the reporter's, uh Paige's, article yet?" she asked.

"No, I haven't yet. Does it spell out anything in particular?" Clay replied.

"It pretty much lays out everything. He gives the name of *Operation Sundown*, which up to this point was not divulged. He also addresses the attempt on the emperor and the reason the *Ticonderoga* was off the coast of Japan. He also talks about the special operation team but doesn't mention any names, thank God."

"Why not mention the names?"

"Because the Navy never told any of the family members what their fathers and grandfathers did to die in action."

"What.... why wouldn't we have told the families?" Clay asked.

"Because we simply didn't want them to know what we asked those men to do. It was felt at the time that the mission was better left to stay a secret, so we just told them that they died in action but nothing specific," the Major responded.

"I don't understand, why not come clean back then?"

"I don't know the reasoning. But can you imagine what it would have been like for those family members to learn that we sent their sons on a suicide mission only to learn that we had a way to end the war sooner that would have saved them all."

"I guess they'd feel like they lost their loved ones for no good reason, and the Navy was to blame."

"Exactly. I know it doesn't make sense today but back then things were different, they just wanted to keep things secret."

"I guess I get it, but it's been a long time, I would think their relatives today would understand what their father's and grandfather's did."

"Maybe, but too much time has passed."

"Okay, so what's our next step?" Clay asked.

"It looks like this Paige guy is setting up for another article. We need to find out what he now knows or what he's found and stop him from printing anything more,'" she responded.

"Bev, we can't do that. You know it's against the law to force this guy from reporting what he's uncovered, accurate or not."

"Figure it out Clay. Whatever he has could significantly create waves in the relationship between us and Japan. We're going to have to run some interference with this story as it is, but I'm worried about the ramifications if Paige finds something even more compelling about the operation and reports it without us knowing what it is."

"I'll do my best, but I can't promise anything. This guy's good and I don't think I'll have any influence on what this guy wants to report."

"Do what you can," she said.

'Yes ma'am," replied Clay, then the phone went silent.

Matthew came back with a full plate and plopped down at the table. "So, how'd it go?"

"Well, Austin pretty much spelled everything out about *Operation Sundown*, so we'll need to find out what else he knows and try to convince him not to report on it," Clay replied.

"Are you serious? You know this guy. Good luck on trying to stop him in doing whatever he wants to do."

"Well, those are our orders."

Matthew reached for his plate and looked over to his boss. "She never lets you off easy, does she."

Clay didn't say anything, got up and went to the buffet.

CHAPTER

62

It had been a while since Chris and Robert had moseyed over to Cindy's house and the curiosity about what Austin had uncovered was more than they could handle. After all, they were the ones that got this story going.

"Should we impose?" Robert asked.

"I don't think they'll mind," Chris said. "Besides, it appears that our timing has never been good so why not keep with our track record."

They both walked over to Cindy's house with the sole purpose to see what more Austin had found from John's journal. They had read his article and were curious as to what the final story would be about.

It was just after noon when Chris and Robert knocked on the door, and as usual, they didn't come empty-handed.

"Hi, how are you guys doing?" Cindy asked in a cheerful voice.

"We're doing great. We wanted to see what y'awl were up to," Chris replied.

"Come on in," Cindy said. "Austin, Chris and Robert are here," she yelled.

Robert handed Cindy the plate. "We brought some sandwiches for lunch,"

"That's so sweet, thank you," she replied.

Chris and Robert noticed that the place was free from the stacked books that had been scattered about and were neatly back on the shelves. Austin came around the corner drying his hands with a towel.

"What are you up to Mr. Fixit?" Robert asked.

Austin chuckled, "Well, just trying to get the water to stop leaking in the shower."

Robert smiled. "Getting pretty comfortable around here, are you?"

Austin grinned, "Guess so."

Chris chimed in. "So, we read your article. I can't believe what we were up to back then."

"I know, John's journal is pretty revealing so far," Austin responded.

"It looks to me like you covered everything. Well, I guess the one thing that I didn't get was who were the men that were with John. If you knew who they were, why didn't you let everyone know?" Chris asked.

"You know, I struggled with that. I don't know, I thought they'd be lost in the story of the mission. I feel that we owe them something more, but I didn't know how to craft it yet. Besides, it could be the first time that the relatives of these guys will have learned about what they did," Austin replied.

Robert reached for a sandwich. "You're right about that, I guess. I wonder how they'll react when they learn that their family members were part of an OSS special operation in Japan. I'd think they'd be proud of that fact."

"Maybe, but from what I've found, none of them were recognized for their bravery. I don't know, I just think these men never got their due," Austin said.

Cindy had gone to the kitchen and returned with a tray with glasses of her sweet tea. "Well, there's two military officers here that want to recognize Papa John in some way," she said, as she put the tray down.

Chris's eyebrows raised. "Military Officers, really?"

"Yeah, their IDs indicate that they're with the Army," Cindy replied.

"I think they're really here to find out about what I know about *Operation Sundown*. Frankly, I don't think they knew anything until I put it in print. They claim they want to give recognition to John for being the last living World War two veteran, but I think they have something else in mind," Austin said.

Cindy took a sip of tea. "Well, I hope not. They seem like nice men, and I think they want to do something special for Papa John."

Austin felt guilty about not taking Cindy's perspective seriously and rephrased his opinion. "I agree, I think they want to recognize Papa John."

"That's the least they could do given the significance of being the last veteran," Robert interjected.

"Yeah, and what's so important about *Operation Sundown* anyway. It's not like anything can be that big of a secret anymore. Geez, everything's an open book today with the internet and all," Robert said.

Austin grinned. "It's funny you say that."

Robert took a bite of his sandwich and with his mouth full mumbled. "What?"

"The internet. I typed in *Operation Sundown* when I read it in the journal. Nothing popped up and my computer went dead. At first, I thought I had done something wrong, but the damn computer just died. It finally came back after about an hour. That's when I felt that whatever John was telling me must've had some truth to it."

"Could've been something wrong with your computer," Chris questioned.

Austin shook his head. "Could've been but it hasn't been that long ago and now two Military Officers come knocking on our front door. I think there's a bit more than coincidence here."

"So, what the hell is so big that the government is spying on you and sending people down here? You think that they think that you discovered something that they think is important?" Robert queried.

Everyone looked at one another trying to follow Robert's string of logic. Then Cindy and Austin glanced at one another.

Chris noticed the glance. "So, what's so secretive?"

"We think that John could have had something at one time that was valuable to Japan and the US government wants to find out what it could have been," Austin replied.

"Well, what did Papa John have?" Robert asked.

"That's it, we don't know. We don't even know if he ever had anything at all. It's just a guess on our part based on what I've read in the journal so far. In all honesty, I haven't finished the rest of the journal, so who knows? But having two military guys come here leads me to believe that Papa John had to be in possession of something at one time, now we just have to figure out what it was."

Austin glanced over to the journal sitting next to John's chair. It was time to find out what mysteries would unfold.

CHAPTER

63

In typical fashion, Clay didn't say anything on the drive to Cindy's house. He was mulling over what the Major had said and trying to figure out how he was going to deal with Austin. He knew that it he needed to get some information and yet, he was ordered not to divulge anything, it was a conundrum at its best. Matthew was accustomed to his boss's silence and despite the need to say something, he thought it best to let him think, at least for the moment.

Finally, Matthew decided to get the conversation moving. "So, what's going to be your approach?"

"I'm not sure yet. I don't think that laying our cards on the table will be enough," Clay said. "We need to make a connection of some kind. I just don't think there's anything in common that will show him that we're on the same side."

"Cap, in all honesty, we're the ones that have orders to basically shut him down."

Clay shrugged. "Yep, those are our orders."

Austin looked at his watch when he heard the car drive up. It was exactly five o'clock. "Well, I have to give it to 'em. That military training pays off, they're right on time."

"I'll go make some more tea. I know Matthew really likes it," Cindy said.

The doorbell rang, Austin walked to the front door and greeted them. "Good afternoon gentleman." He reached out and shook Clay's and Matthew's hands. "Please, come on in."

Austin motioned to Clay and Matthew to sit on the sofa.

Matthew noticed how different the place looked with the books not stacked throughout the room. "I see you put all your books back on the shelf."

"Yeah, it got pretty crowded in here." Cindy came in with a tray of glasses filled with her tea and looked over at Matthew. "I know how much you like my tea."

"Thank you, ma'am." Matthew took a glass from the tray.

Clay took a glass as well and took a sip. "This is really good."

Austin took a glass and put it beside him on the table.

"I read your article Austin and will say it's rather revealing," Clay said.

"Thanks, I think that it clearly spells out what I've concluded was *Operation Sundown*."

"Well, it's very interesting and specific," Matthew responded.

Austin sat back in John's chair. "It's certainly been an eye-opener to see what we were up to back then. Going after the emperor was ballsy for sure and I can appreciate that if the operation was successful, we'd have likely ended the war without the A-bombs."

"Your right, it may have ended the war, or it may have extended it if the Japanese military took a tactic of revenge. As you know, their army was fanatical and swore they'd never surrender. I guess it was best that we never succeeded in the operation," Clay said.

Austin leaned forward. "Tell that to the men that died on that mission."

Matthew and Cindy glanced at one another; they could sense a chill in the room, there was a sudden silence. It was only a fleeting moment, but it felt like several minutes.

Clay nodded. "I understand but a lot of men died in the war Austin. Those men were among many who lost their lives on the beaches and in the islands during the Pacific War,"

"I get that, but it wasn't but a few months later that we dropped bombs on Nagasaki and Hiroshima. If we wanted to take out the emperor, why not just drop one on Tokyo?" Austin queried.

"There were a lot of decisions being made at that time. Clearly there were some good and bad ones, but the war's over. We've been allies of Japan for decades. We'd like to keep the relationship as tight as it is now," Clay responded.

"As tight as it is now, that's interesting Captain. Has my article done something that would jeopardize that relationship?"

Cindy could see the tension starting to rise again and interjected. "Clay, how do you like the tea?"

"I like it a lot. We don't have this up in DC," he said.

Matthew sensed that Austin had figured why they were there and decided to take a different approach. "How did you figure that the *Ticonderoga* was off the coast of Japan?" Matthew asked. "All our records at the time showed that it was in port during May of forty-five."

Austin leaned back in John's chair again. "Well, truthfully, I had some information that showed that what we tried to convince people to believe wasn't true. We deployed the *Ticonderoga* for the *Operation Sundown* mission and gave everyone to believe that it was somewhere else."

"That's true, we have an article with the *Ticonderoga* in port at Pearl, but it was really the *Yorktown*. It was the same carrier class so no one would have been able to distinguish the two," Clay said, then he took another sip of his tea.

"Really?" Austin said.

"Yes sir, Cap here discovered that the article's photo wasn't the *Ticonderoga*. He enlarged the picture that was published only to discover that it was the *Yorktown*. We were just as surprised when we found this out."

"So, are you telling me that you two were trying to figure out the *Ticonderoga* story as well?" Austin asked.

"Well, when I read your article, I decided to do some research on the ship's whereabouts on the timeline that you printed. When we started to dig, we found some inconsistencies in our records," Clay said.

Austin sat up in the chair. "So, you guys were in the dark about what *Operation Sundown* was all about?"

"Well, I guess you can say that. We actually found out about the mission by accident. We did a search in one of our file rooms that holds archived information about the Pacific campaigns and found the files for the *Ticonderoga* and *Yorktown*. The May nineteen forty-five files were empty except for one notation. It said *Operation Sundown*. That's when we started to do a bit more research and then things started getting crazy," Matthew said.

"What do you mean crazy?" Cindy asked.

Clay cut in; he wasn't certain they should be sharing the information, but he needed to get something from Austin. "Your article was the catalyst to start our investigation into *Operation Sundown* and figure out what information you had come across and how you came to get this information. As you might guess, the Japanese government wasn't aware of our actions back then, and despite the fact that we were at war, we have been concerned that the information you've provided could be the start of some tensions between our governments."

Austin shook his head. "That doesn't make sense. What tensions could there be now? So, we didn't tell them about the attempt on the emperor. They had our guys' bodies that died over there, they could've put two-and-two together and figured it out. So why the concern now?"

Cindy frowned. "Can I ask you Clay, why are you so interested in this? I get it, it's your job, but really, why are you here?"

Clay sat back in the sofa and rubbed his temples. Cindy could tell that she hit on something.

Clay looked over at Austin. "You know it's funny in a way. I've always been a student of the *Ticonderoga*, but it's been a while since I had thought about that ship. When your article came out it kinda got me thinking again."

"About what?" Austin asked.

Matthew could feel the tension ease a bit.

"About my grandfather. He served on the *Ticonderoga* at the same time your grandfather did," Clay said, as he looked at Cindy and then back to Austin.

"I never got to see or even meet him, he died during the war, so when your article came out it started to resurrect some memories." Clay looked down recalling his conversations with his grandmother. "I have only one picture of him when he joined the Navy. In a way, my grandfather was the real inspiration for me getting into the military."

"I'm so sorry, how did your grandfather die?" Cindy asked.

"You know that's the frustrating thing. My grandmother told me the story of when the Navy came to let her know about his death. Honestly, we don't know how he died. My mom's still around but she doesn't recall anything. She always wanted to know more about her father, but there was nothing that we could ever find out. I'm just disappointed that she has so little of her dad to remember," Clay said.

Cindy put her hands on Clay's leg. "I'm so sorry. I'm sure your grandfather was a great man."

"Thank you. I'm sure he was, as was your grandfather."

"Where was your grandfather from?" she asked.

Clay sat up and smiled. "He was from New York. A city boy, born and raised in New York City."

"What was his name?" Austin asked.

"Francis Balboa." Clay chuckled. "The one thing my grandmother told me was that he was quite the talker; he loved to chat with anyone who would listen."

Cindy gasped and looked over at Austin.

Austin's face took a serious turn. "Did you say Francis Balboa... Frank Balboa?"

Clay noticed Austin's expression. "Yeah, why?"

Austin shook his head. *Jaws*, he muttered.

CHAPTER

64

The room was quiet as things started sinking in. The irony was not lost on Austin or Cindy, and they thought the coincidence seemed too unbelievable to have been determined by chance. The silence sent a message to Clay, he was puzzled and curious by their behavior. Matthew surmised there was something significant as well, given Austin's expression. Whatever he said, rattled them.

Clay frowned. "Why did you want to know my grandfather's name?" he asked.

Austin shook his head in disbelieve. *Shit, this is too surreal.*

"Frank Balboa was your grandfather?" Cindy asked.

Clay looked at them. He didn't understand why they were acting the way they were. "Yeah, why? Do you know something about him?"

Austin walked over to the kitchen table, picked up the journal, walked back to the chair, pulled out a photo and handed it to Clay. He stared at it but didn't zero in on anyone in particular, however after a few minutes something familiar started to emerge. He didn't say anything and continued focusing on a face. It didn't take long before it sunk in. "This is my grandfather, isn't it."

"Yes, it is," Austin said.

Clay cleared his throat. "Wow." He stared back down at the photo and then handed it back. "I've never seen this before."

"Those are the men that were the team for *Operation Sundown*."

Clay looked at Austin wondering if everything he was saying was real, but the photo certainly included his grandfather.

Austin continued. "He was part of the operation that you've been sent down here to find out about."

Cindy and Matthew looked at one another. They had both felt the tension building between Austin and Clay but started to see a connection occurring.

"Never saw this coming," Clay said.

Austin chuckled, "Neither did I."

Clay shook his head. "Geez, I can't believe this. To say, 'what are the odds' would be apropos I guess."

"Your grandfather and mine were very good friends. They relied on one another and were there for each other," Cindy said.

Clay didn't know what to say. He had come down here with orders to find out what Austin knew and prevent him from printing anything that could be detrimental to the Japanese and American relationship. Now he finds out that his grandfather was part of the operation he was investigating.

"Take a few minutes. This is probably a lot to digest," Austin said, then handed the photo back to Clay and left for the porch.

Matthew started to lament about the oppressive Florida heat, which Cindy found comical. Clay got up, grabbed his glass of tea, and walked out to the front porch.

Clay pulled out a neighboring chair at the table where Austin was sitting. "I guess this wasn't what either of us were expecting," he said.

"You can say that again," Austin replied.

Clay handed the photo back to Austin who momentarily stared at it. "These were the men that risked their lives to try and put an early end to the war. Not sure why the Pentagon felt the need to send you down here. I get it now that you didn't know anything about the operation but now you do. So, Clay, what's really the reason that you're here?"

Clay sipped his tea. "You know, Matthew's right, this stuff is really good."

"Well, it's that southern thing that makes it so good," chuckled Austin.

"You know, everyone that I've met around here has been so hospitable and welcoming. I can understand why people who come here don't leave," Clay said.

Austin smiled; that was his intention.

Clay cleared his throat and took another sip of tea. "Listen, in fairness I owe you an explanation. Matthew and I initially didn't have any clue about *Operation Sundown* but later were given the basis of the mission."

Austin nodded his head. "Yeah, I figured that you were pretty much in the dark."

Clay mulled over his next move; he knew the consequences but needed to get Austin to understand the bigger picture. "What I want to tell you is confidential," he said.

Austin frowned. "Okay?"

"I was sent down here to find out where you were headed with your final article and determine whether it would yield any information that could be embarrassing to the United States and if necessary, stop you from printing anything."

"Well, not sure what in the world I would have, or that I would report that would be that significant to drive any wedge in our relationship with Japan."

"Well, from what we understand, the team may have taken something that is significantly important to the Japanese government. Honestly, no one knows whether that's true or not, but it's been something that's been festering since the end of the war. The funny thing is that while the Japanese government makes these assertions, they won't tell us what they think we have," Clay said.

"So, your grandfather and John, and the rest of the team, reportedly have something that could drive a wedge between our two governments that have been allies for years?" Austin asked.

"Yep, that pretty much sums it up."

Austin pondered whether he should say anything about what he and Cindy had uncovered in John's journal, but something changed when he saw Clay's expression when he found out about his grandfather being part of the team.

"Give me a minute." Austin walked back into the house.

Clay looked out over the street; he saw moss hanging from the large oak trees. The shade made the temperature comfortable. He felt a quiet solitude that he hadn't experienced before. He remembered Gladys's comment about people wanting to stay once they've visited. Clay smiled, *she's right about that.*

Austin returned after a few minutes with John's journal. He sat back down at the table and flipped it open to a page that he had tagged.

"When Cindy and I were going over some of the notes that John had written, we came across something that didn't initially pop out. It wasn't until you guys came down here that we took a second look at things." Austin showed Clay the journal page where John had written the notes. "It appears that during the operation the team was spotted and attacked by a number of Japanese soldiers. During the retreat and melee, the team took off with something that had been in a box of some kind. They had no clue what it was and thought it may have been something important. After all you don't have a column of Japanese guarding a box. Anyway, as it turns out your grandfather and John were together and grabbed the contents of the box as they headed back to a rendezvous point and...." Austin paused and cleared his throat. "Well, let's just say, that Papa John references picking something up."

"Did he say what it was, do know where it is?" Clay asked.

"That's just it, we have no clue whether he left it on the ship when he got back or whether anything exists at all. I haven't finished the journal yet but so far nothing has been mentioned."

"Wow, well then I guess there may be some merit to the Japanese assertions."

"Maybe, but it's just assumptions, that's all," said Austin.

"Is there anything further that you can tell me about my grandfather,"

Clay said when Cindy and Matthew came out from inside the house.

"Matthew and I have been talking and we were thinking that it'd be great if we got together tomorrow for dinner," Cindy said.

Matthew smiled and with anticipation in his eyes said. "Yeah, it appears that Cindy here makes a great meatloaf."

Austin chuckled and wondered whether Cindy knew how to cook anything but a meatloaf. "I can tell you that it's out of this world," he replied.

Clay shook his head. "I don't know, we certainly don't want to intrude."

"Actually, it'd be a great opportunity to learn more about the details of *Operation Sundown*," said Matthew in a tone that all was but pleading.

"Well, sure, we'd love to if it's not an imposition," Clay responded.

Cindy smiled at Clay. "Then it's set. Tomorrow at six o'clock."

Matthew grinned with excitement. "That's a date."

"And with that we should be going," Clay said.

Austin got up and shook Clay's hand. "Look forward to getting back together."

"Me too. I'd like to learn more about my grandfather if you have anything else."

"Sure, we'll talk."

Clay looked over at Matthew and pointed to the car.

Austin watched them drive down the street. He stood there thinking about his earlier interactions with Clay who he now saw in a different light. He also knew that what he would have to tell him about his grandfather would be difficult, but for now he wanted him to think of his grandfather as a part of a team of heroes, the rest would come later.

CHAPTER

65

It was late in the evening and Major Whitestone was alone in her office. She had been busy working on some defense appropriations that were having difficulty working its way through the Senate Subcommittee. She hated this part of the job; it was mind-numbing work, and she never liked the politics side of her job. She was also wondering what more Clay had found out about Operation Sundown. She reached for the phone to call him when her desk phone rang.

"Major Whitestone," she said matter-of-factly.

"Major, please hold for the Secretary of Defense," came the voice from the other end.

Shit, she mumbled to herself. She hadn't finished her work on the appropriations bill yet and figured that was the reason for the call.

"Beverly!" came an enthusiastic voice. She hated the fact that the Secretary took it upon himself to address her by name versus by rank. She had earned the title Major and was bothered by some civilian politician who earned his position by way of political contribution to the president's campaign.

"Yes, Mr. Secretary, what can I do for you?"

"Just checking in to see how things are going," he said.

"Doing fine. It's late Mr. Secretary. I'm surprised your calling me about how I'm doing."

"Well, I was really interested in knowing what you found out about that article that spilled the beans on *Operation Sundown.*"

"I have a few my people down there doing some digging as we speak."

"Great, glad to hear it. Is there any update?"

"Not yet sir. I'll let you know as soon as I get anything."

"I need to know something pretty soon," the Secretary said. "I had Japan's Ambassador here making some inquiries about the operation and what additional information we can provide."

"Well, the reporter that wrote the story laid out the details. I'm not sure whether we need to provide anything further beyond telling them that there was a war on." She hoped that she didn't come off as too sarcastic but, at the moment, really didn't care.

"Yeah, in the end I think they understand that. Their more curious to find out whether we have anything further that we could provide about that operation,"

"Sir, with all due respect, what are they asking us to tell them?"

"That's it, the little bastard won't tell me shit. He just wants to know if we have anything more that we can tell them. I told him that as far as we know, we don't have jack! Not sure if he knew what I meant but I didn't care."

Bev smirked. She appreciated the Secretary's candor. "Sir, whatever they think we have must be something, for them to get this involved in some off-beat story from a reporter."

"You'd think they'd just come out and say it but their being cagey about all of it. I can't believe I'm wasting everyone's time on this. Just let me know if you find out anything."

"Yes sir, will do." Bev hung up the phone and reached for her cell.

Clay had just returned to the hotel thinking about the evening. He was still stunned by everything that occurred and began to feel a connection with his grandfather; something that he hadn't felt before.

"Cap, that had to be one of the weirdest things to happen," said Matthew as they walked through the lobby.

"I'd say that would be an understatement," Clay responded.

"Where do we go from here?"

"Not sure at the moment," Clay said, then he felt his cell phone vibrate in his pocket and answered the call. "Yes ma'am."

Matthew glanced over to see the waitress serving again. He was glad that Clay's phone rang and strolled up to the bar.

"Did you find out anything material?" the Major asked.

"I haven't found anything significant yet but we're going over for dinner tomorrow and I should be able to get some more details."

"I just got a call from the Defense Secretary who had a meeting with the Japanese Ambassador. It appears that their government is rather antsy about this whole thing, and he wants us to find something out soon. Put whatever pressure you need to get some information from Paige so we can get this bullshit wrapped up."

"I'll do my best, but I think that in the end this will just be a story about the men that went on that mission. By the way, do you have any idea who these men were?" Clay asked.

"Not a clue. Clay, they were just men doing their duty, just like you and me," she said.

Not a clue, Clay thought. Up to a few hours ago he had a similar attitude. "Did the Secretary ask the Ambassador what the hell they think we have?" he asked.

"From what he tells me, they haven't told him a thing. Like you and I discussed, whatever it is, if it's anything at all, must be significant for them to be this hush about it."

"I'll do my best."

"I know you will."

Clay hung up the phone. He wasn't sure where he was going to go with Austin. He really wanted to find out more about his grandfather then he did about whatever Japan was worried about. He recalled the picture that Austin had handed to him. Other than the old photo his mom had given him, he had never seen another picture of his grandfather. He was taken by how happy he looked to be with the men of Operation Sundown. It was something that he could tell his mom. He hoped that Austin would be able to tell him how his grandfather died.

CHAPTER

66

The evening breeze was a bit humid but when mixed with the rustling of the trees and the sound of crickets, it didn't matter. Austin sat on the porch sipping his tea that he'd become quite fond of. His days of bourbon and boozing were over. It had been a difficult transition, but he realized drinking to forget the past only worked in fleeting moments. What he wanted now was to focus on his future and hoped that Cindy would be a part of it. He was worried that his quick proposal may have been premature. They hadn't talked about it since he asked and worried that she may have had second thoughts. He knew he hadn't done things the right way and was kicking himself for jumping the gun like he did. It wasn't long before Cindy came out to join him.

"I can't believe how things have moved so quickly," Cindy said.

"I'd say that was an understatement," Austin replied.

"It's just unbelievable that Clay's grandfather was Frank Balboa. I just about fell out of my chair when he said his name."

Austin appeared disinterested. "Yep, that was really something alright."

Cindy frowned. "Are you okay?"

Austin took a sip of his tea. "I know it's been a pretty tumultuous time with everything that's happened but...." He paused to form the right words. "I know that we've been somewhat distracted, but I wanted to make sure you knew how much I loved you."

Cindy smiled. "Austin, I love you too. I hope you know that."

He was relieved that she hadn't wavered. "Well, we haven't talked much about things since I asked you to be Mrs. Paige."

"Yeah, I guess you're right, but you've been pretty busy, and I figured that when the time was right, we'd talk."

He felt a cool breeze suddenly cross his face and remembered a similar feeling at Mandy's grave. He thought that perhaps she was trying to tell him something.

Cindy rubbed his arm. "Is everything alright?"

"Actually, everything's perfect," he replied.

They both sat in silence for the moment letting the sound of the evening rule the conversation.

Austin reached into his pocket. "I want to give you something." He looked down at his closed hand without looking up.

Cindy's expression noted concern. "It's okay," she said in a quiet tone.

"When Mandy was young, I'd say probably nine or ten, she was in an art class. She had so much energy and was full of excitement back then. She was really good at art, and it seemed to be her passion at the time. Well, anyway, she had found a piece of circular glass with a hole in the middle, she worked on smoothing it out for weeks. It was an array of colors that she said reminded her of how happy she was to be my little girl."

Cindy rubbed his arms.

"Needless to say, I was blown away by what she made and kept it for all these years." He opened his hand. "I know that she'd be so happy for you to have this."

Sitting there was a beautiful glass ring filled with colors that even in the evening lights, brightly glistened.

Cindy looked puzzled until she realized what he was doing.

"I know this isn't what you were expecting but until I get things all finished up here, I thought it would do for an engagement ring."

Cindy's eyes filled with tears as he put the ring on her finger. Then she started crying. She got up and hugged him and then sat down wiping tears from her eyes.

"It's absolutely beautiful," she said, as she continued wiping her eyes. She put the ring on her finger. The rainbow colors danced as she turned her finger against the lights of the front porch. "It's just beautiful," she repeated.

Austin chuckled. "Well, I'm glad it fit; I was worried. When Mandy gave it to me it only fit my pinky finger."

Cindy laughed. "Well, it seems to fit me just fine."

She sat there for a while admiring the ring. The significance of it all was overwhelming. While she hadn't ever known Mandy, she felt a unique connection.

Austin watched as she rolled the ring around on her finger. He was happy that he had gone back to his room in Middlebury to fetch it from his drawer. He hadn't looked at it since Mandy died but knew she'd be happy to see it worn.

Austin was taking in the moment. Since he came to Florida, he had stopped drinking, found new energy in his writing, fallen in love, and was getting married. But he was about to uncover something that would affect everyone he knew and have such a historical significance that it would affect two nations in a way that he could never have imagined.

CHAPTER

67

The table was set, and the house smelled with the scent of spices that made the mouth salivate. Cindy had worked for most of the day preparing the meal. Austin had only gotten halfway through the fifth journal and was slowly examining each page. John's handwriting was getting difficult to read and he wanted to take his time, so he didn't misunderstand anything.

"I'm telling you; you're killing me with the smell of that meatloaf," Austin yelled from the living room.

"You like it?" Cindy shouted from the kitchen.

"Yeah, I do but I don't want to wait to get some."

Cindy came around the corner holding a fork with a piece of meatloaf on the end.

"Here you go mister antsy pants," she said, as she put the fork in Austin's mouth.

"Geez, that's good," Austin mumbled trying to talk while chewing on a hot piece. "Just out of curiosity, do you know how to cook anything else besides meatloaf?"

"Oh, you just wait, I have a bunch of things up my sleeve."

"Can't wait to see what you got."

Cindy slapped Austin on the arm and turned back to the kitchen to finish up the dinner.

Austin laughed and returned to the journal when his cellphone rang. "Hey Anthony, what's up?"

"How are things going down there?" Anthony asked.

"Good. Some interesting things are unfolding," Austin replied.

"Like what?"

"Well, like I had thought, we're on target with *Operation Sundown*. I've been visited by two military officers from the Pentagon that validated the operation's purpose."

"Military officers, is that what you were referencing when you said that you'd get the validation for your story?"

"Yep."

"Shit, I can't believe that you've stirred the pot that much. Why did they send officers down there?"

"I think they want to know what more I know about the operation."

"What could be such a big deal that the military brass has to be involved?" Anthony asked.

Austin didn't want to break Clay's confidence by telling anything more. "That's what I'm working on." He also didn't want to divulge the connection between Clay's grandfather and John; at least not yet.

"Man, that's a big deal to have the Pentagon involved with this. Be careful, we don't need them meddling in our story."

"No worries, I can handle things down here." *Meddling, you have no idea,* Austin mumbled.

"Well, we need to get things wrapped up. When do you think you can get me the last article?" Anthony asked.

"Can you give me some time to put it all together?" Austin responded.

"What's 'some time' mean?"

"A couple of weeks?"

Anthony didn't say anything, and he knew he was pushing things. He wasn't sure how long it would take to determine if John had really taken anything.

"Okay, but that's it. I need this done and you need to get back here. I miss you man. It's not been the same."

"Got it. Miss you too."

Austin hung up the phone. His world had changed since he left Middlebury and now he needed to figure out how to let Anthony know.

Cindy came around the corner from the kitchen wiping her hands on the apron she was wearing. "Who was that?"

"Anthony," Austin answered.

"What did you tell him?"

"Only that we've had some Pentagon visitors and that we've validated that purpose of the operation and what John's team executed during the war."

"Did you tell him that Papa John may have taken something?"

"No, I didn't want to get into that, at least not yet."

"Good."

"Why, are you concerned about something?" Austin asked.

"I don't know, maybe," she replied.

"What would you be concerned about?"

"Well, I like Clay and Matthew. I think they're really nice people and now that Clay's grandfathers in the mix, I don't know, I just think that in some weird way Papa John wanted all of this to happen."

Austin shrugged. "Maybe you're right." He wasn't into the paranormal thing but something in Cindy's voice resonated inside. What are the odds of all the connections happening as it has, he thought. Well then John, talk to me.

CHAPTER

68

ustin opened the journal and started slowly going through each page. He knew he needed to get things wrapped up, but he also wanted to ensure that he didn't miss anything that John had written, and the writing was getting more difficult to read. Cindy was in the kitchen and by the clanging that was going on, she was hard at work with the final touches of the dinner.

Austin sat back in John's chair and started reading. He flipped the pages to see that he was close to the end. He was particularly interested to see if there was anything further about what had been scooped up when John and Jaws were trying to escape the battle. He was certain that was why Clay and Matthew were here. He started:

> I've never gotten over why we had to lose the team for this stupid mission. I saw the war end a few months afterward. Why were we sent in there if there was an option? It pisses me off that I had to lose my captain, my team, my friend for this chicken-shit operation. I'm just pissed at them all. I should have died with my team. Why did I make it back? I just don't understand.

Austin was struck by John's note. He had only known him as a sweet man who cared for his family and friends. He certainly had mellowed over time, but he was clearly bitter when he first came home. He continued:

> *I'm going home to marry Evy. She's the only one that will be able to understand me and what I've gone through. I hope that I can be the same man that I was when I left. I'm scared that I've changed after all I've seen. Please God, don't let me lose her. Help me forget it all.*

The war had taken a toll on John, and it was clear that his memories were slowly fading. Austin wondered how it had to feel to be in that Japanese village that night. He had never been in the military and had no perspective of how a man could feel after being in combat. He continued reading.

> *It makes me sad that I was the one who had to represent those friends that I lost. The Navy never gave the families anything. Why me? Why was everything kept from them. It's so sad that we never existed.*

Austin stopped and took a big breath. He was reading things John had documented over time. He could see the tone start to change as he continued.

> *It's been a long time. I've never reached out to the families of my team. They should know how their loved ones died. Why did they give me everything? They should have gone to the families. They just dumped them on me, it just doesn't make any sense. I was the last. Did they expect me to explain things. I'm getting too old, and my memory of things is starting to go. I need to let them know what heroes they all were. They should know.*

Austin was trying to figure out when John was jotting down his thoughts. He hadn't dated anything but by way of handwriting, he could tell that there were significant gaps between each entry.

> *I'm alone now. I lost Evy and the memories of her, and my team are getting harder to remember. I wish I had Jaws here to talk to. I wish I had them all here to talk to. I figure that I'll be joining them soon.*

Cindy quietly came around the corner to check on how Austin was doing. "How are things going?"

Austin jumped; he was engrossed in John's notes and wasn't prepared for the interruption. "Okay," he said.

Cindy glanced at the clock. "They should be here pretty soon."

Austin nodded and continued reading.

It's been years. I need to make it right. Operation Sundown needs to be told. The truth needs to be told.

Austin stopped again and took a deep breath. Something was evolving and he knew that the next few pages would be revealing

I've seen too many wars since World War II. Why do people find it necessary to kill each other? I don't understand but I know I have to make things right. I know my time is coming to an end soon. I was bitter and mad for so many years. So much so that I refused to admit my mistakes and come to terms with what I did back then. We were at war, and I was young and stupid but it's time to make it right. They're extremely important, I know that now. I shouldn't have kept what I took, I should have returned them, but I didn't. It has to be made right. I'm too old and too ashamed to do it myself. Someone has to do it for me. I'm so sorry for what I did, please tell them that I'm sorry.

Austin's heart started pounding. John did have something. *Shit, I can't believe this,* he mumbled.

He was at the next to the last page; he turned it and sat frozen. He just stared; it was if he could sense John standing next to him. He felt a sudden warmth come over his body as if someone draped him with a warm blanket and was having a hard time catching his breath. The only words on the page were hard to read and looked to have been written with a weak hand as if struggling to get them on paper, but it was clear enough to make out.

Make it right.

CHAPTER

69

Austin sat in the chair; he couldn't move. He felt as if John had come back and whispered in his ear. He looked back down again at the words written on the last page. *What'd you mean, make it right?* he mumbled. John knew that someone would ultimately find the journal. *Why didn't you just tell me? Why the cat and mouse game? Why did you wait?* He was so immersed in thought that he didn't hear Cindy come into the room.

"Austin…. Austin are you here!" she said, with emphasis.

"Yeah, sorry, yeah, what?"

Cindy pointed to her wrist as to show the time. Austin looked at his watch. "Shit, it's almost six," he said.

"Well, they were right on time last time, I'll bet they'll be on time this time too," Cindy said.

Austin was so focused on reading the journal that he didn't notice that Cindy had set the table and put a beautiful flower arrangement in the center.

"That looks nice," Austin said.

"Well, I was going to have you help but you looked so into that journal that I didn't want to bother you. By the way, did you find anything interesting?" Cindy turned and darted back into the kitchen.

"Yeah, found some interesting things."

Austin didn't want to get into the details and as was predicted, it was exactly 6:00 when he heard Clay and Matthew pull up.

Austin put the journal down, but his mind was still on what he had read. He was trying to sort things out when Clay and Matthew rang the doorbell.

Austin opened the door to see them standing there with big grins on their faces. "Good to see you all. Come on in."

Clay handed Austin a couple of bottles of wine. "I hope you like Red. I figured with meatloaf; red was the right wine to have."

Cindy came from the kitchen and took the bottles of wine. "Thank you so much, a red will go perfectly."

Matthew rubbed his hands together and put his nose in the air. "Cindy, if your meatloaf is as good as it smells, this is going to be one awesome meal."

"Well thank you, and it will be," she replied, as she darted back in the kitchen.

Clay and Matthew retreated to the living room and took a seat on the sofa. Clay noticed that the journal was open. "So, anything new?"

"New?" Austin responded.

Clay pointed at the journal. "Yeah, wasn't sure if there was anything revealing."

Austin looked at the journal and shrugged. "Oh that, nothing much."

Cindy came around the corner and hugged Clay and Matthew. "We're so glad that you could come tonight," she said. "You guys feel like family now."

Austin was surprised by how quick they all bonded despite their first encounter but then Frank and John were like brothers, so it almost felt like everyone was family.

After a bit of small talk, they all sat down at the table. Austin was still focused on what he had read and was trying to put some logic to it all. Cindy poured the wine in all the glasses save Austin's, who had water in it. Clay picked up on it and surmised the reason.

The dinner went well with complements to the chef throughout the meal. Austin was watching the interaction between everyone but was so immersed in thought that he seldom engaged in conversation. Clay noticed it but didn't say anything; he could see that something was distracting Austin and given their recent interaction, it was out of character. Cindy and Matthew were hitting it off so much, that neither took notice of Clay and Austin. It wasn't long before Austin noticed that Clay was focused on him.

"You're pretty quiet Austin," Clay said.

"Huh, what?" He had been thinking about the last words in the journal and hadn't realized that he had disassociated himself from the group. "Oh, yeah, sorry, I was just thinking about something."

Clay was perceptive, he figured that Austin finished the journal and something was distracting him. "So?"

Cindy and Matthew picked up on Clay's inquiry and stopped their conversation. The room was quiet as attention was suddenly directed at Austin; the words *Make it right* kept swirling around in his head. He crossed his arms on the table and looked at Clay. "Your grandfather was a great man," he started.

Clay stiffened, he wanted to know more about his grandfather but hadn't figured it would be now. "I always thought he was," he said.

"He and John were close. They bonded when John pushed your grandfather out of a plane," Austin said.

Clay's expression turned to shock. "What!"

"Well, not without a parachute. Apparently, your grandfather needed some convincing and John helped him. Regardless, from that point on they seemed to be inseparable. The operation team nicknamed your grandfather, Jaws."

Clay laughed. "I'll bet it had to do with something about him being a talker."

"Yep, you got it."

Cindy and Matthew were sitting watching the conversation. They knew

284

their role at this point was nothing more than being the audience.

"Anyway, your grandfather and John were together when all shit hit the fan that evening."

Austin went on to describe how *Operation Sundown* had failed. Clay was glued to every word. He knew some fundamentals of the operation but was clueless as to the details.

"Your grandfather and John made it out together, but both were wounded in their escape. They had made it to the boat that they used to get them to the operational point, but your grandfather had been hit too many times. He died in John's arms as they headed back to the *Ticonderoga;* he was buried at sea. I'm so sorry that you had to hear it from me, but your grandfather was one of a kind. John never forgot about him."

Clay sat there for a moment. He had been seeking answers for years, now he finally got them. "Thanks," he said.

Cindy excused herself from the room. Matthew sat in silence, there wasn't anything to be added and he thought it best not to.

"You know, it's sad that my family wasn't given the opportunity to learn this back then. I'm not sure why it was necessary to keep all of this from us. At least my mom will know how her dad passed. She probably won't understand why, but now she'll have something, as sad as it is."

Cindy had gone into John's room. She reached up and grabbed the box from the shelf where she had found the fifth journal. She wasn't in any hurry, she opened it and slowly looked through the contents. She could hear the muffled sounds of Austin and Clay talking but paid no attention to anything. When she initially opened the box, she pulled several things out, but she had only one mission that evening and that was finding the fifth journal. This time was different, now she was looking for something just as important. It didn't take long for her to find it, and then some.

Clay had a relieved look; he finally had some finality to the questions about his grandfather. "I could never have imagined that things would have unfolded as they have. I can't thank you enough for giving me the final story of my grandfather. It's something that I never thought I'd have."

No one took notice of Cindy's return. She sat down at the table with something that she clearly had bundled in her hands. Clay turned and looked.

She slowly put a few of the items she had collected on the table in front of him. Clay stared at the items; everyone could see his expression change. It was subtle but he was clearly moved. There in front of him were a Purple Heart and a set of dog tags.

"These are for you," Cindy said. Clay picked up the dog tags to see his grandfather's name on them. It was the same for the Purple Heart. She also had something additional that no one saw coming. She reached out and placed four Purple Hearts on the table: one for each member of *Operation Sundown*. Austin, Clay and Matthew looked at one another.

"These have been in Papa John's box for all these years," she said. "What other secrets do you think still exist?"

Clay saw the look on Austin's face. He was good at reading expressions. "You know something, don't you?" he said.

CHAPTER

70

The dinner table was quiet. The scene was surreal with the Purple Hearts and Dog Tags seeming to reset the mood. The enjoyment of the food and chatter that had ensued at the beginning was now tempered by a realization that something more was to be revealed.

"So, what did you find out?" Clay asked.

Everyone's attention was directed toward Austin. It was clear that something was on his mind. He got up and went to get the journal.

"You finished it?" Cindy asked.

Austin didn't say anything as he sat back down at the table and opened the journal. He started reading the passages that John had written. He could see Cindy's expression change as she heard her grandfather's words. She closed her eyes as if hearing him talking. Clay and Matthew were glued to every word, Clay in particular. The Major had told him of Japan's suspicions, now he'd find out if they were valid.

"Make it right," Austin said, as he ended and closed the journal.

No one said anything; they simply let the words sink in.

"Did he mean for you to make it right?" Cindy asked.

"Well, I'm not sure he meant me, but he knew that someday, someone was going to find the journal and assuming they read the first four, would have figured that he had come back home with something that he shouldn't have."

"Shit, so we do have something of Japan's," Matthew said. "But what?"

"Whatever it is, it has to be so valuable that the Japanese are worried that it'd disappear," Clay responded.

"What?" Cindy asked.

"The Major told me that they wouldn't tell our defense secretary what we were looking for, but they're clearly interested in Austin's story. They probably think that you figured it out and have whatever they're looking for and may not divulge it," Clay said.

"So that's why you were sent down here, right?" Austin asked.

Clay didn't say anything. He knew that Austin already knew the answer.

"So, they think we'd steal it!" Cindy exclaimed.

Clay shook his head. "Well, yeah. But I told them you both weren't that way."

"Well, we're not!" Cindy said with emphasis.

"I know, I know," Clay replied.

Austin sat there watching the interaction but was more focused on what John had written. He now knew that John had come home with something but was trying to figure out why it was such a mystery. "What I don't understand was why he wouldn't have told me from the start."

"Well, I'm guessing that he didn't know you well enough to do that," Matthew said. "I mean trust takes time to build."

Matthew glanced at Clay. Austin felt that Matthew's statement had more to it.

"I guess, but I remember John confiding more and more in me. I'm just surprised that he didn't ultimately tell me everything. Instead, he told me to look for the fifth journal when they took him to the hospital," Austin said.

"I think he would have told you before he…." Cindy's voice trailed off.

Austin reached over and patted Cindy's hand. "I know."

"Well, we'll never know his agenda now, but he clearly wants to make amends," Matthew said in a matter-of-fact way.

"I know Papa John, he would definitely want to make things right," Cindy replied.

Clay sat in silence with his eyes closed as he rubbed his forehead.

"What's on your mind?" Austin asked.

"Read back that last paragraph. The one that talks about the mistake he made; how he wanted to make things right," Clay said.

Austin opened the book and started reading. He was halfway through.

"There STOP!" Clay exclaimed.

Austin stopped.

"Read that last sentence again."

Austin started reading it and suddenly stopped; it hit him. "Shit!"

Clay and Austin simultaneously looked at one another and smiled.

"What!" said Cindy.

Matthew knew that Clay and Austin were on the same page. He had seen his captain's expression when he hit on something big and now Austin had the same look.

Austin looked back down and read the sentence slowly, *"They're extremely important, I know that now."*

"Whatever he had…. has, there's more than just one thing," Clay said.

"Cindy, where's that box you found?" Austin asked.

"Just a minute." She went into the room and came back with the box and opened it at the table. They all got up and looked inside. It took only a few minutes but except for some bundled letters that they opened and examined, there was nothing material to point them in any direction. Cindy took some of the letters to read, they were what John had sent to Evy while he was on the ship.

They all stood around the table looking at the box as if something magical would soon emerge. Austin sat back down and looked at the journal again.

"Okay, we know that whatever he has, it has to be multiple things, right?"

"Right," Mathew replied.

"Okay, we can agree on that," Austin said.

Clay watched the interaction as he pondered what the next clue could be. "He obviously didn't know what he had at the time he took it. He had to have written that years later," he said.

"So, at some point after he came back, John must have done some research or something to ascertain what he really had, don't you think?" Matthew asked.

"Son-of-a bitch!" Austin yelled, as he slammed his hand on the table. He looked at Cindy and then at the wall of books neatly placed on the bookshelves.

CHAPTER

71

The evening rattled everyone. The discovery that John was in possession of something at one time was not in doubt, whether he still had it, was. It was clear that the governments of Japan and the United States wanted and needed information to put to rest whether anything still existed at all. They knew that John had done some research to figure out what he had, and given Austin's reaction, they knew where to start. They all looked over at the shelves and concluded that the answers laid within one of those books.

"So, the answer we need is over there?" Matthew asked.

"Yep," Austin replied.

"Wow, that'll take forever to go through all of those."

Cindy stared at the shelf and said, "All we need is to find the right one."

Clay gave a nervous laugh. "Well, the right one is mixed with hundreds of 'em, but I'm game."

Austin shook his head in disgust. "Shit, I should have known better!"

"What?" Cindy asked.

"I put the damn book that I carried around with me back in one of the stacks."

"What book?"

"It was one that I initially pulled that had a red tag hanging out of it. What an idiot, I can't believe I did that." Austin said. "Well, the good news is that it's already flagged."

"Thank God!" Matthew said.

Clay stood up and placed his hands on the table. "Okay Mr. Reporter, what are we looking for?"

They all headed to the bookshelf; Austin patted Clay on the back as he passed.

"Well Captain, the book we want will have a tab sticking out from the top. It has a place marker that John apparently used to flag a spot that had what he was looking for."

They all gathered in front of the shelves looking up and down at the hundreds of books and then at one another.

Matthew shook his head, inhaled, and blew out a big breath. "By the looks of things, it could be a long night."

Austin pointed everyone to a section of the bookcase. "Okay, you start there, you start over there."

"Aye, Aye," Matthew said, he started pulling books from a corner of the shelf.

"Any particular book binder, color or anything in particular we should be looking for?" Clay asked.

"I just remember a red tag sticking out of the top. It had something to do with Japanese artifacts or history. The title is Japanese Antiquities or something like that. Trust me, I'll know it when I see it," Austin replied.

With four people looking through everything, the task should have been easy; it wasn't. They were skimming the books on each shelf, but nothing was immediately evident, and the enthusiasm began to turn to concern.

"I know it's here," Austin said. "It has to be."

"I put all the books back. I don't think that I missed anything," Cindy said.

Austin and Clay had finished their sections and started back to the table. Cindy had finished hers and was sitting on the floor wondering whether she may have misplaced that particular book.

"I don't know," Austin said. "That's the only book that I remember that had any reference to what we need to be looking for."

"So, we'll keep looking," Clay responded.

Austin turned. "We have no choice. Maybe the tag fell out."

The room was quiet as they became resolved to going back and start looking again. They hadn't noticed that Matthew had still been on task.

"So, what did you say Cap, when you said you should start from the back," Matthew said from the corner of the room.

"What?" Clay replied.

Matthew smiled and held up a book. "I should've started from the back." There it was the book with a red marker sticking out of the top. "It says *Artifacts of the Emperor.*"

Austin looked at Clay. "This guy deserves a promotion."

Clay chuckled. "Don't push it."

Matthew handed the book to Austin; he set it on the table and opened it to where the marker was placed. They all gathered around him and watched as he started reading through the content of the page. It was dry reading but suddenly something popped. *They're extremely important,* he mumbled.

"What?" Cindy replied when she heard Austin mumble.

Austin started reading out loud.

> *"There are three highly regarded treasures of the Imperial Family. They consist of a sword, a mirror and a jewel and were housed in three sacred sites around Japan. Japanese history states that the Mirror and the Jewel were used to lure Amaterasu, the Japanese Sun Goddess, out of hiding. The Sword was a gift to Amaterasu as an apology for tricking her into leaving her hiding place.*

Amaterasu is a significant God for the Japanese people. Her descendants came down from the heavens to rule the Japanese people; she is the highest deity in Japanese mythology. The treasures have been part of the Imperial Family dating back to 1000 B.C. They have never been seen by the Japanese people and are only accessible to the Emperor of Japan."

Austin flipped a few more pages but nothing stuck out and nothing further referenced anything in multiples.

Clay ran his hand through his hair. "You don't think, do you?"

"Man, if this is it, well, geez, how big would this be," Austin said.

"I could see why Japan would be pissed off at us if we had their stuff," Matthew said.

Cindy turned and looked at Matthew. "But how grateful would they be if we returned it."

Austin stood holding the book. "That's if anything is here at all."

They all sat at the table soaking in what Austin had just read. Everyone glanced at one another not sure what to say.

Austin pointed at the box on the table and then turned to Cindy. "How did you know to find that?"

"Well, I found it on the top shelf in his closet," she replied.

"Yeah, but how did you know to look there?"

Cindy thought for a moment. "Just a minute."

She went into John's bedroom, opened the drawer of the side table, and pulled out the folded article. She walked back into the room and gave it to Austin. He unfolded it.

Cindy said. "I saw this and noticed that Papa John had a box under his arm. I remember seeing that a long time ago and just started looking and found it on the shelf in his closet."

Austin stared at the picture. "This trunk that he has his foot on, I've seen this before. I think this is the trunk in the picture I showed him that I had found in one of the journals. I remember him telling me a story about how he locked himself inside when he was trying to scare his fellow shipmates."

Matthew glanced at the picture. "What, he locked himself inside that?"

"Yeah, a different story for a different day," Austin said.

Austin looked back at Cindy. "This trunk, do you ever remember seeing it?"

"No, never have."

"If he brought back the box then it stands to reason he may have brought back the trunk. Do you remember anything about when your family brought John to this house?"

Clay and Matthew were sitting there watching the interaction; it was best to let the investigative reporter to do what he does best.

Cindy pondered a moment. "Well, I wasn't here when he moved in. I know they got rid of a lot of stuff and told me that they stored some of his things."

"Stored, do you have any idea where they may have stored anything?" Austin asked.

"No, I really don't. We don't have much storage in these old houses," Cindy said.

Austin frowned. "Old houses?"

As if everyone had concluded the same thing at the same time, they all looked to the ceiling.

"The attic," Austin muttered.

CHAPTER

72

The group walked around the house to find where any access would be. Cindy hadn't ever taken notice of an attic since she moved in to take care of John. She had no need to find it and she wasn't particularly fond of crawl spaces anyway.

With four people walking around the house looking up at the ceiling, it didn't take long.

"Got it!" yelled Matthew who had disappeared into the garage.

They gathered under the access door and glanced at one another. This could be where Japanese artifacts dating back thousands of years were stored. They stood there wondering if they were about to discover history or find another mystery.

They were all looking up at the ceiling when Clay said, "Well, someone's gotta get up there."

"I'll go," said Matthew, with enthusiasm.

Austin waved off Matthew. "If you don't mind, I think I need to do this. If John had intended for me to find this, then I have to be the one to fulfill his wishes."

Cindy rubbed Austin's arm.

Clay glanced over at Cindy. "Ladder?"

"Over there," pointing to the corner of the garage.

Clay found the A-frame ladder, opened it up and placed it under the access door.

"Well, here we go!" Austin climbed up and removed the door. He popped his head up to take a look. "Well, I can tell no one has been up here for years."

"What's up there?" Cindy asked.

"A lot of knickknacks, some clothing material of some sort and a lot of eight-legged friends."

Cindy shuddered. "See, that's why I don't do crawly spaces."

"Hey Cindy, do you have a flashlight?"

"Yes, I'll get it."

It wasn't long before she returned and handed Austin the flashlight, he climbed up in the attic.

Everyone had gathered directly under the access door waiting for some feedback. They could hear Austin maneuvering around things and occasionally heard an expletive that likely was a result of the eight-legged friends he was encountering.

"Anything!" Clay yelled.

"Not yet," came the muted reply.

Quite a bit of time had transpired, and they could hear Austin moving deeper into the ceiling. Everyone looked at one another seemingly to indicate that perhaps their assumptions of finding something were wrong. Suddenly...

"Got something!" came a muffled voice from deep in the ceiling space.

"Did you find the trunk?" Clay asked.

"I think so," came the reply. "I need some help."

"Got it Cap." Matthew bolted up the ladder.

Several minutes passed as Cindy and Clay heard the banging and scraping of something being moved along the ceiling.

"I have no idea how your parents got this up here," Austin said, as he got closer to the attic entrance.

It wasn't long before Austin and Matthew emerged with a large trunk. They got it down to the ladder and to the floor. Austin started brushing the dust from himself and hoped that none of the eight-legged friends hopped on for a ride.

The trunk spoke to the World War II era. They all stood around looking down as if it was going to speak to them. Austin bent down, dusted off the top of the crate and tried to lift the lid; it was locked. He pulled the latch a few times, but it didn't budge.

"I guess we can pop this off with a screwdriver," he said.

Clay looked over to a bench that had a few tools scattered about and picked up a screwdriver and handed it to him. He tussled for a few minutes, but the latch didn't move.

"I guess, I'm going to have to bust this open." Clay found a hammer that was conveniently located on the same bench and handed it to Austin. He took a couple of hard hits to the latch, but it simply didn't move.

He wiped some sweat from his brow. "I can't believe it. It's too old to be this stubborn."

"I guess asking if there is a key somewhere would be a dumb question," Matthew asked.

"After this many years, I doubt whether it still exists," Clay said.

Austin put the hammer down and looked around the garage. "I'm just going to have to bust this open with something harder."

"If what we think is in there, is in there, I'm not so sure we should be banging it up," Clay said.

"Good point," Austin replied.

"Wait a minute!" Cindy said and then ran back into the house.

She bolted into John's room and opened the drawer in the table next to his bed where he had kept the folded article. *If he kept the paper, then maybe he kept the key,* she said to herself with a sense of conviction.

She was in a hurry and pulled everything out of the drawer. There was no key. *Come on Papa John. Don't do this to us,* she mumbled. She reached back in the drawer and started feeling around. *Bingo!*

Austin was still trying to pry open the latch with the screwdriver hoping that a few hard tugs would do the trick; they didn't. Cindy came rushing back out and handed him the skeleton key that she found stuck against the back of the drawer.

"Where did you find this?" he asked.

"It was in the same drawer as the folded article."

Austin held the key, looked up at everyone. "I guess this is the moment of truth."

He slowly put the key in the hole and quietly whispered, *Okay Papa John, here we go.* He turned the key, the latch clicked. He looked up at everyone again. Everyone's faces spoke to anticipation. He slowly opened the lid. The latches squeaked as if protesting. The lid crashed against the back of the trunk. The contents looked as if they were elements of a time capsule from 1945. There were old newspapers with headlines referencing the status of battles during the war. A navy uniform was smartly folded. There were several pictures of the *Operation Sundown* team. He handed a few to Clay to sort out; they included more pictures of Frank with Papa John. Some were of them posing and some included candid shots of them horsing around. Clay smiled as he flipped through them.

Austin was sensitive to the age of the items and slowly lifted each of them from the trunk. And while everyone was pleasantly surprised by John's collection, the real reason they were looking seemed to be alluding them. It was clear that they were getting to the bottom, and nothing was standing out.

Austin handed Clay more photos and looked back down to pull out a few more newspapers. He lifted the last of the papers when he noticed something. It was a silk blanket with faded red trim. There were illustrations of Japanese characters painted on the blanket. It was neatly tied at each end with gold rope that had not faded over time. As if handling a newborn baby, he slowly lifted the blanket from the trunk and put it on the worktable. Everyone looked at one another, their expressions said everything - the moment of truth. He slowly untied the golden ropes and pulled back the front of the wrap. Cindy gasped and the hairs on everyone's arms stood up. Wrapped in a small, beautiful cloth was a jaded jewel. A similar cloth contained a small round mirror in an old frame. And next to them laid a plain sword that clearly looked to be from the ages. All the items seem to give off a glow as if expressing joy of finally being found.

They all stood there looking at the sheer beauty of the items. Even though they knew what they had was centuries old, the weight of the find was overwhelming.

Austin stared at the items. "You know, with the exception of the Emperors of Japan, no one has ever laid eyes on these."

No one said anything, they knew the significance of what Austin said. They also knew they had a huge responsibility.

"Now what," said Matthew.

CHAPTER

73

The enormity of the find started sinking in. They had the most sacred relics of the Japanese empire and had to figure out what to do with them. The other concern was their protection and figuring out how to return them to their rightful place.

Austin slowly wrapped the items back in their respective covers. He lightly tied the golden cords on each end of the blanket and, as he had done when he took the items from the trunk, gently placed them back inside and closed the lid. He locked it with the key and handed it to Cindy.

"We need to put this trunk somewhere," he said.

"Papa John's room," Cindy replied. "That's where we need to put it."

"Agree," Clay responded.

Austin and Matthew picked up each end of the trunk and slowly walked it into the house and to John's room. After years of being tossed around from ship to shore and house to house, Austin and Matthew treated it with care. After all, Japanese history rested in their hands.

They all gathered back around the table and sat there for reflecting on the moment. Austin put his hands on the journal and smiled as he recalled the words *make it right*.

"To Matthew's point, what do we do next?" Austin asked.

"I need to make a call to the Major and let her know what we found," Clay replied. "That makes sense."

"Austin, you can't write about this, at least for now?"

"I know. It's hard not to but I don't want John's legacy to be tarnished by people thinking that he stole something this important from Japan. We need to get this right."

"I'm not sure how this is going to unfold, but the US government needs to take it from here," Clay said. He was concerned how Austin would take this, after all, if it wasn't for him, nothing would have been found.

"I understand."

"Excuse me," Clay said, as he got up and walked outside.

Clay pulled his cell phone from his pocket and punched in the Major's number.

"Clay?"

"Bev. We found it."

"What?" she asked.

"We found it Bev. We have what the Japanese have been looking for."

"What is it?"

"Well, actually, it's not an 'it', it's more a 'they'."

"Come again."

"We found the sacred items of the Japanese Empire. It's a sword, a mirror and a jewel dating back to one thousand B.C."

"You mean you found a bunch of antiques and that's what our governments have been at odds about?"

"Well, what if Japan had our original Declaration of Independence. We'd be pretty pissed off don't you think."

"Good point," she said. "Listen Clay don't let those items out of your sight. If they're that important, I can imagine that there will be a lot of sensitivity to their security. After all, we don't want to lose them again."

"Understood," Clay replied. "Bev, you can't tell anyone what we found. All we should say is that we have what their looking for."

"Why can't I say anything?"

"We've done research on these items. They're sacred to the Japanese. No one has ever laid eyes on these things except the emperor. I'm sure they don't want to know that four average Americans did something that no Japanese person has ever done."

"But they'll know that you all have seen these things."

"Likely, but the less we say, the better."

"Okay, I guess I get it."

"Thanks."

"Great job Clay. I'm happy that I have you taking care of this. Kind of like old times."

"Yeah, I miss those days, Bev."

"Me too. I'll call you later when I find out what to do next."

Clay clicked off the phone and smiled.

Clay walked back into the house. Austin, Cindy, and Matthew were in the living room talking about the evening. Austin and Matthew were reliving their experience in the attic and tried to make Cindy squirm as they described the size of the spiders they saw. Both did their best as the size of the creatures kept getting bigger with each story.

"Would it be okay if Matthew and I stayed here until we get this Japanese thing resolved? The Major has asked us to keep an eye on the crate and I think it'd be better to have it stay here than try to move it somewhere else."

"Sure, you can stay in Papa John's room," Cindy said. "Matthew, you can stay in the other bedroom."

"Thanks," Clay responded.

"What did the Major say?" Austin asked.

"She's going to check with her superiors, and she'll let me know what the next step will be."

303

"Guess things will be buzzing up there," Cindy said.

"Well, we have two countries that have been pointing fingers at one another for decades. I guess this is where diplomacy will rule," Clay said.

"I'm sure it's not that big of a deal."

"You may be right."

The Major made her calls. It wasn't long before the Japanese government was informed of the find. Austin, Cindy, Clay, and Matthew had done something that two governments had been unable to do for years. They all thought their involvement was over. They had no idea about what was to happen next.

CHAPTER

74

C lay had sent Matthew back to the hotel to fetch all their belongings and bring them back to the house. While Clay trusted Austin and Cindy, orders were orders, and he was going to stay with the trunk until otherwise told differently. Austin and Clay had retreated to the porch while Cindy went inside to finish cleaning the kitchen. They sat at the table and exhaled; the evening had taken a lot out of them.

"Well, this has been the most exciting meal I've ever had," Clay said.

Austin chuckled and shook his head. "You can say that again."

Clay glanced out the front porch and reflected on the evening. Then he decided it was time to change the moment. "So how did you and Cindy meet?"

Austin smiled and raised his eyebrows. "Well, it's a pretty short story actually. I was sent down here to do John's interview and was introduced to Cindy by my brother-in-law, who lives across the street." Austin pointed to Chris's house wondering if he'd see two sets of eyes peering out at him. "To say I was tongue-tied when I saw her would be an understatement."

Clay smiled. "I can understand that."

Austin grinned and leaned forward in his seat and leaned on the table. "I can't explain it, but it felt like we had been waiting for one another for a long time. I don't know, things just feel right when we're together."

"Well, I can tell you, you both seem to be great for one another," Clay said.

"Yeah, it's kind of a comfortable feeling being here. She's been so strong and supportive. I didn't realize how much I needed that." Austin leaned back. "I had someone several years ago, but things happened that were more than we could have imagined. I guess, we weren't strong enough for each other and well…," his voice trailed off.

Clay nodded. "Well, I can say that you both seem very happy."

"Yep, we are." Austin looked back at the kitchen window and whispered. "We sure are."

"So, what's your plans? Are you staying after you get everything wrapped up here?"

Austin leaned back again and looked around. The breeze had picked up and the rustling of the tree limbs made crackling noises. The sound of the wind through the leaves created a soft whisper as if sending a message to the evening skies. He closed his eyes and felt the breeze, then opened them and smiled. "Yeah, I think I am," he said. It was the first time he had actually told himself that with any certainty.

Clay looked around taking in what Austin was seeing. "I understand why you would," he said. "And what about Cindy, I guess she's excited about you staying?"

Austin laughed. "Funny, I haven't really said anything specific, although maybe it's a moot point, I asked her to marry me."

Clay smiled and reached out his hand. "Well son of a gun, congratulations! That's just fantastic!"

Austin shook his hand. "Actually, you're the first person I've told."

"Well, I'm honored."

Austin hadn't had any close friends. Anthony was the closest friend he'd had and appreciated everything that he had done for him for all these years, but something was different with Clay. Despite their rough start, they seemed to be cut from the same cloth; buttoned up macho men that despite their veneer, had hardships in their lives that neither would admit to anyone.

"And you?" Austin asked.

Clay frowned. "What?"

"Anyone special in your life?"

Clay chuckled. "Well, once perhaps but that's been a long time ago."

"Really?"

Clay looked down at the table, smiled and talked as if reminiscing. "Yeah, it's been a while and I thought that feelings would fade over time, but I guess that was wishful thinking."

"Trust me, time doesn't heal all wounds, I don't care what they say," Austin said.

Clay looked up. "Yeah, I guess you're right about that."

Austin didn't say anything. Silence filled the gap and gave Clay time to reflect. "Yeah, I had someone at one time, but things got complicated and, you know, it ended." Clay gazed out to the street again and looked as if his mind was far away.

"So, tell me about the Major." Austin said.

Clay sat back with a puzzled expression. "What?"

"The Major," Austin repeated.

Clay shook his head. "How did ya... "

"I'm a reporter Clay, I can pick up on things that others can't see, even themselves."

Clay knew Austin was on target and could have denied everything, but he would have seen through that too.

"Yeah, the Major. Well, that's kind of a long story."

"Got time."

Cindy finished up in the kitchen and came outside. "So how are things going out here with you two?" she asked.

"Your soon-to-be husband seems to be a very perceptive person," Clay said.

"Well well, Mr. Paige. So, you finally told someone."

Austin just shrugged. Cindy was pleased that he felt comfortable enough with Clay to give him the news. She had seen the two of them get closer as they worked together, so she wasn't surprised by his move. Cindy went behind Austin and gave him a kiss on the cheek.

He reached up and stroked her hair. "Clay here was about to tell us about the Major."

"The Major?" she asked.

"Well, there's not much to tell," Clay replied.

Cindy wrapped her arms gently around Austin's shoulder and leaned her head against his. "Do tell," she said.

"Well, in short, we had gone to school together at West Point. I was a bit of a rebel back in the day. I know that's hard to believe." Cindy and Austin chuckled. "Anyway, Beverly was a smart, ambitious soldier, certainly more than me. Unfortunately, I had some issues when I was at West Point that almost got me tossed out."

Austin and Cindy sat in silence letting Clay continue.

"Unfortunately, I had a propensity for libation."

"Libation?" Cindy asked.

"Well, let's just say I partied a lot. Regrettably, drinking started turning into a habit more than the occasional social event."

Austin saw that it was difficult for Clay to say and could understand why.

"Well, to say that Bev saved my career would be an understatement," Clay continued. "She helped me through that part of my life. She basically got me back on track."

Austin felt Cindy squeeze him. He started to reflect on what he had gone through.

"When we both graduated from West Point, we were assigned to the Pentagon to do some strategic work for military operations. We did some secret reconnaissance work together for the Afghanistan invasion." Clay stopped for a moment and smiled as he remembered their past. "It was all pretty cool stuff, but I had the bug to get into combat. I guess that was just some macho bullshit in the end."

Cindy came around Austin and sat in the chair next to Clay.

"Bev and I had gotten really close." Clay didn't elaborate, he figured that Austin and Cindy would understand what that meant. "Anyway, I told her that I wouldn't go but I had put in for a transfer and didn't tell her. When my orders came in, I left for Afghanistan despite her objections. A few years had passed and although we kept in contact things just faded."

Cindy put her hands on Clay's arm.

Clay patted her hands and nodded; he knew she could understand. "Well, I guess that God can play funny games. As it turned out, I got wounded and they sent me back to the Pentagon and, wouldn't you know, I ended up in the same division as Beverly. Only she was the Major and I was the captain." Clay chuckled at the serendipity of it all.

"So, what did she say when you came back to the Pentagon?" Cindy asked.

"Nothing. She's never come to my division and interacted with me for two years."

Austin shook his head in disbelief. "Two years? You can do that?"

"The Pentagon is so big and cumbersome that you can get lost in the building for two years and no one would be the wiser."

"Wow, never would have thought that," Austin replied.

"Anyway, this little task got us talking again and kind of rekindled things. I wish I could make it better, but I don't think she'd every trust me again."

Cindy gave Clay another pat on the arm. "Well, you know people do forgive."

"Maybe, but they don't forget. Funny, she never married and neither did I. Honestly, I never thought I'd find someone like her again, so I never tried. I guess she didn't either. When we saw each other after so many years, it seemed like time had stopped. She looked the same as she did the day I met her. I just wish I could turn back time and make things right."

"You can't, but you can start to make it right now," Cindy said.

"I wish," Clay responded.

Cindy's expression turned serious. She looked into Clay's eyes as to emphasize a point. "I've seen too many people live in the past. They dwell on things that happened, things they've done, and nothing changes. They think it's all over and then, something or someone comes along that changes the narrative. You were sent back to the Pentagon for a reason. Now you have the chance to change your narrative and only you can rewrite it."

Clay didn't say anything. He thought it an impossible task to try and make it right with Beverly, but Cindy had a point.

The lights of a car lit up the porch as it pulled into the driveway. Matthew had returned with their luggage. Austin and Clay got up to help bring everything inside when Clay's cell phone rang. He pulled it from his pocket and looked over at Cindy and Austin who turned to see who called - they knew who it was. Cindy smiled and held out her hands, one flat and one with an imaginary pen; she started pretending to write.

Clay knew what she was saying. He punched the phone. "Beverly?"

310

CHAPTER

75

Things were moving fast. The Japanese government had put together their contingent of government officials and an Imperial designee who would handle overseeing the artifacts and transporting them back to their origin. The emperor was made aware of the find, yet no one knew what his involvement would be; there was always secrecy when it came to the Imperial family.

Austin, Cindy, Clay, and Matthew were unaware of the frenetic activity that was underway. The morning was uneventful as they all got up and started their day.

"So, what do you think is happening now?" Matthew asked, as he sipped his second cup of coffee.

"Probably a few government officials talking to one another I suppose," Clay responded.

Austin didn't say anything as he held his coffee cup and watched the interaction between Clay and Matthew. He figured that his involvement was nearing an end when his phone rang. "Shit!" he said.

"What?" Matthew asked.

"This is my boss: I owe him an article that wraps up this whole investigation."

Clay looked over, "We can't put anything in writing yet, at least not until we find out what the next step is."

"But he already knows that we've been doing some investigation. He's going to want to know what we've dug up," Austin said. "I can't bullshit him."

"Is he trustworthy?" Clay asked.

"No one I would trust more."

"Okay, but we need to keep this out of the press for now."

Austin answered his phone and explained what had occurred so far. He didn't go into a lot of detail and was pleased with his bosses sensitivity for secrecy, but he pushed him to get something drafted as soon as possible. Anthony knew that once the word got out about the Japanese artifacts that it would be hard to contain the story.

"So?" Clay asked, as Austin hung up the phone.

"He understands but wants me to get something written so that we can be the first to tell the story."

"Okay, that's fair. I'll just need to convey that to the Major so that she's in the loop."

Cindy entered the room with a platter of pancakes and sausages. "You know you can call her Beverly."

"Man, that's what I've been smelling," Matthew quipped.

Clay looked up a Cindy and smiled.

Matthew looked over at the two of them. "Beverly, huh, I guess that you've sort of spilled the beans on that."

Clay didn't say anything.

Everyone was enjoying their breakfast and reliving the night before. Although no one said anything, they were all waiting in anticipation as to what would happen next. They figured that things were likely buzzing in

Washington and Tokyo but weren't aware to what extent. It wasn't long before Clay's phone buzzed.

"Hello," he said.

"Is this Captain Hughes?" said the caller.

"Yes," Clay replied.

"Please wait for the President," came a voice from the other end.

"What?" Clay asked, wondering if he heard correctly.

"Please wait for the President of the United States."

More due to reflex and military formality, Clay immediately shot out of his chair standing straight. Austin, Cindy, and Matthew sat in shock wondering what had gotten into him.

He held his hand over the phone and whispered, "It's the president."

"Captain Hughes?" came the voice.

"Yes sir," Clay replied, hoping his voice hadn't gone up two octaves. He was clearly nervous.

"I understand that you've found something that belongs to the Japanese Imperial Family," the President said.

"Yes sir, well in fairness, this was found by an investigative reporter. We were just here to assist in the recovery."

"Well, kudos to him and yourself for locating these items. The Prime Minister of Japan has asked me to convey his sincerest appreciation for what you've done and will be sending some people to pick up everything. I've asked that you remain in charge of the items until they get there."

"Thank you sir, I will keep them safe."

"You said a reporter tracked these items down?"

"Yes sir.'

"What's their name?"

"Austin Paige."

Austin, Cindy, and Matthew were listening to Clay's responses. Austin was startled when he heard his name mentioned.

"Certainly Mr. President," Clay said and then handed the phone to Austin.

Austin's eyes widened as he reached for the phone. As did Clay, he stood up.

"Hello?"

"Austin, I want to thank you for locating the Japanese artifacts. That was great work indeed."

He had seen and heard the president on television but impressed when he heard him in person. "Thank you, Mr. President, but I had a lot of help from others."

"Well, how many people helped you?"

"Sir, there were four of us but there were others that helped as well."

"Are they all there with you?"

"Well, the principal team is here with me now?"

"Well let's get them on the phone. Can you put me on speaker?"

"Yes sir." Austin handed the phone to Clay and whispered that the president wanted to be on speaker. He didn't want to try and figure it out himself, he was worried that he'd accidently hang up on the President of the United States.

"Sir, you're on speaker," Austin said.

"Who am I talking to?" the President asked.

"We have Captain Hughes, whom you've talked to, Lieutenant Broadmeyer and Cindy…." Austin lost his thought for a second and forgot Cindy's last name. He could feel his face heating up with embarrassment.

"Cindy Paige," he bolted out. Cindy quietly giggled.

"Well, you all deserve the nation's appreciation for locating these artifacts. As you know, these missing items have caused controversy since the end of the war. Thanks to your efforts and tenacity, we'll be able to reunite these items to their rightful place."

"Thank you Mr. President," everyone said in unison.

"Tell me Austin, I'm curious, I understand that you found these items in an attic. How did they get there?"

"Mr. President, it was Cindy's grandfather who had secured them to keep them safe until they could be returned. Even though he held onto them for so many years, he was determined to see them back in their rightful place. Unfortunately, he passed not too long ago and wasn't able to personally tell us where anything was, although we were able to piece together the story," Austin said. He had his fingers crossed.

There was a silence on the phone. Austin knew he had spun the story a bit and wondered if the president believed him. The last thing he wanted was to have John thought of as ill intended. Austin and Clay looked at one another waiting to hear what was coming next.

"Cindy, I am sorry to hear about the loss of your grandfather. What was his name?"

"Thank you, Mr. President, for your condolences. My grandfather's name was John Anderson, we called him Papa John."

There was a pause. "Wait, did you say John Anderson?" the President asked.

"Yes sir," Cindy replied.

"Wasn't he the last living World War two veteran?"

"Yes sir."

"Someone told me about this. Was anything special done at his funeral?"

"Mr. President, we had a small service up in his hometown of Buffalo."

"Buffalo, why isn't he in Arlington?" he asked.

"He wanted to be buried, next to his wife," Cindy replied.

"I completely understand. But the last living US veteran of that war is significant. Let me look into this. Again, I want to thank you all for everything you've done."

"Thank you, Mr. President," everyone said in unison.

"Goodbye." And with that the phone went silent.

Everyone looked at one another for a moment wondering what just happened.

"Shit that was cool," Matthew said, breaking the silence.

Everyone laughed in relief.

Austin looked over at Cindy. "And you wondered if your life was going to be boring."

"Cindy Paige!" she said, as she slapped Austin on the arm.

"Guess I was a bit premature," Austin said.

"What, you two getting married?" Matthew asked.

"Yep," Cindy replied.

"Shit, I'm always the last to know anything."

They all chuckled as they sat down to finish their breakfast. Cindy had retreated to get the pot of coffee to warm up everyone's cup that had cooled down. It wasn't too long before Clay's phone rang again.

"Hello Beverly?" Clay said. He didn't say anything, but everyone could hear the muffled voice on the other end.

"What!" he exclaimed. "Are you sure about this? Okay, yes, we certainly will be here. Yes, we can do that. Okay, sure, we'll talk shortly." Clay hung up the phone and looked at the three of them all focused on him. "Well, if things couldn't get any crazier. I've been informed that the Prime Minister of Japan will be coming here with his entourage to bring back the artifacts. He's combining this with his trip to meet the President. He wants to personally thank us for what we've done for them."

Cindy bolted from the chair. "I have to clean the house!"

CHAPTER

76

The next few days were busy with arrangements being made for secret service and security. Most concerning was the status of the Japanese artifacts. Given the decades that they had been missing, the Japanese government wanted assurances that the items wouldn't disappear again. And given their concern that the word could get out that they were all in someone's bedroom, the Japanese government was looking for what measures were being taken to secure the artifacts. It wasn't long before that answer came.

Clay's phone had been ringing since the find. He was principally talking to Beverly as she was being directed by the Secretary of Defense and he by the President's office. Everyone had been sequestered in the house as things around them were happening that were out of their control. It was organized chaos at its best.

Clay's phone rang, he listened as more directions were provided. "Bev, don't you think that's a bit overkill?" He listened more. "Okay, you're the boss," he said, as he chuckled and ended the call.

He turned to Austin, Cindy, and Matthew and held up his hands in exasperation. "Well guys, they want to have the street blocked off with security and will be flying a helicopter over head from time-to-time to ensure that things remain quiet here."

"Quiet!" Matthew exclaimed. "Security on the street and helicopters? I don't think quiet will be the rule."

"I don't think Fort Myers has seen anything like this since Edison moved into town," Cindy said.

"Bet he didn't have helicopters flying overhead," Matthew replied.

A few hours passed when there was a knock at the front door. Cindy got up, walked to the front of the house, looked out the side window and saw two serious looking men in uniform standing on the porch. She slowly opened the door and peered around the corner.

"Ma'am, is Captain Hughes here?" the military officer asked.

"Yes, just a minute." Cindy closed the door and locked it. She figured that he was a legit military officer but didn't want to take any chances.

Clay came to the door and opened it.

"Captain Hughes?" the officer asked.

"Yes."

"Sir, my name is First Lieutenant Cross, we're from the Florida National Guard. We've been ordered to secure these premises and will be posting guards outside and at the entrance of the street. We have also contacted the local authorities, so they know that we're here. They don't know why, that's confidential, but we wanted them to know that we're taking orders from the Pentagon and not them."

"Understood Lieutenant, thank you." Clay closed the door and shrugged at Cindy. "Guess we're locked in for a while."

Clay turned and looked out the window. He could see two National Guard soldiers standing on either side of the door and figured they were as many standing at the street entrance. He also noticed two gentlemen walking across the street. "Cindy?" Clay said, as he peered through the curtains. "We have some visitors. Do you know them?"

Cindy looked through the window. "Yep, we know them. I've been wondering what was taking them so long."

Clay didn't say anything, he figured he'd find out soon enough.

Cindy opened the door as Chris and Robert slowly walked to the front door. The two officers standing at either side of the door looked serious. "They're with me," she said to the two soldiers. They nodded.

Chris and Robert walked in slowly looking around thinking that something terrible must have happened for there to be two military men standing at the front door.

Robert had a concerned expression. "What's going on?"

Clay and Matthew turned the corner.

"Chris, Robert, this is Captain Hughes and Lieutenant Broadmeyer," Cindy said, as she pointed to them.

Clay and Matthew reached out and shook Chris and Robert's hands.

"Nice to meet you," Clay said.

"Chris and Robert are our neighbors. Actually, Chris is Austin's brother-in-law," Cindy said.

"Well, ex-brother-in-law but that's not important," Chris corrected.

"Oh yes, Austin did mention that you lived across the street. Very nice to finally meet you," Clay responded. "Please call me Clay and this is Matthew."

Austin turned the corner after hearing everyone talking.

"Military, what in the world did you get yourself into?" Chris asked.

Austin laughed. "Well, you know all that stuff we've been talking about, you know, the Japanese artifacts."

"Yeah," Chris said.

"Well, we found 'em."

Robert's expression turned to shock; his eyes widened. "No shit!"

Clay made a quick glance at Austin. His expression said everything; *can they be trusted.*

"Clay, these are the guys that got the ball rolling. If it weren't for them, we'd never would have found out about Papa John being the last living veteran and likely, the artifacts would have never been located," Austin said.

Clay looked relieved. "Okay, well we certainly appreciate all your help," he said.

Austin looked at Chris and Robert, his face turned very serious. "Guys, you can't tell anyone about what we found. If you do, you'll have to answer to the two military personnel out front."

Chris and Robert looked at one another.

Robert glanced at the front door. "Seriously?"

Austin stared at them and laughed, "Just kiddin', but I am serious about the secrecy thing."

"Shucks, I wanted to see what those guys would do," Robert said.

"Seriously!!" Chris exclaimed.

Austin and Clay told Chris and Robert about the way the artifacts were discovered and apologized that they could not show them the items. They told them about how sacred the artifacts were and the need to keep them secure. Then they continued with the story about the call from the President. They both stood astonished by how things had happened over such a short period of time. It wasn't long before Robert noticed something.

"What's that?" Robert asked, pointing to Cindy's hand.

"What?"

"What's that ring on your finger. It's beautiful."

"Oh, this," she said. She looked over at Austin.

Chris put his hand over his mouth. "No way!"

Cindy nodded.

Chris got up and hugged Austin and then Cindy. "Man, that's awesome!"

It didn't take long before it registered with Robert. "When, where?"

Austin looked at over to them and smiled. "Well, nothing formal. It was a ring that Mandy had made for me years ago. It's not a diamond; I figured I'd get that later on."

Cindy looked down at the ring and rolled it around with the fingers on her other hand. "Really, I think this is beautiful. Don't get me another ring," she said. "Well, I mean not another engagement ring, but I'll take the other one."

"Does Anthony know?" Chris asked.

"Not yet, but I'll tell him soon," Austin replied.

"He'll be happy for you both."

Clay and Matthew watched the conversation unfold. It wasn't long before Clay's phone rang once again. He got up and went into the kitchen. "Hey Bev, how are things going up there?"

"It's been crazy Clay. I can't believe what attention this is all getting up here," she said.

"Tell me about it. I've had a conversation with the President, we have military personnel guarding the street and outside the front door and we have a helicopter flying around. I think we've woken up this sleepy little town."

"Well, it's going to get a bit worse."

"What now?"

"Along with the Prime Minister of Japan who will be stopping by to meet you and to take possession of the artifacts; the Defense Secretary will be with him. To say there's going to be a lot of security would be an understatement. Also, the Press has caught wind that something is happening there so be prepared."

"Does the Press know why the Prime Minister and Secretary are coming?"

"No, but they'll find out, I'm sure."

"Okay, I'll do my best to keep the chaos to a minimum."

There was suddenly an awkward silence on the phone. They both knew why but neither wanted to be the first.

"You know Bev, I'm sorry about what happened years ago. I was an idiot, but I figured you already knew that. I just wish I knew then, what I know now; maybe things would have been different." He paused and then let it out. "I miss you."

There remained a silence. Clay thought that he had misinterpreted the moment.

"I guess I didn't understand things either. I was trying to keep you with me and didn't take into consideration what you wanted and probably scared you off. I've lived with that since. I should've been more understanding and I wasn't," Beverly said.

"I know this is probably a stupid thing to ask but, do you think we can forget about the past and maybe try this again?" Clay asked.

"I'd like that. I'll have to make some changes in our reporting relationship, but…. yeah, I'd like to try again. And, for the record, your still an idiot," she said.

Clay laughed. "Yes ma'am, still an idiot. I agree Major." Clay shook his head and grinned. "Talk with you soon Bev."

"Yeah, talk soon," she said, then ended the call.

Cindy had been standing next to the entrance of the kitchen doorway. She hadn't purposively listened in and just heard the last bit of conversation. Clay slowly put the phone in his pocket and smiled. He turned and saw Cindy smiling back. He wasn't sure how much she overheard but it didn't matter. He was starting to rewrite the narrative.

Clay walked back into the room and let everyone know what was about to take place in the next few days. Given the significance of the dignitaries, everyone was starting to get anxious about what was to occur.

CHAPTER

77

A few days passed and the anticipation was palatable. Even Clay and Matthew, who each had been in combat situations, were a bit taken by everything that was taking place. Austin completed the final article that had included the rest of John's activities with *Operation Sundown* and took liberties in describing how he had acquired the Japanese artifacts and how they were recovered. This was to be a memorial to the last living war veteran and the men of *Operation Sundown* and, in the end, how John wanted to do his part to give respect and honor back to the Japanese people.

Austin gave Clay the draft. "Let me know what you think?"

Several minutes passed when he handed it back to Austin. "This is really good," Clay said. "I really appreciate what you said about my grandfather. It means a lot."

"You know, those pictures of Papa John and your grandfather. I bet your mom would like to see those," Austin said.

"Shit, with everything that's been going on, I never thought of calling her about this. Geez, I'm an idiot." Clay disappeared to the back of the house and made the call that he always hoped to make.

Austin grabbed his phone and went to the front porch. He passed two soldiers, who were different but no less intimidating, and sat at the table to call Anthony. It didn't take but a few rings for Anthony to answer.

"Hey boss," Austin said, before Anthony could answer.

"Hey man, what's going on down there? Anything more than what you told me before?" Anthony asked.

"Too much, but I finished the article."

"Great, when can we go to print?"

"I figure that as soon as the Prime Minister takes the artifacts, we should get the story out on the internet."

"Prime Minister?"

"Yeah, the Prime Minister of Japan will be here to take the artifacts back and the Defense Secretary will be joining him. I'm not sure why he's coming but I assume it's to have some U.S. presence when the transfer is made."

"Wow, I guess you've really created some excitement down there. I can only imagine what's been going on."

Austin paused for a moment and thought it a proper time. "Hey Anthony."

"Yeah."

"Listen, I wanted to let you know something."

"What?"

"I've asked Cindy to marry me."

There was silence. Austin wasn't sure what Anthony was thinking, hopefully something good.

"Wow, that's sudden," he said.

"Yeah, I guess it is."

"Okay, let me get this straight. I send you down to do a story on a veteran. You end up discovering ancient Japanese relics, you get two governments involved, then the Prime Minister of Japan and Secretary of Defense are coming to meet you and, to top it off, you're getting married."

"Oh, did I mentioned that I had a conversation with the President of the

United States," Austin said, hoping he didn't sound like he was gloating.

"Why of course you did, just a casual conversation with the President," Anthony replied.

Austin was a bit nervous; he figured that Anthony was being sarcastic but the silence on the phone was concerning. He wasn't sure what was coming next. He finally broke the silence. "Are you okay?"

He heard a laugh. "Just yankin' your chains," Anthony replied. "Man, I can't send you anywhere without you making something big happen."

Austin chuckled with relief but figured the next thing would not come off as well.

"Listen, I know this might be difficult, but I've decided that I want to stay down here."

"Well, I'm not surprised. When I met Cindy, I figured that you two were meant for each other. I would've been surprised if you told me anything different."

Well, that wasn't what I was expecting, Austin thought. "I'll come back up for sure to get things settled there before I come back down. I guess, you'll want to replace me, and I can understand that."

"What are you talking about?"

"Well, I'd be down here, you're there. I figured you'd want someone up there full time."

"Buddy, have you heard of the internet, email, Zoom. Don't know where you've been but you don't need to be here to do the job."

Austin paused for a moment. He'd put a lot of pressure on himself with the decision to stay in Fort Myers and hadn't given thought about alternatives.

"You're my best reporter; clearly you can get things done. Why in the world would you think that I'd put you out to pasture? You're an investigative reporter, you dumb ass, so you do the investigating and I'll do the publishing."

Austin nodded. "You got it, boss."

They chatted for a few minutes before disconnecting. Austin smiled, he felt that he'd finally found peace.

CHAPTER

78

I t didn't take long, and as was predicted; the Press were starting to gather at the entrance of the street. The neighbors started to wonder what all the commotion was about. Some called Cindy but she convinced them that it was simply a follow-up to John's passing. She hoped that he would have received a grander ceremony but, for the moment, she had to use him as a ruse.

It wasn't long before they received the call they had been waiting for.

"Yes, thanks for letting me know. Yes, we're ready," Clay said, as he clicked off his phone and looked at everyone. "Well, it's time. They're on their way."

Cindy stood and pressed down her dress. "What do I do? Do I say anything? How do I look? Am I alright?"

"You're fine. You look great," Austin said. He was just as nervous but did a better job of hiding it.

"Listen, this will be quick. The Prime Minister will likely say a few words and then they'll take the artifacts. I'm sure it'll be an in and out sort of thing," Clay said.

"Yeah, I can't imagine that it'll be that big of a deal," Matthew added.

They had been hearing the whirling sound of the helicopter passing over for a few days, but it was typically a quick flyover, this time it sounded as if it was hovering above them. It was the sign that things were starting to happen.

Clay's phone rang again. "Hey Bev. Yep, all set. You got it." Clay hung up. "They're just around the corner."

The neighbors had been hearing the noise of the helicopter but when it stalled over the house, they all came out into their yards. Some had talked to others and conveyed what Cindy had told them but the sheer size of the activity cast doubt on the legitimacy of her story. It wasn't long before the blue lights of the local sheriff's office and military vehicles turned onto the street followed by a line of black Chevy Suburbans with dark tinted windows. Cindy looked out the window to see some of the neighbors talking to one another. She glanced across the street to see Chris and Robert sitting on their front porch taking it all in like it was an unfolding movie. They all walked out to the front porch as the motorcade stopped in front of their house. They saw the flags fluttering on the front of the cars: half were the Japanese, the others American. The security personnel jumped from the front seat and opened the back doors. Out came what they assumed was the Japanese Prime Minister, who was wearing a black suit and red tie. He was followed by a robed man who looked as if he were a Monk of some kind.

"The Prime Minister is shorter than I thought," Cindy whispered to Austin.

"Don't tell him that," Austin replied. Cindy giggled; it lightened the moment.

"Who's that guy in the robe?" she asked.

Clay and Matthew who had been in casual dress since they arrived in town were now in their formal military uniforms.

Clay leaned over and whispered. "My guess is that he's from the Imperial palace."

As with the first, men opened the doors of the second set of Suburbans that had the American flags affixed to them. Out came a tall man dressed in a gray suit and blue tie. Clay immediately recognized the Secretary of Defense. Out of deference, the Secretary followed the Prime Minister up the sidewalk to the front of the house. It was a good thing; the Secretary would have eclipsed the Prime Minister if he had led the group.

Austin grabbed Cindy's hand. "We made it right, Papa John," he whispered loud enough for the four of them to hear.

Cindy squeezed Austin's hand. Clay and Matthew snapped to attention and saluted as the Prime Minister walked up the stairs. He smiled and reached out and shook everyone's hand.

"It is very nice to meet you," he said in clear, perfect English.

"Very nice to meet you as well," Cindy said.

Clay saluted. "Mr. Secretary, very nice to meet you sir." Matthew saluted the Secretary as well.

He smiled and shook everyone's hand. "Pleasure to meet all of you as well."

The Prime Minister looked to the robed gentleman standing next to him. "Please let me introduce you to the Lord Keeper of the Privy Seal of Japan. He is the one that will take possession of the items. There will be a small ceremony in accordance with the Imperial tradition and then we'll be out of your hair."

Cindy giggled; she was impressed by the down-to-earth comment by the Prime Minister.

He turned and winked at her. "May we come in?"

"Please, we'd be honored to have you in our home," she said, as she led the way.

Austin followed. He recalled when he and Cindy sat on the bench by the river lamenting about what their lives would turn out to be. Now he was following her, the Prime Minister of Japan, the Defense Secretary, and an Imperial Monk into her house. *Man, how things have changed.*

Cindy guided them to the living room and motioned for everyone to have a seat.

"May we have the opportunity to see the items?" the Prime Minister asked.

"Yes, certainly, please let me show you the way," Austin replied and pointed to John's bedroom.

His heart started to race as he thought about how much faith was put with the group when they revealed that they had discovered the artifacts. For a moment, he was concerned that perhaps what they found were just Japanese souvenirs that John picked up. They had described the items to the Pentagon and figured they had done the same with the Japanese government, so he figured them to be authentic, but *'what if.'*

Austin pointed to John's crate. He had emptied everything except the artifacts. The Prime Minister looked to the Lord Keeper and bowed. The Lord Keeper returned the bow then leaned over and lifted the latches that Clay unlocked as the entourage was entering the street. He bent down and lifted the items from the trunk and placed them on the bed. He looked at the Prime Minister and Austin with an expression that each understood. They turned their backs as the Lord Keeper unfolded the cloths that held the items. He started chanting which signified that everything was authentic. Austin let out a breath.

The Prime Minister and Austin retreated to the living room where the Defense Secretary was in conversation with Cindy, Clay and Matthew. Cindy had tears running down her cheeks which concerned Austin.

"Is everything okay?" he asked.

Cindy nodded yes but couldn't speak. The Secretary turned. "The President has asked me to convey his request to honor John at his grave site in Buffalo. He wanted me to tell you it's only proper to recognize the last living veteran for his service to our country."

Austin smiled, "Please tell the President that Papa John would have loved that."

The Prime Minister sat down on the sofa and chatted with the group. He was amenable and very comfortable to talk to. He thanked everyone again for finding the artifacts and did not discuss anything as it related to their disappearance or recovery. He was just happy that he was able to reunite them with his country. He talked about their historical significance to the Japanese people. It wasn't long before the Lord Keeper came from the room. He walked over to the Prime Minister and whispered in his ear.

"The Lord Keeper asked if it was permissible to return the artifacts in the trunk?"

Austin looked to Cindy. "I think Papa John would have been honored to have his trunk used in this way," she said.

Austin smiled, *indeed he would.*

The Secretary motioned to the military guards that were standing at the front door to come and take the trunk to the Prime Minister's Suburban. The two guards walked into the bedroom and came out carrying the trunk as if it were a coffin followed by the Lord Keeper who was chanting all the way to the vehicle. They slowly walked in unison and placed the trunk in the back of the Japanese Suburban. Everything was done in a respectful manner. After decades of controversy over the artifacts that had been going between the two nations; the matter was finally resolved.

The Prime Minister bowed to the group as they all gathered on the front porch. He reached out and took Cindy's hands. "We were enemies when we were at war. We are friends now. I know your grandfather was a great man and I would have been honored to have said this to him."

Cindy choked; her voice cracked, "He would have been honored to have called you his friend," she said.

Austin sniffed trying to hold back any signs of emotion; it was difficult, but he held fast.

The Prime Minister shook everyone's hand and returned to his Suburban.

The Secretary waited until the Prime Minister entered his vehicle and then turned and shook everyone's hand. "I can't thank you all enough for what you've done. We're glad that we've been able to put an end to this issue. Great work: all of you," he said. "And Cindy, we'll be in touch very soon to make arrangements for Buffalo."

"Thank you so much," she replied.

Clay and Matthew had little to say but were happy that it was over. They all remained on the porch as the entourage started leaving.

"Well, I guess that's the end of that," Matthew said. "Got any sweet tea?"

Everyone let out a laugh.

"Yes I do," Cindy replied.

Clay and Matthew turned and went inside but Austin and Cindy remained on the porch to see the last of the vehicles leave the street. It was noticeably quiet; there was no more circling helicopter. They looked down the street; the crowd of neighbors who had gathered on their lawns slowly retreated into their homes. They looked across the street to see Chris and Robert flashing a thumbs up. Austin reached out and put his arm around Cindy and she him. A gust of cool wind blew, and like Austin had experienced in the cemetery in Middlebury, Cindy thought she heard a whisper from Papa John… *thank you, now be happy.*

EPILOGUE

The autumn leaves made the surroundings look like a painted picture. The day was cold and cloudy which was typical for this time of year in Buffalo. The cemetery took on a regal look with flags fluttering on the graves of former soldiers. There was a stand with a large picture of John and Evy with the Purple Heart and Distinguished Service Cross attached to it. Austin looked around to see hundreds of people standing in thick overcoats; many were military, others were Press and many were just people from Buffalo paying their respects. He took Cindy's hand and walked her to her seat. Across from them and about fifty yards away were seven smartly dressed military men standing at attention with rifles perfectly held across their chests. Not too far away were Clay and Matthew, who were in their formal military uniforms. Austin held Cindy's hand throughout the ceremony that was led by the Secretary of Defense. The bugle played Taps followed by the military soldiers firing their rifles in the air for the twenty-one-gun salute. The Secretary came over and gave Cindy a tri-folded American Flag, and thanked her for John's service to his country. She smiled and thanked him for the recognition.

It was a moment fitting of a hero. Something that Cindy felt her grandfather had been all his life, both in the Navy and as a family man. As the ceremony ended, people started departing. Many came by and shook Cindy's hand and thanked her for allowing them to be able to show their respect.

Anthony walked up to them both and looked at Austin. "You know, I'm really going to miss you."

"Going to miss you too," Austin replied.

"Not you, you old lug, her," Anthony said.

They all burst out with a laugh. "Just kidding, I'll miss you both." Anthony grabbed Austin and gave him a big hug and did the same with Cindy. "Take care of him," he said, as he looked at Cindy.

"I will," she replied.

Anthony started down the hill, turned and pointed at Austin. "And you! You know I'm still your boss. Right!?" He shouted.

Austin smiled and gave him a thumbs up.

Matthew came and whispered in Cindy's ear. She smiled and kissed him on the cheek. He shook Austin's hand and left. Clay had been standing nearby waiting for the right moment. He walked up to them and turned to introduce an officer who, like Clay, was in formal military attire.

"Austin, Cindy, please let me introduce you to Major Whitestone," he said.

The Major smiled and reached out her hand, Cindy put her arms around her and gave her a hug. "Beverly, it's so wonderful to finally meet you," she said.

"It's so nice to meet you too," Beverly replied. "And thank you for everything." She looked at Clay; Cindy smiled. Then she shook Austin's hand, smiled, and mouthed, *thank you*. She walked to the car and left Clay standing looking at Austin.

"What, you old crusty captain," Austin chuckled.

"There's someone else I'd like you to meet," Clay said.

He reached out and took the arm of an elderly lady who was dressed in a pink overcoat with a bright blue scarf wrapped around her neck. "Mom, this is the gentleman I told you about who found the information on your father."

She was frail but strong enough to give Austin a hug. He hadn't noticed it when she approached but he did after she stepped back. In her hands were the dog-tags, Purple Heart and Distinguished Service Cross that had been awarded to Frank Balboa.

"Thank you so much," she said with a quiet voice.

Cindy reached out and took Clay's mom's hand. "Your father was a hero, you must know that," she said.

"I know, thank you."

Austin held Cindy's arm as they both watched Clay and his mom walk back to their car. After he helped his mom into the seat, Clay turned and stood there looking back at them, smiled, held out his hand, one flat and the other as if holding an imaginary pen. Cindy smiled; she knew what he meant... he had rewritten his narrative.

All the men of Operation Sundown were posthumously given the Distinguished Service Cross for their valor during battle. Austin had also sent the families the Purple Hearts that had been in John's box all these years. The families had not had any information about their fathers or grandfathers, and had it not been for Austin's article, they may have never known about their bravery and service to the country.

Several months passed. Austin and Cindy were sitting on the front porch. Austin had bought a couple of rocking chairs to add to the porch experience and even though it was winter now, he loved the idea of sipping sweet tea while sitting in shorts and a short sleeve shirt. He hadn't had a drink of alcohol for months and had no desire to drink again.

"They're not doing this in Middlebury right now, I can tell you that," Austin said, as if bragging about it.

"I guess not," Cindy replied.

He was also enjoying his newfound fame. The news article about John, *Operation Sundown* and the recovered Japanese artifacts had preceded all other news organizations and he was being recognized for his outstanding investigator work. He had been contacted by CNN, MSNBC, FOX, and other large networks to join their teams, but he declined. He was just fine staying with the *Town Register*. He waved as he saw Chris and Robert walk onto their porch, they waved back. They were both now involved with organizing Austin and Cindy's wedding and were taking great pride in designing the perfect event.

Austin was holding Cindy's hand as they rocked in unison in their chairs. His eyes were closed and was taking in the moment when his cell phone rang. He didn't recognize the number and had thought about just letting it go to voicemail.

"Who's that?" Cindy asked.

"Probably SPAM," Austin replied.

"Well, it may not be, shouldn't you answer it?"

He rolled his eyes as he picked up the phone. "Hello?"

"Austin?"

"Yes."

"This is the Secretary of Defense," came the reply.

Austin frowned; he wasn't sure he heard correctly. "What?... Who is this?"

"Austin, this is the Defense Secretary."

Austin stopped rocking and sat up in the chair. "Sir, what can I do for you?"

"Glad you asked, I have a job that needs someone with your investigative skills. Are you in?"

"Uhm, sure... I guess, is it that important?"

"Important enough!" Then the Secretary said in a commanding tone. "Pack your bags; I have a helicopter on its way."

ACKNOWLEDGMENTS

Those who were instrumental in supporting the work in this novel are many. First and foremost is my wife Cindy, whose undying encouragement kept me focused and who so fervently believed in me and in this story dedicated to her father.

To John Biffar and Dave Beaty of Dreamtime Entertainment, who provided creative feedback, and Roberta Voelker, who was my proofreader and first to read the initial draft, and who, after finishing, gave me a 'thumbs up' on the story. Also, to my publisher, Diane Lilli, whose insight, feedback, and support made publishing *The Last of the Greatest Generation* a reality.

And, a final acknowledgment to my former father-in-law, Robert "Shorty" Gallagher, who also served in the Navy during WW II and who passed at the age of 96 on February 10, 2023.

CPSIA information can be obtained
at www.ICGtesting.com
Printed in the USA
BVHW041426140623
665887BV00008B/820